MMC

AFTER
THE
FALL

·

AFTER
THE
FALL

A NOVEL

KYLIE
LADD

•

DOUBLEDAY

New York London

Toronto Sydney Auckland

DD

DOUBLEDAY

All rights reserved. Published in the United States by Doubleday, a division of Random House, Inc., New York, and in Canada by Random House of Canada Limited, Toronto.
www.doubleday.com

Originally published in Australia in paperback by Allen & Unwin, Crows Nest, in 2009.

DOUBLEDAY and the DD colophon are registered trademarks of Random House, Inc.

LIBRARY OF CONGRESS CATALOGING-IN-PUBLICATION DATA
Ladd, Kylie.
    After the fall / by Kylie Ladd. 1st U.S. ed.
        p. cm.
    First published: Crows Nest, N.S.W. : Allen & Unwin, 2009.
1. Married people—Fiction. 2. Adultery—Fiction. 3. Domestic fiction. I. Title.
    PR9619.4.L335A69 2010
    823'.92—dc22
    2009042318

ISBN 978-0-385-53281-5

PRINTED IN THE UNITED STATES OF AMERICA

10 9 8 7 6 5 4 3 2 1

First American Edition

For Craig.

Always.

And only.

Trip over love, you can get up.

Fall in love and you fall forever.

— ANONYMOUS

AFTER
THE
FALL

·

KATE

·

I had been married three years when I fell in love. Fell, tripped and landed right in the middle of it. Oh, I already loved my husband, of course, but this was different. That had been a decision; this was out of my control, an impulse as difficult to resist as gravity. Mad love, crazy love, drop, sink, stumble. The kind of love where every little thing is a sign, a portent: the song on the radio, his Christian name staring up at you from a magazine you're flicking through, your horoscope in the paper. Normally I don't even believe in horoscopes, for God's sake. Love without holes or patches or compromises, soft as an easy chair, a many-splendored thing.

At first I enjoyed it. A fall is a surrender; you can't help it, you didn't plan it. Maybe you could have been more careful, but it's too late for that now—you might as well enjoy the swoop and the speed, the unnerving sensation of having your feet higher than your head.

I fell in love with a man who had hair like silk. A man who said my name as if he were taking communion, who looked me in the eye while we made love, and even again afterward. He fell too, and there we were, clutching each other as the hard earth hurtled up to meet us.

That's the thing about falling. It doesn't go on indefinitely, and it rarely ends well . . . plunge, plummet, pain. Even if you get straight back up, even when you regain your footing, after the fall nothing is ever quite the same.

LUKE

•

Okay, it was the sex. Or, okay, it was love. When Cress insisted we see a counselor I knew the question was bound to arise: Why did I do it? Why had I betrayed her? I couldn't work out which answer might be better received, so I turned to my best friend, Tim, for advice. Given that Cress was also going to be at the session I had to be careful. Did I say it was love, and appeal to her romantic side? Cress is the most sentimental soul I have ever met, and I had a hunch, ridiculous as it may sound, that pleading love or one of its lesser forms—a crush, infatuation—would be a better defense than straight lust. Then again, given that she was such a romantic, maybe even mentioning the word risked alienating her completely—love, I suppose, being the sort of thing reserved for one's wife. The alternative was to plump for sex, but would that leave Cress forever paranoid about the hoops she herself wasn't jumping through in the boudoir?

Either way I was doomed, though I was hoping Tim could come up with something plausible. Predictably, though, he just looked shocked. If Cress is the most sentimental person I have ever met, Tim is the most naive. Or the most moral—I'm not quite sure what the difference is. "Just tell the truth," he sputtered, looking moist and uncomfortable, checking his watch when he thought I wasn't looking. "How much longer do you want the lies to go on?"

Well, indefinitely would have been nice. For seven months I was the happiest man in the world. Who wouldn't have been? Two beautiful women whose faces lit up when they saw me, one always available if the other was elsewhere. I'll admit it was good for the ego, but that was just the fringe benefit, never the aim. And for that reason I can't feel guilty about it: nothing was planned or premeditated. I feel guilty enough about the conventional things, of course—guilty as hell for hurting Cress, even some residual Catholic remorse for breaking my vows. Up till then I'd believed in them. But I never felt guilty for loving them both. Parents claim that they love all their children equally, and no one doubts this. Why can't it be the same for adults? Maybe I'm rationalizing what I did, but in a lot of ways I think everything that happened would have been far more objectionable if I had stopped loving Cress, transferred my affection rather than shared it.

In any event, Tim was no help, and I ended up telling the counselor that the whole thing had just happened. That sounds pretty lame for someone in advertising. I'm meant to be good at making words do as I please, but I could tell no one was fooled. Not Cress, sitting sniffing on one side of the office, eyes skittering away every time I glanced in her direction; not the counselor, mouth narrowing skeptically as she heard me out. Goaded by their disbelief, I abandoned any thought of appeasement and went on the attack. Forget love or sex . . . I blamed loneliness, frustration, all those long nights that Cress worked, then was too tired to talk, never mind touch, when she finally did get home. Bad move. My wife spent the session in tears and I wondered if I shouldn't have just gone with lust and been damned.

I don't know. It *was* love, and it *was* sex, and it was fate and karma and reincarnation too. It was an epiphany and an epitaph. There, I'm making the words work now.

CARY

·

I don't think about it much. No, really. What's there to think about? It happened; it's over; I'll survive. What's the point in talking about it? It's not going to change what took place. I mean, I made my decision too, and now I'm going to live with it—all this blathering around in circles isn't my style.

I grew up in the country. Sometimes I think about moving back there, though I know there's little work. What appeals, though, is that out there you just *do*. You don't debate, or discuss, or try to weigh up every angle. . . . There isn't time for it, and it's never helpful. You come off your horse or your bike; you get up, brush yourself down and get on with it. No point wondering if you'll ever ride again—it's not an option; you have to. It might hurt, but bruises heal. Bones too. Even hearts.

CRESSIDA

·

For ages after I found out I tormented myself, wondering when it had started. Not the sex, which was too much even to contemplate. Not even the kissing, but the thought, the desire, the possibility. They'd always clicked; that much was evident to anyone with half an eye, but it's still a fair stretch from flirting to fucking, particularly when you're both married to other people. That's crude, and I apologize. Luke would be shocked to hear such language from his virgin bride.

No, what I want to know is if such a thing can truly just happen, as Luke so ingenuously told the counselor. Surely people don't go around just falling into bed with others on a whim? Not, as I seem to be reiterating, if they are otherwise legally wed. Did they discuss it? Or did they just know, the way I sometimes know when I see a patient for the first time that he or she is going to die? It's something about their faces: something blurred or unfinished. There's no sense of the adult version lurking underneath, maybe because they will never grow old. I'm invariably right, though I wish I weren't. I'd rather not know at all, in case I then don't try hard enough with the ones I'm sure won't make it. Self-fulfilling prophecies frighten me.

When I first found out about that kiss, though, I wasn't frightened. Angry, yes, but I never felt threatened. It didn't even occur to me that this might spell danger. That probably sounds silly, but I knew my husband and the games he played. Luke is a flirt: a man who loves women and attention in equal measure, and preferably together. We had some stormy scenes over it when we were courting. It never did sit easily with me, but after a while it's amazing how one can adjust. Then too, I guess once I knew he loved me I could see it for the sport it was. It even validated me in some crazy way: he would spend all night at parties charming these beautiful women, succeed, and yet still leave with me. And after we did leave he would be so aroused by the thrill of the chase that we would rarely make it home without pulling over into some darkened street to heave and tussle on the backseat of the car . . . my hair caught in static cling on the seat belt, my toes pressed hard against the misted windows. Those nights were the grace notes of my marriage. I truly didn't care where the desire had come from as long as it was spent on me. And it was, wholeheartedly.

Luke is a golden boy, one of those the gods have smiled upon. Everything comes easily to him, or at least it appears to. Head prefect at school, valedictorian at university, a cushy job full of long liquid lunches and long-legged girls. Even his birth was blessed: after three daughters his parents were longing for a boy, and hey, presto, that was exactly what they got. Golden too in his coloring. A classical gold: hair the color of a halo in a Renaissance painting, eyes the blue of the Madonna's robe. Rich, vibrant colors. He isn't particularly tall or well built, but he stands out in a crowd.

Actually, I'm blond myself. I'm also good-looking enough, I suppose— I had to be to have attracted his attention in the first place. But my eyes are brown, my skin is fairer and my hair much lighter, a pale imitation of his, as if it has been washed once too often or left out on the line too long. When we stood next to each other it was *his* hair, *his* features the eye was always drawn to, as if he'd sucked all the color out of mine. My parents thought we looked like brother and sister, and my friends used to tease me about the beautiful blond babies we would make. I wanted children, and God knows I thought about them too. But try as I might I could never quite see them, their faces as hazy as the faces of the patients I knew would die.

KATE

·

It wasn't as if I stopped loving Cary, not in the least. People don't believe this, but I did love them both, and at the same time. Luke claimed he understood, but then he would, wouldn't he? We agreed with whatever the other said, as lovers do. Luke even admitted that he still loved Cressida, something I found profoundly irritating, though I was professing the same attachment to my own spouse. He used to justify it by comparing us to parents, able to love multiple children equally. I was never convinced by that—like so much of what Luke said it had surface appeal, but didn't stand up to closer scrutiny. The love for something you've made and must protect is surely different from the love that wants to possess, devour, exclude? No, for me it was more like when you hear a great song for the first time. For weeks you walk around humming it to yourself, unable to get it out of your head, playing only that one tune out of your entire collection. It doesn't matter that there are loads of songs you love, whole albums that resonate deeply with you—they can wait. That's not a great analogy—Luke is the one who is good with words.

Maybe a better illustration would be a migraine. One moment you're well; the next you're in so much pain you can't open your eyes. Everything is changed. Nothing exists except the throb and fret between your temples, though underneath it all you're still perfectly healthy. I sometimes think I had a migraine of the heart. I suppose you could call it infatuation, though to me it was stronger than that. *Eclipse* might be closer to the mark.

It was a different story with Cary. When we tell others how we met he likes to joke that there were fireworks from the word *go*, though in truth it took me almost a year to fall in love with him. Still, there *were* fireworks. We met at the Melbourne Cup. Cary's not a big fan of the races, but I love them. Dressing up, champagne, lots of men in suits . . . what's not to like? Usually I went with a group from school, but this year was different. Cup Day fell in the middle of our finals, and everyone else was staying home to study. I'd thought I probably should too, but when Joan called and offered me a spot in her parents' marquee I couldn't resist.

Joan and I were childhood friends—or childhood allies, anyway. We weren't really similar, but had been thrown together by pushy mothers who partnered each other for doubles and thought how sweet it would be if their daughters did the same. Neither Joan nor I was even into tennis, but we quickly formed an alliance. I'd tell my mother I was practicing with Joan; she'd tell hers the same. We'd then go shopping or to the beach, where Joan would sunbake with her sneakers on so her tan lines would collude with her story. The ruse worked well, though our parents always wondered why we never made it to the second round in any of the tournaments they were forever entering us in.

Increasingly, though, as we got older, we spent more and more of our supposed practice time apart. Eventually, we gave up the game altogether. I did like Joan, but I never felt completely at ease in her company. Maybe it was because the friendship had been forced on us, or because, with her careful grooming and precise sentences, Joan always made me feel messy. I thought about declining her invitation, but the alternative of staying at home, trying to study while simultaneously resisting the urge to contact the guy I was in the throes of breaking up with at the time, was too terrible to contemplate. Besides, there were going to be free drinks.

It was one of those typical Melbourne days that can't make up its mind. I've been to the Cup a few times, and it seems it's always either scorching or pouring, never anything in between. That year, it was both. The morning had dawned hot and unsettled, and was quickly ambushed by a fierce north wind that pushed the temperature into the nineties before lunch and played havoc with sundresses and scarves. I didn't know many of Joan's family or friends, and as the day wore on, the atmosphere under the canvas became more and more stifling, till I felt that I was drowning in dead air and dying conversation.

By four o'clock I'd had enough.

"I'm going to place a bet," I told Joan. "There's one more race, and I need some fresh air."

"Do you want me to come?" she asked, fanning herself with a form guide.

"No, you stay here. It might take a while. I'll have that, though," I said, plucking the guide from her fingers.

"Put something on for me then," she said. "Are you feeling lucky?"

Though the big race was over, outside the crowds still heaved and surged. If anything, they were even worse, turned manic and unpredictable by too much sun and alcohol. The wind threw dust in people's faces; whipped up the skirts of women passed out on the lawns. Men laughed and nudged one another at the sight, then turned their backs and had another beer. A cool change wasn't far off. I really did plan to place a bet, but the queues for the bookies were so long that I gave up as soon as I saw them. Instead, I decided I'd watch the final race. I'd been there since nine without seeing a horse, and it would kill some time before I headed back to the tent.

I pushed my way to a spot by the fence, picking my way over prone limbs and through the middle of picnics. The horses were going into their barriers on the other side of the track, small black dots with no idea that they were the excuse for such bacchanalia. A man on my left swayed and laughed, belching uncomfortably close to my ear. I stepped back to avoid him, bumping into another suit.

"Sorry," I mumbled, briefly conscious of the warmth of his chest.

"That's okay," he said pleasantly; he was possibly the only other person along the rail who wasn't drunk. "Are you all right?"

Before I could answer him, a loudspeaker screamed the start of the race. As one, every head along the fence swiveled to the left, craning to catch a glimpse of the pack as they came around the turn and along the straight toward us. Just then the wind swung around violently, suddenly freezing where a minute ago it had been hot. The change moved up the course almost in line with the horses, the sky rapidly darkening, a few drops beginning to fall. I watched its hasty progress: women clutching desperately at their hats; tents sinking inward, then filling with air as if they were breathing; the crowd at the turn running for shelter as the first thundercloud burst. As the field galloped past, the change was upon us too, almost as if the horses were dragging it along behind them like a great silvery sheet. The rain hit, and I turned to flee.

Of course, I didn't get far. Everyone had had the same idea, and the lawns were in chaos. Almost immediately I knocked into two people, and tripped over a third. Then my heels caught in the wet turf, and I broke one wrenching them free. I stood there cursing, dripping wet.

"Hey—are you all right?"

It was the guy from the fence, repeating his question of ten minutes ago. I held up my broken shoe in mute reply.

"Come on, then," he said, tugging my hand as the rain beat down. "Can you walk?"

I swear I tried, but with one high heel and one bare foot I could barely manage a hobble. The fence guy suddenly lunged forward, scooped me up over his shoulder, and carried me at a run through the pelting rain, expertly dodging gamblers and debris. I wondered if I should scream, or pummel his back. Instead, I started to giggle.

He jogged like that for a good five minutes, me jouncing inelegantly over his shoulder. Past the bars, people lined up five deep trying to get in; past the restaurants and the awnings and the public toilets, all suddenly bursting at the seams. When he slowed down we were in one of the small lanes of stables at the back of the racecourse.

"I used to work here when I was studying," he said, depositing me gently onto a bale of straw in the comfortable gloom of what seemed like a feed shed. "Mucking out stables, cleaning tack . . . It was that or wait tables, and I liked the company here better."

He held out a hand, warm and large. "I'm Cary," he said.

"Kate," I replied.

"Sorry—I didn't ask you where you wanted to go. I thought we should both just get out of the rain. Is there somewhere I can take you?"

We looked out at the rain, now coming down in sheets. I thought of the tent, its stale air, the stagnant conversation. Joan would be waiting for me, her skirt still pressed, lips pursed as she checked her watch.

"There's nowhere I need to be," I told him.

Girlfriends have looked at me askance when I've told them this story. There I was, they point out, soaked to my skin, no doubt freezing, perched on a hay bale in some dingy shed at the back of a racecourse with a total stranger. Wasn't I scared? Apprehensive? Or at the very least uncomfortable?

Well, no, on all counts. The way Cary sat beside me, careful not to make any accidental contact, told me that he meant me no harm. Plus he loaned me his jacket, which was as wet as the rest of our clothes, but stopped the chill. We talked, and he told me he was a geneticist at the Royal Children's Hospital; he had been at the Cup with a group of colleagues before they got separated in the crush on the lawns. At one stage he ducked out briefly and returned, improbably, with some strawberries, a tea cake and a rather warm bottle of wine.

"They were just about to throw it away," he said, gesturing in the direction of the corporate tents. I didn't care—I was suddenly starving. We ate and talked, laughing as we passed the bottle back and forth between us. Occasionally I thought of Joan drumming her fingers, ringing my cell phone and giving up in disgust. I hadn't charged it before I left home, and it lay lifeless in my bag, fogged with moisture. But the parking lots would be boggy now, if not flooded. They wouldn't be leaving for a while yet.

Around us I could hear movement . . . horses being boxed for the night or prepared for the trailer ride home; the low, reassuring tones of grooms soothing nervous animals. It was dusk, then dark. The rain had stopped. Cary pulled me to my feet and I felt a pang of disappointment that our idyll might be over. But he simply wanted me to see the city skyline, lights left on in the office towers hovering in the distance like fireflies. After its long day, Flemington was almost still.

"I love it like this," said Cary, almost reverently. "Quiet, returned to itself. That relief you feel at the end of Christmas Day when everyone's gone back to their own homes."

I wasn't sure that I knew what he meant, but it didn't matter. Cary's hand brushed against mine, and without really knowing who initiated it we were leaning toward each other. As our lips touched there was a burst of sound and the sky lit up around us. Fireworks, probably part of the package at one of the corporate tents. I gasped as a flotilla of blue and white sparks floated gently to earth around our heads; then Cary was kissing me again, his mouth tasting of strawberries and cinnamon.

CARY

·

Kate can't help but give the romantic version. She swears she's a realist, but I've seen how she pouts when other women get sent flowers; how her eyes cloud over at diamond commercials on the TV. I'm not big on flowers, but she got her jewelry and a husband, and for most women that would have been enough. Marriage isn't just about romance, is it? It's about family and companionship and teamwork, not just bouquets and fireworks. The advertising industry has a lot to answer for.

Still, that November night when we met did have its share of romance. Kissing Kate under a sky full of Catherine wheels is a memory I'll take to the grave, no matter whom I'm buried beside. But she didn't mention that the feed shed smelled like horse piss and wet straw, that the hay bale scratched, that the drenching had left us both freezing and her eye makeup was halfway down her face. I wonder if she remembers, or has she conveniently blotted those things out? A woman who claims she's a realist but still checks her love horoscope in *Cosmopolitan* is a dangerous mix: she'd rather die than ask for what she wants, but she'll sulk when she doesn't get it. Although sulking would have been the least of my worries.

Yet when people ask how we met I tell a version just like Kate's. No stink, no scratches, just champagne and pyrotechnics. I guess I'm as guilty of romanticizing as she is, though at least I know how it really was. Deep down she probably does too.

LUKE

·

As winter draws a gray cloak around Boston I find myself thinking more and more of Melbourne. I wouldn't call it homesickness. Maybe it's simply that the adrenaline of the sudden move here, the shell shock of packing up and relocating to an unknown city half a globe away, is wearing off. And really, there's no particular place I miss as I pick my way to work on footpaths obscured by salt and grit and snow. Rather, it's the feel. Sunlight on the back of my neck on the days I used to cycle to the office, the suburbs slipping past in a fog of dewy lawns and people walking dogs. The city as ripe and fresh each morning as the apples wrapped in tissue paper at the Queen Vic market.

To be honest, I resisted those suburbs for a long time. When Cress and I first married we had an inner-city apartment, not far from the one I'd rented in my bachelor days. Both places were tiny, but I loved them, loved the city and the energized hum that was the backdrop of each day. Later, when the lease ran out, we moved to a four-bedroom home that her sister had chosen, Cress being too busy at work to house-hunt. I'd argued against its size; Cordelia had calmly informed me that we'd need those rooms for children before too long. Cress proposed a compromise: we'd stay in the city if I could find a house equal to her sister's offering. I looked, but such a thing didn't exist, of course, at least not within our price range. Some compromise.

I'm adjusting to Boston. It's good to be back in a city, good to have left behind the constant lawn mowing and gutter cleaning of a suburban home. The locals are friendly, better educated than most Yanks, more sophisticated than most Australians. I guess that comes from being forced to spend so many months indoors, from having to entertain themselves with books and movies and restaurants rather than just sport.

One thing I'm still getting used to, though, is snow. Snow is funny stuff. Most of the time it is ugly and difficult, turned black and brown and yellow by the actions of passing cars and dogs. It goes slushy or icy, coagulates with grit and ends up walked into every shop or office in town, melting into grimy puddles. But when it is freshly fallen, white and pristine, it looks wonderful. Snow softens the edges on everything: buildings, litter, noise. For some reason it's far less cold when it snows, and I've come to anticipate those days as a respite from the cruel bite of the usual negative temperatures. Underfoot, really fresh snow is crisp and makes a squeaking noise as you walk on it, just like sand on the beach. Maybe that's what makes me think of home.

CRESSIDA

·

I wasn't quite a virgin bride, but I almost made it. That seems an incredible thing to admit in this day and age, and for a while I was as ashamed about my pure prenuptial state as I would have been by its converse just a century earlier. Certainly friends have looked surprised when I tell them—not that it's the sort of thing you put on your résumé. *Relatively unsullied: only one sexual experience prior to marriage.* Considering I was twenty-seven at the time, who'd believe me?

That isn't quite true either. Really, I'd had my fair share of sexual experience; it just hadn't quite reached the natural conclusion. Nothing was consummated; the deed wasn't done. Penetration, I mean, to be blunt. For all those years I remained intact, then threw it away less than forty-eight hours before my wedding. I'm a doctor; why do I find this so hard to talk about, for goodness' sake? I reminisce about falling in love and end up using words like *penetration* and *intact* instead.

I wasn't always so clinical. When I first met Luke I even eased up on my studying for a while, much to the horror of my parents. My father is a doctor too, an anesthesiologist. It's an appropriate choice, given that bedside manner has never been his strong suit. All those years spent sitting by comatose flesh have atrophied his social skills, nothing for company but the hiss of the gas and the plink of machines. He's polite, but small talk is like Japanese to him, and etiquette as useless in his world as calligraphy. I never felt pressured to study medicine, but I never considered any alternative either. Somehow it was just communicated to us that that was what we would do, the fact inhaled with the scent of furniture polish in our carefully tended home. We all followed in his footsteps, my two older sisters going into rheumatology and dermatology, respectively. Joints and skin . . . I wanted something a little more personal.

Pediatrics was a natural choice, as I'd always loved children. "That's lucky, because you married one," jibed a friend when she overheard me saying this once at a ball. I laughed dutifully but was slightly stung, though a quick glance at Luke illustrated her point. In the corner, a band was trying to pack up, having finished their set. Luke, however, had a microphone, and despite the best efforts of their female singer he wasn't going to give it up. A little drunk, but higher still on the crowd around him, he circled the stage, alternately posing as Mick Jagger, Elvis Presley, Bono—responding to any suggestion that was thrown at him. In between he'd return to tease the singer, crooning at her in character so that the anger left her heavily rimmed eyes and she became as giggly and light-headed as the rest of them. I have to admit, it was funny—he's always been a showman. In the end I think the drummer got tired of waiting around, grabbed the mike and the girl and hustled them both off the stage. Luke finished his act without even looking embarrassed. The singer, of course, was still trying to catch his eye.

KATE

•

I'd love to be able to say that after that magical first kiss Cary and I fell hopelessly in love, then had sublime sex, the perfect wedding and babies straight out of a diaper commercial. But it wasn't quite like that. For one thing, at the time we met Cary was interested in someone else, a girl at work whom he had been hoping to see at the Cup. I was embroiled in a pretty painful breakup myself. We exchanged numbers and chatted on the phone once or twice but nothing really came of it. The evening of Cup Day had been magical, but that was the problem—it was so exquisite it seemed like a dream, not something that could stand up to daylight. When I spoke to Cary on the phone he seemed withdrawn, even uninterested. And after a few how-are-yous, what was there to say? It wasn't as if we had a history, or even mutual friends to talk about.

Still, I was a little piqued when it appeared that nothing would come of the whole encounter. I had found Cary attractive and interesting, and thought the feeling was mutual. Plus it seemed a terrible shame to waste such a romantic story. On my way home that night I was already dreaming of how one day I would tell our children that their parents met in a rainstorm and kissed under a sequined sky. Despite herself, even sensible Joan was quite taken by my tale, once I had apologized about a hundred times for being so late. I dined out on the story for a few weeks, and I have to admit it was embarrassing when nothing eventuated. But that was all. I wasn't crushed by it, and after six months it was difficult to believe it had ever really happened.

That might have been it if it weren't for glandular fever. My best friend, Sarah, was getting married, and my ex, Jake, had also been invited to the wedding. The three of us had met in college, where we all began in classics. We still moved in roughly the same social circle, though *ellipse* was perhaps a better term, given how hard Jake and I worked at avoiding each other whenever our paths crossed. I'd remained single after our breakup, though I'd heard through the grapevine that he was seeing some blond Amazon whom no doubt he'd bring to the wedding. Knowing that I'd hate to be there alone while Jake was flaunting his new chick to all our friends, Sarah had suggested I attend with her cousin.

I agreed immediately. Ryan and I had met a number of times over the years, at Sarah's family beach house and her various birthdays, and we got along well. Better yet, he wasn't planning on taking anyone to her wedding. Maybe he was gay, I wondered, and was cheered by the prospect—at least that way he was less likely to pick up at the wedding and leave me all alone.

It all sounds a bit sad and desperate, doesn't it? I guess in truth it was, but I was still a bit sad and desperate about the way Jake and I had ended. Ryan was the best face I could put on it . . . at least until he called to tell me he'd just been diagnosed with glandular fever.

I hung up the phone in a panic. It was the night before the wedding, and the outlook was grim. Who would be available at such short notice?

I was toying with the idea of asking Joan what her brother was doing when I thought of Cary. Cary looked okay in a suit. He was easy to talk to and respectably employed. Even if I had to explain the situation to him, he seemed nice enough to go along with me for a night. I dug around in my purse for his number, still scribbled on a scrap of napkin from our impromptu picnic on the hay bale.

The phone rang five times before it was answered by a machine.

"Hi, this is Cary, and here's the beep." I liked the message. No theme tunes, no zany sound effects, no time wasting: just concise and to the point. No games, I thought to myself as I stammered out something about please calling me urgently. You'd always know where you were with this one. Then I went to bed at the ridiculous hour of eight thirty, depressed, thinking about how at the same time the following night I'd be sitting alone in a sea of couples, adrift and unclaimed.

Jake was introducing me to a woman with breasts the size and color of cantaloupes when the phone rang. Relieved, I turned to look for it, then woke up confused and angry when it wasn't in my handbag. For a moment I lay there disoriented until it dawned on me that somewhere a phone was still ringing. As I retrieved it from under my clothes on the floor the digital clock flashed eleven twenty.

"Hello?" I mumbled, still half-asleep.

"Hi, Kate. It's Cary." The voice at the other end was wide awake, confident, even amused. When I didn't immediately respond he prompted, "You called me earlier tonight."

"Oh, God, yes, I'm sorry," I said, sounding dazed even to my own ears. "I just woke up," I added, aware that I was effectively admitting that I had no life to be sound asleep before midnight on a Friday.

"If you want I can call back some other time," he offered.

That brought me around. "No, no, don't hang up," I practically begged. "I have to ask you for a favor."

To his credit Cary didn't burst out laughing at the whole sorry tale of Ryan, the wedding and the glandular fever.

"When did you say this was on again?" he asked, just as I was wondering whether to mention my nightmare of the cantaloupes in a play for sympathy.

"Tomorrow," I said despondently, hating to sound so pathetic.

"Okay," he replied. "What time?"

"Okay?" I almost shrieked. "You mean you can do it? You don't have something else going on?"

He laughed. "I do have something else going on, but I can cancel it. It sounds like your need is greater. And I even have my own suit. I bought one when I got married."

I felt dazed again. "You're married?"

"Does it matter?" he asked. When I didn't answer he took pity on me and said, "No, I just wanted to see how badly you needed a date. It must be pretty serious if you still didn't turn me down."

"It is," I conceded. My pride was well and truly gone by now, but I was so grateful to have a foil for Jake and his melon-endowed partner that I hardly cared. We agreed that Cary would drive over to the house I shared with a friend; then we'd take a cab from there to the ceremony.

"Good night, Kate," he said, as we hung up. His voice was sweet, almost wistful. "It will be lovely to see you again."

For the first time in weeks I suddenly found myself looking forward to the wedding. Jake could bring whomever he wanted. I would be safe.

CARY

·

To tell you the truth, it was Cressida I was interested in at first. I'd seen her in the corridors at work, her light blond hair rippling down her back as she walked, a stethoscope slung loosely around her neck holding it in place. It was amazing hair, and to be honest probably not all that appropriate for a hospital. But as far as I know she was never once told to tie it back, not even by the carbuncled old professors who usually took such delight in petty administration. My guess is that they enjoyed looking at it every bit as much as the rest of us. Once she came to a meeting in scrubs, her hair hidden under a green cloth cap, and there was a palpable sense of disappointment in the room.

We all looked at Cressida. I wasn't alone in that. Her iridescent hair and medieval name made her stand out, even when she was a student. But despite all the attention she had never relied on her charms to make her way. Hospitals are like country towns, and I would have heard about it if she slept around. No, the astonishing thing was that she really did seem as pure and unsullied as that sheaf of blond locks. She went out, I guess, but not with any of us. Not, that is, until persuaded by Steve.

Steve was the guy I shared my lab with at the time. He's noisier than I am, so every year he got the job of lecturing the med students for their six hours of genetics, and I got the job of setting and marking their exams. It was a system that suited us both, particularly Steve, who'd turn his last lecture into a forum at the local pub and use the opportunity to chat up that year's talent. Steve was gregarious and well liked, but even I was surprised when he told me he had managed to persuade Cressida and some of her friends to join the group of genetics staff who were planning a picnic at the Melbourne Cup.

He watched me carefully as he told me the news.

"Really? Are you sure?" I asked when he mentioned her name in the group of student attendees. Cressida had always seemed friendly enough, but distinctly unattainable.

I'm not a gambling man. I'm always weighing up chance and probability for the families who consult me; it's what I do for a job. I work with odds every day, and I know that they're rarely on your side. So I don't like to bet, but I went along to that picnic in the hope I'd see Cressida.

I didn't. I couldn't imagine her there anyway, among the debris and the debauchery; couldn't imagine her at ease between the girls with vomit in their hair and the boys wearing top hats and board shorts. Steve thought he had seen Cressida in the crowd, but wasn't completely sure. Had she even turned up? It hardly matters now, I guess. By the time our paths crossed again years later and we finally did become friends I was married to Kate and she was seeing Luke.

KATE

•

I love weddings, always have. I'm not usually a romantic, but there's something about all that unbounded optimism, people hugging one another and toasting the future, that gets me every time. And the enormous power of those words, which are so well-worn but never fail to move me: *With this ring I thee wed, with my body I thee worship.* . . . *With all that I have, and all that I am . . . till death do us part.* It's the idea of giving oneself up so utterly to someone else, to something else, something bigger, more meaningful and grander than you both.

So I guess I was in the mood to fall in love. I was certainly in the mood to cry and feel sentimental and drink too much, all of which probably contributed to the former. And there was a ready-made target in Cary, who stood smiling on my doorstep at exactly the time he had said he would be there.

It was good to see him again. Cary isn't stunning in the way Luke is. His hair is ash blond to Luke's gold, his eyes gray and calm. He doesn't make women turn around and look back over their shoulder when they pass him in the street, but he's tall and slim, and has a friendly face. As soon as you meet Cary you feel relaxed, comfortable, as if the two of you went to primary school together or something. Not much upsets him. He wasn't at all concerned about being a rent-a-date or spending an evening with strangers, and because he was so unself-conscious I soon felt that way too.

We got to the church a little early, a first for me. I was trying to talk to Cary above the strains of the organ when in the middle of a chord the music suddenly stopped, and I turned to see Sarah materialize at the back of the church. I think I might have gasped, then immediately turned it into a cough so as not to embarrass myself. She looked transformed. *Radiant* is a cliché for brides, but radiant she was, as if there were candles under her skin. I had the sudden urge to touch her, to see if she was real.

As she came down the aisle I felt Cary take my hand and gently stroke it. The service murmured in the background while his fingers moved lightly but purposefully over knuckles and wrist, making velvety forays along the five digits, faintly resting on the nail bed before retracing their path. There was a daring and a tenderness in the movements that stopped my breath, made my blood grow thick and languid, banished thought altogether. I felt that were I to look down, his passage would be marked on my skin, like henna on the hands of an Indian bride. When I glanced toward Cary he was looking straight ahead, to all appearances intent on Rick's declaration to Sarah, though to me this was now only a sideshow compared to the three-ring circus in my lap. Cary's touch was intimate, but not really sexual. Rather, it was a hypnotism, a promise, an opiate that both aroused and calmed. I was caught completely unprepared as the happy couple paraded back down the aisle, retrieving my hand with both haste and regret, feeling it burn and pulse at the end of my arm like a phantom limb.

Outside the church someone tapped me on the shoulder and I jumped, nerve endings still tingling. It was Jake, with a nervous-looking brunette in tow.

"Thought we'd better get the introductions over and done with," he said, tugging his partner toward him. "I'm Jake," he continued, looking at Cary curiously, "and this is Samantha." Samantha smiled, but I was the only one who noticed. After all my fears she was just an average girl, like me.

"And I'm Cary," said my partner, reaching across to shake Jake's hand. "Did you go to college with this bunch? I don't think I've heard Kate mention your name."

I nearly snorted with laughter at his cheek, but managed to smile innocently at Jake instead. Jake, however, was not so easily discomforted.

"Yeah, I know her pretty well. Most of the guys here do," he replied in a tone that hinted at more than my sociability.

Cary, bless him, was unfazed. "Then they'll know how lucky I am to be here with her tonight," he said smoothly, putting one long arm around me as if he had been doing it all his life.

"How long have you two known each other?" asked Samantha.

"Since last summer," Cary replied, smiling down at me fondly. "There were fireworks from the minute we met."

And from then on I was hooked. I don't think I spoke to Jake the rest of the night, and he would have had to screw Samantha on the bridal table to get my attention. Cary and I drank champagne, we talked, I introduced him to my friends, and after dinner he held my hand again. When I met up with Sarah to compare notes in the bathroom she laughed at how flushed I was, and when we embraced at the end of the night she whispered, "Keep him," in my ear. I didn't need to be told. When she arrived back from her honeymoon ten days later his car was still parked outside my house.

LUKE

·

Cressida's family had a beach house, of course, but I was surprised to learn that Cary's did too. Actually, it was more of a shack, and on a lake, though one so vast that it could have been the sea. The property was in the north of the state, not far from where Cary had grown up amid the flat wheat-lands. Usually that part of the country was in drought, but this year it had rained, and for the first time in memory the lake was almost full. When Cary discovered that I was as keen a water-skier as himself, the first time they came over for dinner, he promptly invited Cress and me to join them for the approaching Easter break.

"Hey!" I remember Kate protesting through my acceptance. "I thought we were going to catch up with Rick and Sarah?"

"We can do that anytime. You know I never get a chance to ski," Cary said, then turned to Cress and me. "She's not all that keen unless it's about a hundred degrees, and even when the weather is right, skiing's not legal unless there's a third person there to keep watch. So I've got my boat sitting in the garage, and it gets out about once a year when I can talk some mates into coming." He turned to Kate. "Say yes—I don't think I've seen you in your bikini all summer."

Kate giggled, slightly shrill from the champagne. "Well, it's not my fault if you're always spending your weekends off at conferences rather than at home with your bikini-clad wife." She swallowed another mouth-ful, then shrugged. "Okay, then."

I was a bit surprised—Kate had struck me as someone who usually got her own way.

"Is that all right with you?" I asked my own wife belatedly.

Cress replied as she always did: "Sure, as long as I'm not working."

Of course, Cress *was* supposed to be working, but for once she managed to swap her shifts, all except for the last day of the break. We took her car so she could come back to work on Monday, following Cary's four-wheel drive as the city gave way to suburbs, paddocks, unending land. Easter was early that year, midway through March, and hot enough even for Kate. As holidays go, it was close to perfect. Though the four of us hadn't known one another for long, we got on easily. Cress and Cary had worked together on and off for years. At first I found him a bit withdrawn, but he loosened up and relaxed as the days went by. Kate was different altogether—laughing, talkative, noisy from the word *go*. I don't think she was ever completely quiet; even when reading or making her breakfast she would be humming under her breath, occasionally singing a few lines. She flirted with all three of us, Cress as much as Cary and me. Cress is too self-conscious to have ever been a flirt herself, but she responds to it in others and was easy prey for Kate's charms. The two of them couldn't have been more different physically: Cress with her almost Nordic good looks and thoroughbred body, all lean lines and flared nostrils. Kate was slim too, but in a different, more compact way, half a head shorter than my wife, her hair and skin dark.

The days fell into a pattern: regular, comfortable. Mornings were for fishing while the girls slept in, then lunch on the deck before afternoons spent reading or sunbathing on the small crescent of beach near the house. Around four, with the sun still high but the evening calm descending, Cary and I would launch the boat while Cress and Kate tied back their hair and eased into wet suits, squealing as warm skin met rubber still wet from the day before. Kate would usually ski first, too impatient to wait once she was ready. Cary would throw her the rope; then we'd idle as she adjusted herself, the small, sleek head bobbing in the water like a seal's, eyes narrowed in concentration. Behind her floated the bush and the beach, our bright towels on the sand the only man-made items.

Kate, I remember, was learning to slalom. She got out of the water all right on one ski, but then invariably lost control and skidded off over the wake to either side, her slight body jerked straight out of the binding on more than one occasion. This made for some spectacular falls and, hours later, even more impressive bruises, spreading like sunsets on the flesh caught by the rope or the ski as she toppled. "Lean back! *Back!*" Cary would yell over the din of the engine as she emerged from the water, only to groan as once again the ski began to wobble, and Kate received another dunking. But she refused to go back to two skis, despite her frustration. "Just stubborn," Cary said, shaking his head in resignation as Kate nose-dived off our stern for at least the twentieth time that weekend. Finally he'd order her into the boat and I'd drive while Cress skied—elegantly, gracefully, the way she did most things, not even getting her hair wet—and Kate sat shivering beside me in the observer's seat while Cary rubbed feeling back into her battered limbs.

We'd return from skiing as dusk was falling, then sit with beers on the sagging deck until the mosquitoes drove us inside. Spread out at our feet the lake glowed like a mirror, brighter each night as Easter's full moon bloomed. Kate drank straight from the bottle, occasionally pressing the cold glass against her skin to ease sunburn or muscle strain, Cary toying with the damp hair still slicked to her neck. Eventually, someone would start dinner while the others showered and cleaned up.

On the second night Cary excused himself sheepishly after Kate had left for the bathroom, and a few minutes later we heard giggles and shrieks over the thrum of the water. Cress and I exchanged knowing glances and laughed, slicing tomatoes for a salad as the noise continued. But then it went quiet, the water stopped, and moments later I heard a soft, stifled moan.

"That was Kate!" I said, intrigued. I'm always interested in other people's sex lives.

"Mmmm," replied Cress, slicing faster, biting her lip.

There was another low moan, and I reached to turn down the volume of the CD we were listening to.

"Don't," said Cress, blocking my hand, then increasing the sound instead. When I looked at her she was blushing, eyes riveted to the chopping board. "It's none of our business," she added, sounding tense.

"Let's do some business of our own then," I suggested, lifting a strand of pale yellow hair away from her face.

"In here?" Cress asked, shocked.

"Why not? It's not as if they're going to notice."

The noise from the bathroom had risen in pitch, and the water had been turned back on.

"I don't know," said Cress, crossing to the refrigerator for more tomatoes. "There's something a bit sick about their being so overt and your being so turned on by it."

I walked over and pinned her against the fridge, cutting the sentence off with my lips. Caught by static, her hair fanned out across the surface of the door, sparking and crackling as I pressed myself against her. For a moment she resisted, but then kissed me back, giving in with good grace. Try as I might to ignore them, Kate's moans were still faintly audible as I made love to my wife. Dinner was late, and our own showers cold.

CARY

·

Weddings aren't my scene, as spectator or participant. As a general rule I try to avoid them, though when Kate called and begged me to come to Sarah's I agreed at once, thrilled at the second chance. We'd drifted out of contact after that evening at the Cup, though not because I was pining after Cressida. Like any man with eyes in his head I was interested in her at first, but once I met Kate, Cressida was just a pretty face. Guys like me don't end up with women who look like Cressida anyway.

No, what happened was that I lost my nerve. I'm pretty shy, and Kate was like one of those firecrackers that had danced in the air as we kissed, full of light and spark. Usually I'd tag along with Steve, eking out a social life from the students he met or parties he invited me to. On my own I was less confident—I think I called Kate twice before giving up and hoping she'd call me. That strategy eventually worked, though I can't say I'd advise it.

We started going out after Sarah's wedding, effective immediately. I couldn't believe my luck when Kate took me home, and to be honest figured that what came next was a particularly generous thank-you gesture for rescuing her in her hour of need. But the next morning she seemed to want me to stick around, and the next night too. Before I knew it we'd been together for six months, then twelve, and I wasn't even sure how it had happened.

Three and a bit years on we went back to the church for the christening of Sarah and Rick's first child. Kate was one of the godmothers. Afterward we picnicked on Sarah and Rick's sloping back lawn. Kate was on her third glass of champagne when Sarah wandered over.

"Here," she said, thrusting the child at Kate, who took her awkwardly—reluctant, I suspect, to put down her glass.

"So," Sarah said without preamble, sitting down next to me, "enough of us always inviting you two to these things. When are you going to make an honest woman of her?"

I glanced across at Kate, expecting her to howl in protest. We'd never really discussed the future—it was hard enough getting Kate to commit to dinner with my parents in a week's time. Besides, things were fine as they were.

"Good question," Kate said, bouncing the baby rather gracelessly on her lap without looking up. "When are we getting married, Cary?"

"Married?" I said. "I've never thought about marriage."

It was the wrong thing to say, though in fairness I was put on the spot. Kate colored but was silent, her movements gaining in vigor. The infant in her lap shrieked with glee, her head wobbling about on the stalk of her neck.

"Never thought about it?" scoffed Sarah, reclaiming her baby lest Kate do actual damage. "How can you have been together for this long and not have thought about it?"

I shrugged, outnumbered. "Kate knows I want to be with her. I just didn't think the whole white-dress thing was really necessary."

"Well, you never asked," Kate shot back, her eyes finally meeting mine.

"I don't like weddings," I tried to explain, irritated at having to justify myself in front of Sarah. I've always hated scenes. "They're expensive, out-dated, too formal. And a piece of paper won't make any difference to how we feel or whether we stay together."

"Well, you're wrong if you think we'll stay together without it," Kate snapped, her tone making it clear she wasn't joking.

Sarah shushed the baby, though she was already quiet. Though she swore later she'd had no idea what trouble her question would provoke, I was furious at the unexpected interrogation and humiliated by our private business being dealt with in public. It wasn't even as if marriage had ever been an issue before. Early on, in the first rush of love, I'd deliberately not mentioned it for fear of scaring the somewhat flighty Kate. Later, I guess, I'd just gotten settled. It was a ridiculous scene, and for a second I thought about walking out. But Kate is a proud woman, and I knew if I left she would never forgive me. Besides, I'd been sure since the start that she was the one, and if this was what she wanted, was it really such a sacrifice?

Nonetheless, I hesitated for a second, the car keys in my hand biting like tiny knives. Kate's opal-colored eyes sparkled defiantly, the picnic around us gone quiet. Then I put the keys back in my pocket and picked up the half-empty champagne bottle at Kate's feet.

"Okay, then," I said, raising it as if for a toast. "Kate, will you marry me?" The funny thing was that as the words left my mouth I felt my anger leave too, replaced with assurance and the closest I've yet come to joy.

A few people on an adjoining rug turned around to look at us, one of them knocking over a deck chair as she craned to hear Kate's answer.

"Are you serious?" asked my bride-to-be. Then, without waiting for an answer, she leaned over, took my face in her hands, and kissed me until we were both breathless. Through the applause of the watching guests I heard the clink of glasses and the laughter of children playing at the end of the garden.

CRESSIDA

·

It wasn't his looks that attracted me to Luke. I can be sure of that because I hadn't even laid eyes on him when I first started falling in love. It happened over Christmas, at the end of my second intern year. After six years of medical school, then two years in the public hospital system, I was exhausted, and had no greater plans for the festive season than to crash at the family beach house before commencing my pediatrics training in January. The rest of my family was there too, but they'd been in the same boat and understood my fatigue enough to leave me to a routine of sleeping in and long afternoons lying on the sand.

The first note appeared on Boxing Day. After Christmas lunch I'd come down to the beach for a swim, as I'd also done the day before, the first of my leave. Our house was right on the water, with a little beach hut off to one side. My mother had insisted on the hut so that all our beach equipment—buckets and spades when we were younger, sun lounges and umbrellas as the family grew up—could be left there and not transferred inside, where sand might sully her carpets. It was a hot afternoon, and I had gone to the beach hut for an umbrella when I found the note, jammed into the U of the padlock. *To the girl with blond hair and green bikini* it read, the words spelled out in a loose, attractive script. I unfolded it, glancing around. Only a lone geriatric dog walker was in sight. *Merry Christmas!* the note read. *Can I be your present?*

I wasn't sure whether to be flattered by the attention, or terrified that

I had acquired a stalker. On reflection I determined to be neither, and got on with reading my book.

But the next day there was another one. *You're too pretty to stay under that umbrella*, it said. *Can I tempt you away for a swim?* Foolishly, I blushed at the compliment, and again looked around. The beach was rocky, and relatively unpopular. A few families splashed nearby, but there was no sign of my anonymous suitor. I felt annoyed, and more than a bit silly as I scanned the horizon. Was this supposed to be a joke? Maybe tomorrow I'd stay at the house.

But when tomorrow came my curiosity got the better of me. Despite myself, my pulse surged as I approached the beach hut, noticing the now familiar white cardboard wedged into the lock. This time it was wrapped around a small bunch of flowers, pink daisies with faces as yellow as egg yolk. With eager fingers I opened the note, dropping the flowers into my bag. *Hello again, gorgeous*, it said, the tone confident and cheeky. *Can we meet just once? I'm single, straight and on the balcony of the house at the bottom of the cliff—the one with the Spanish roof. Just raise your arm if I can come down and say hi.* I looked up, panicked, knowing immediately the home that was meant. The sunlight was strong, and for a second I couldn't quite pick it out. Then something bright caught my eye, and I could just make out a man standing on the balcony. It was too far away to see much, but I could tell that he was smiling and had an arm raised, his golden hair catching the light like a jewel. Without thinking and despite my better instincts I raised my own arm. Then I stood there waiting, my heart pounding in my ears, while my future husband strolled down the beach toward me.

LUKE

·

Though that Easter break was only four days it felt like forever, the warmth of the sun wrapping my memories in a kind of opiate haze. I'm not a sentimental man, but I often find myself remembering that holiday. On the last morning Cress left around dawn so she could make it to her shift. Though she was quiet, her departure woke Cary, who took one look at the becalmed lake and insisted the three of us head out for a ski. The sun hadn't long been up by the time we got the boat in, and mist lingered on the water like guests reluctant to leave a good party. Kate had to be coaxed into the lake, grimacing as she lowered herself from the back of the boat.

"Now remember," Cary instructed as he lassoed the ski rope toward her, "weight on the back leg, then go with it. Okay?"

Kate just nodded, teeth chattering as ripples lapped at her ski. Cary resumed his seat, looked back over his shoulder, then threw the throttle forward. Kate shot up from the foam, the ski wavering beneath her. For a moment it veered wildly toward the wake and I groaned to myself, sure she had lost it again. But with a monumental effort Kate centered her weight, dug in, then finally leaned back as if there had never been any problem. Her features relaxed and she let out a whoop, frightening the cormorants paddling for fish on the edge of the lake, the flapping of their black wings as they took flight sounding like applause. Cary grinned and gave her the thumbs-up.

Kate made it around the lake then, growing in confidence, zigzagged back and forth across the wake, occasionally unsteady but always recovering. When her thin arms could finally hang on no longer she threw the rope in the air, making a quick curtsy on her ski before it sank beneath the water. We motored back to pick her up and found she was still smiling.

"It all just clicked," she said, thrilled, treading water as she pushed the ski toward me.

"You did look pretty good out there," I said as I plucked it from the lake, then extended my hand to help her into the boat.

"Good? I looked fantastic!" Kate exulted. Then she took my hand, but instead of climbing into the boat she gave a sudden sharp tug. Not expecting it, I was pulled off my feet and headfirst into the water, hearing her laugh as I went under. When I came up coughing she was halfway up the ladder, still laughing. I made a lunge to pull her back in, but she was too quick, wriggling out of my grasp as she scrambled up the rungs to safety, giggling. And that was it—literally, I guess I fell for her. Maybe not immediately, but that was the start of it. For the rest of the day and all the way home in the backseat of Cary's car I sat and tried not to think about the way Kate's thighs had slipped through my hands, like mercury rising up a thermometer.

TIM

•

I thought nothing Luke could do would ever surprise me, until the day he told me he was getting married. Don't get me wrong—Cressida is a wonderful woman: intelligent, refined and undeniably beautiful, and I couldn't fault his choice in any way. I actually even worried about her at first. I wondered how she'd cope when Luke's interest flagged, and anticipated missing her when they broke up, as they were sure to do. When Luke called after they had been seeing each other about six months and said he had some important news I just assumed it was over. But before I could get to the hows or whys he was telling me they were engaged, and asking me to be best man.

I suspect people think I'm jealous of Luke, though I swear that's not the case. I know that next to him I seem drab and unexciting, my mediocrity magnified by his own sheen and poise, like cheap buttons on an expensive suit. But appearances aren't important to me, and Luke's life is far too complicated for me ever to covet it. We are so different that I doubt we would have become friends if not thrown together by the private school we attended, whose classes were seated according to alphabetical order. It meant that Luke Stevens and Timothy Stevenson, who would never usually have moved in the same circles, became inseparable.

A lot of Luke is about surface, but it's a mistake to think that's all there is. By thirteen, Luke's face had already marked him out from the rest of us. Teachers paid him extra attention; he was regularly picked early for teams at recess, though he was no better at sports than anyone else. In tenth grade, when we started dancing lessons, it seemed as if the entire one hundred and twenty girls bused in from a nearby school had eyes only for him, a collective passion that occasionally erupted in name-calling and tears after class. Luke made the most of it—who wouldn't? But he never relied on it. He still did his homework. He still practiced for those teams, when he probably could have gotten away without it. And because we were seated next to each other he talked to me, though I was never in the popular group, and stayed my friend even after we left school.

Predictably, the wedding couldn't have been lovelier. Cressida's family has money but, more important, taste. On top of that, Cressida and Luke made a stunning couple, never more so than on that bright afternoon, when the glow coming off them was almost palpable. They were in love, but the most touching thing was how both thought they had done so well to be marrying the other. "Isn't she just gorgeous?" Luke whispered to me as Cressida came down the aisle, as humbled as if he were the woodcutter marrying the princess. "I still can't believe he chose me," confided his bride later, as we danced at the reception, her voice thrilled and awed in equal measure. If I was ever jealous of Luke, it was on that day. Not because, once again, he was getting what he wanted, or because I secretly lusted after Cressida. No, what I envied was the excitement that they both radiated, the certainty that they couldn't have done better.

And for that reason I expected it to last. God knows, Luke had been flighty with women. But then, he could afford to be, and it was no more than you'd expect from any good-looking male in his twenties. For all his conquests, though, Luke had never before admitted love.

In a funny way, I was kind of relieved when he told me he was getting married. It was exhausting keeping up with Luke's dalliances. Months went by when he would see and/or sleep with five, six or seven different women. I'd find myself having drinks with him and some Monica when I'd seen him the week before with a Kelly, after bumping into a bothered Belinda, moping because he hadn't called. Stupidly, I felt bad for those girls, and if I'm honest probably a little piqued that he invested so much time and energy in them. I had seen much more of him since he met Cressida, and I liked her a lot. She was calm, kind, dependable, and more adult than him, though a few years younger. I thought she was great: a smart choice, a good influence who would save him from AIDS or a palimony suit. I thought marriage would be the making of Luke. And I really did think that nothing he could do would ever surprise me again.

LUKE

•

I did love Cress, and I expected to be faithful to her. I wrote those notes because of how she looked when I spied her on the beach from my brother-in-law's home, indulging in a little voyeurism between courses on Christmas Day. That's pretty superficial, but it turned out I couldn't have picked better if I'd asked for résumés. She was sweet and smart, not just a doctor, but one who treated kids with cancer. I thought my mother would expire from delight when I told her.

I planned our meeting as carefully as any advertising campaign: the notes, the daisies, what I was wearing the day she looked up to the balcony. Later, with Kate, it was a lot more visceral, completely out of my control, which should have told me something. But with Cress I was stage-managing the play. She was the most beautiful woman I had ever seen, so I set out to woo her, guessing that she was the type to be won over with patience, not passion. Years of practice give you an instinct. Three days later I kissed her for the first time in her parents' beach hut, surrounded by rotting spades and damp towels, the smell of seaweed and the ocean thick in my nostrils.

And then the crowning achievement on that conjured résumé: she was still a virgin. I was almost tempted to tell my mother that too, so pleased was I. Though I didn't marry her for it, Cressida's virginity appealed. I've never subscribed to the try-before-you-buy theory, and I knew enough about sex to understand that if you love someone the physical stuff will be commensurate, at least while the love lasts. Of course, love is no prerequisite for good sex, and I'd also learned that. But it's crazy to think that you could be mad about someone and then incompatible in the sack. The chemistry comes first, and well before you take off your clothes. I truly didn't care if she'd had other men before me. I'd had other women and that didn't mean a thing—sex is just sex, not something to be saved or traded like shares. But I think it was the whole mythology of the virgin that appealed—the integrity and strength it implied, the way it made my choice of her seem even more astute.

So I was quite prepared to wait for Cress in that regard. Truth be told, the anticipation was a turn-on, abstinence being about the only sexual technique I hadn't tried. It wasn't complete chastity—I couldn't have borne that—just enough of the taste to make me crave the whole meal. Once we were engaged it seemed we might as well wait, and I thought we'd come to some sort of understanding. I'd kiss and tease and fondle; she'd respond to a point, then push me away. It drove me wild. No one had ever pushed me away before. Each time I tried to get a little further, sure that she would put the brakes on, arousing us both in drawn-out, months-long foreplay. It was all building up to one hell of a wedding night when, two evenings before the big day, she suddenly gave in. I was so used to her stopping things that I just kept going, and before we knew it that was that.

To be honest, I think we were both a little disappointed. Not by the sex, but the fact that it had happened: my climax was an anticlimax. And then there was the question of contraception. I hadn't used it, and I assumed Cress hadn't either—it wasn't as if she had ever needed it before. I spent the entire day leading up to our wedding worried about becoming a father rather than anticipating being a husband. I knew Cress wanted kids—of course she did, with her job—and I supposed I wanted them too, just not yet, or anything even approximating yet.

By our rehearsal that evening I couldn't bear it.

"You look nervous," said Tim, when I met him at the church.

"You don't know the half of it," I muttered grimly as he steered me inside.

At the far end of the church Cressida was laughing with her bridesmaids. In a floral-print dress and wearing no makeup, she looked about twelve years old. For a second I felt a stupid urge to turn and run.

"You're doing the right thing," Tim reassured me. "Heck, if I meet anyone half as good as—"

"I'm scared I've gotten her pregnant," I hissed, cutting him off midfantasy. Even through my panic I almost laughed at his expression. Tim must have had sex by now, I thought, but you'd never know it.

"How?" he asked, loudly enough to make a bridesmaid turn. I just rolled my eyes. Perhaps he hadn't after all.

"Hello, hubby," said Cress, almost skipping over and taking my arm. She looked flushed, and I wondered if she felt all right. Before I could kiss her, the minister cleared his throat and asked us to kneel. We mouthed words after him for twenty minutes, then approached the altar to practice signing the register.

"Cress, last night . . ." I whispered over the organ's drone.

"Was perfect," she finished for me, giggling, "even if it means I can't wear white tomorrow."

"Did you use anything?" I demanded, aware even as I did so how bald the words sounded.

"What?" she replied dreamily, practicing her new signature. My name looked alien coming after hers.

I was opening my mouth to ask again when the priest indicated we should proceed back down the aisle of the church, and the moment was lost. Anyway, what could I do? Cress was so excited that I didn't have the heart to push it. The odds were low, I told myself. Cress shouldn't have her big day spoiled by my panic.

I needn't have worried. Driving home after drinks with the wedding party, Tim revealed that he'd overheard the bridesmaids chatting as Cress and I pretended to sign the registry. One of them had remarked that Cress had lost weight, putting it down to prenuptial nerves. The other had agreed, adding that she'd probably been lucky not to gain any, given that she had recently gone on the pill. I felt ridiculously relieved—relieved and ridiculous. Of course Cress would have done something like that. She was a doctor, after all, as well as being one of the most organized and efficient people I knew. I stared out the window, cursing myself for overreacting.

"Can I ask why it mattered so much?" Tim said, choosing his words carefully as he steered around a parked car. "I mean, even if the timing wasn't ideal, you are still getting married."

He was right, but I didn't know myself.

CRESSIDA

•

After our wedding I called in to the hospital. Not to work, though Luke joked that I would no doubt get talked into drawing some blood or doing a discharge, and end up missing the reception. No, I had promised a number of my patients that I would come in so they could see me in my wedding dress. Little girls love the notion of a wedding, of the handsome prince on horseback and a happily-ever-after, particularly when their own likely ever-afters are so bleak. My bridesmaids came in too, with some confetti for the children to sprinkle and a pretend wedding cake my sisters had made, iced in pink and white and topped with silver balls. Luke begged off, saying he had things to organize at the reception. I didn't mind—I know he can't bear the smell of hospitals, though I have to say I've never noticed it. It was probably better for the girls that way: imagination is usually far less disappointing than reality. For a start, he didn't have a white horse.

I'd experienced a disappointment myself just a couple of days before, when I'd finally lost my virginity. Luke never pressured me about sex. I knew he desired me, but when I admitted my inexperience he seemed intrigued, charmed. I would have given in much earlier if he'd really wanted, but he always seemed to draw back the moment any real heat arose between us.

When it did happen it wasn't what I'd expected, though I'd had twenty-seven years and a medical degree to help me prepare. It was clumsy and rushed, more awkward than I'd ever anticipated. I didn't know if I was meant to help guide him into me, or lie as still as I could. I didn't know how I should move or how long it should take or quite how much mess there was going to be afterward. For all that, though, it was wonderful. I felt in some primal way that now I belonged to Luke forever, that by entering me he had become me. I understood why marriages were void without consummation, and the power in the act that for centuries had made it taboo for the unwed. Luke, of course, had more experience, but I could swear he felt the same. After all, it was our first time with each other, and on that basis we were equal. It wasn't what I expected; it was much, much better.

I'm sure some of the bridesmaids felt a bit silly at the hospital, but I was walking on air. People turned to look at me in the corridor; nurses I worked with dabbed their eyes. Usually I'm not one for attention, but I have to admit I enjoyed that hour at work. The best part of all was the children. I think they truly believed I was a fairy princess; even the boys were edging over to touch my gown or stroke the pearls sewn onto my veil. One little girl who was finishing a round of chemotherapy asked if I could grant wishes, but seemed happy to accept a slice of wedding cake instead. Her mother smiled at me, and told her daughter to put it under her pillow, so she would dream of her future husband. I left the hospital light-headed with joy, and with no more need of dreams. I had my husband, my prince. My happily-ever-after was just beginning.

CARY

•

Once I'd popped the question Kate didn't muck around. The next morning she went out and chose her own ring, having asked me in passing over breakfast if I wanted to come. I had a paper to prepare for work, so I declined, assuming that we'd go another day instead. But when I got back from the hospital that evening she handed me a small emerald-green box.

"I hope you like it," she said offhandedly, not really meeting my eyes. Then she wandered off to make a cup of coffee, as if the whole thing were merely a tedious detail.

For a second I was confused, never imagining she'd have selected anything without me. Hell, it had taken her five weeks to choose the color of her new car, and by the time that was decided she had changed her mind about the make and model as well. Kate's the sort of woman who gets dressed at least twice before leaving for work, four or five times for a big date or important meeting. On the days I got home before her I'd find discarded outfits stepped out of in the hall and bathroom, a litter of shoes kicked under the bed in haste. My house was never as neat once Kate moved in.

She came back with the coffee, steam curling in her hair. "Well?" she asked shyly, leaning up against the door frame. I opened the box. Against the mossy velvet, stones sparkled like small fires, like the eyes of a wild creature. Opals. Had I had a chance to think about it, I would have chosen a diamond, something hard and bright and indestructible. I guess it would have been a solitaire, on a plain band, something beautiful without being flashy. Something, I now saw, altogether too pedestrian and impersonal. Instead Kate had gone for opals: luminescent, moody opals. Even as I took the ring from the box the colors shifted, subdued one minute, shimmering the next.

"Isn't it gorgeous?" Kate said, swooping on the ring like a magpie.

"It's not what I would have chosen," I admitted. Seeing a frown begin, I quickly added, "It's a lot more beautiful."

"I knew it!" she crowed, holding her hand up to the light. "Tell the truth—you wouldn't have gotten around to it for weeks, would you? And when you did you wouldn't have looked past diamonds." Her words were mocking and affectionate in equal parts, and she leaned across to kiss me as she spoke. "Lucky I took matters into my own hands then."

Lucky indeed—my choice would have been sure to disappoint. In my defense I pointed out that things were unfolding far more rapidly than I could ever have expected. Twenty-four hours earlier I hadn't even thought about getting married, yet now I had a fiancée and she had an engagement ring. I was impressed by Kate's choice, but something irked me too. For more than three years I'd loved this girl, slept and laughed and fought with her. I thought I knew her, every intricate, irrational facet, and yet I would have gotten it wrong if I'd chosen her ring. It wasn't just that, though. Why couldn't she have waited for me to come shopping with her, or even to propose, for that matter? Why did it all have to be so impetuous?

KATE

•

"Seventeen," I told him, after some quick mental calculation. There was silence. Outside, a light rain started to fall on the slate roof of Cary's house.

"Seventeen?" he asked. Though it was too dark to see I felt him sit up in bed. "Are you sure?"

"Well, eighteen now, I suppose," I replied, wishing we were at my place. We'd been going out for about three months, but almost invariably ended up staying at his house, which was bigger and had more food in the fridge. My own roof was tin. I loved lying under it at night when the rain was falling, the staccato patter of small drops and gurgle of water in the congested gutters lulling me to sleep. Cary's roof was mute, and I imagine the spouting was cleaned regularly.

"And I'm number eighteen?" he persisted.

"Eighteen you are." I giggled, sleepy despite the lack of aqueous sound effects. "Does that get you the key to the door? Or do I keep that for number twenty-one?"

"Kate!" he protested, reaching for the light. I tried to stop him, but wasn't quick enough. Unrelenting glare filled the room.

I covered my eyes, though not before I'd seen the aghast expression on his face.

"What?"

"Eighteen! That's a whole bloody football team."

"So it is." I was struck by the image, imagining my ex-lovers lined up for a team photograph, arms oiled and crossed, shoulders dipped menacingly toward the camera. The thought made me smile. "I wonder what position you'd be? You're not really the full-forward type . . . maybe a wing. Can you run?"

"Don't sound so pleased, for God's sake."

"Why not?" I asked, cuddling into him with my eyes still tightly shut.

"It just seems an unseemly number of . . . partners, that's all."

"Well, you asked. How many have you had then?" Suddenly curious, I peeped up through my fingers.

"Not *that* many, that's for sure," he said petulantly, staring straight ahead.

"How many?"

"Enough," he mumbled.

"How many?"

"Five," he said, then looked over at me as if he'd just revealed he had AIDS or liked country music.

"Five's okay," I said, covering my eyes again. "Turn out the light."

"Okay? It's not even a third of your total."

"It's enough for a basketball team. Besides, you seem to know what you're doing." I meant the comment as a joke, a compliment, but his face flushed and for a second I feared he was taking me seriously.

"Still," I went on quickly, "there's a lot you can learn, so let's get started."

I rolled over on top of him and kissed the faint freckles lurking above the bridge of his nose.

"Hey," he protested, "I'm not finished talking."

"I am, though," I said, turning off the light. Cary tried to stop me but instead knocked over a stack of journals piled on his bedside table. They clattered to the floor, bringing the lamp down with them. With a great show of self-restraint he didn't even jump up to retrieve them. Not immediately, anyway.

I'm still not quite sure what bothered Cary more: the actual number of my lovers or the fact that I'd had more than him. I hate that question anyway. What does it matter, as long as you're both healthy and taking precautions and not messed up in the head about the whole thing? Still, when Cary asked I wasn't as wary as I should have been. I really liked him—really, *really* liked him—and so I wanted to be honest. I've lied about sex before, and it never works out. There are some things you can lie about, but sex isn't one of them. Sooner or later with sex you lose your composure, drop your guard and then it's too late to pretend. *So that doesn't really do it for her. So he does like it if I dress like that.*

The other thing was that Cary was four years older than me. Ergo, he probably assumed we would have at least been competitive in the numbers stakes, though I wasn't surprised that I was so far out in front. Unlike me, Cary's quite shy. He warms up beautifully, but he is a slow starter, and he's not much good at making the first move. Years after we met he confessed that he'd been quite taken aback that I slept with him on our first date, and left to his own devices would have waited at least a month before trying his luck.

"Our second date," I corrected him. "I didn't sleep with you at the Cup."

"Of course not," he'd replied, looking slightly shocked. "We'd have hardly gotten away with it at a racecourse."

I didn't tell him, but I'd gotten away with worse. In the stands during a rock concert. At the courthouse, with a guy I met on jury duty. A racecourse would have been quite manageable.

But while I wasn't going to deny it, I wasn't necessarily proud of my tally. Most of it was fun, but some of it was silly, or dangerous, or because I was drunk. Even worse, at least twice it had been out of politeness, so I could get home or go to sleep without a scene. The actual number was immaterial; how many of those I had genuinely cared about would have been a better question.

So when Cary said five I was perfectly fine with it, even if he wasn't. One would have been fine, fifty would have been fine, but five was just right. Knowing Cary, as I was beginning to at that time, he would have found out their full names and where they lived, something that couldn't necessarily be said of all my conquests. He would have seen that they got home safely, sent flowers or called the next day. He would have made sure, as far as a man ever can, that they enjoyed the experience as much as he did. Or if he didn't enjoy it, he would have let them down gracefully, tactfully, not let the phone go silent for weeks or start avoiding their eyes at the office. Five was too few not to have exercised some care in selection, some restraint, some integrity. Maybe I'm romanticizing things, but I think not. Five was perfect. Besides, I meant it when I said he knew what he was doing.

CARY

·

For all my initial reluctance I enjoyed marriage more than I expected: saying "my wife" in conversation, coming home to a place where she always was. We'd lived together for about a year before Kate pushed me to propose, but for some reason being Mr. and Mrs. made it different. Kate got rid of most of my bachelor furniture, planted an herb garden and painted the kitchen. When I asked her why she had never bothered with these domestic improvements before the wedding she hesitated and then blushed, something my wife rarely did.

"I wanted to be sure it was worth the effort," she admitted. "That I wasn't going to go off you and then end up not living here anyway."

Note that she hadn't allowed for the possibility that I might go off her, as she put it. I only laughed, used to Kate's forthright ways by now. At least she was honest.

My father adored Kate from the moment they met. I wasn't surprised—Kate was drawn to men, and vice versa. With the exception of Sarah, all her close friends were male. My mother, however, was more reserved, suspicious of Kate's small frame and profession, worried about her own prospects of becoming a grandmother.

"She's certainly different from your other girlfriends," she told me as I scraped the plates after our first dinner together. "Opinions on everything! And working with bones—what sort of job is that?"

"She's an anthropologist, Mom," I replied, though Kate had already explained this.

"It's too creepy for words, if you ask me—handling bits of dead people all day."

"They've been dead for centuries," I replied calmly. "She cleans the bones, figures out where they're from and what they can tell her. It's tricky work."

My mother sniffed, unimpressed. "She's not a career woman, is she? I should have guessed that she wasn't the sort to be burdened by a family."

That was my mother all over—one minute doubting Kate's suitability as a partner, the next bemoaning the fact that she wouldn't be providing grandchildren. We heard my father laughing loudly at something Kate was saying in the other room.

"Well, I hope you know what you're doing, because you'll have your hands full with that one," she said, snapping the oven door shut as she removed the pudding.

I didn't know, I wanted to tell her, but that was half the fun.

Fortunately the relationship improved from there. Kate learned to tone down her views and her voice when we visited, and my mother softened once she realized Kate was a permanent fixture. When I called to tell her we were engaged she seemed genuinely delighted, albeit as cautious as ever.

"I hope it's not going to cost you a fortune," she warned after some teary congratulations. "Girls these days have such romantic notions."

This from a woman who named her only son after a movie star.

"It's okay, Mom," I reassured her. "It won't be a big do."

That was my hope, anyway—but, of course, I hadn't reckoned with Kate.

KATE

·

"Why him?" Sarah asked me once, after Cary and I had been together for almost two years. For a moment I was offended, thinking she was doubting my choice. But her face, when I turned to confront her, was as guileless as porcelain, her voice tinged with interest, not judgment.

I sighed. It was a valid question, so why was it so hard to answer?

"Because I love him?" I ventured, the words sounding insipid even to my ears.

"Zzzt," Sarah replied, imitating a buzzer. "Not enough information. Why do you love him?"

We were having lunch in Grattan Street, opposite the museum where I worked, sipping our coffees at an outdoor café in the March sunshine. I know it was March, because after four blissfully quiet months the surrounding tables were filled with students from the nearby university, and it had taken forever for our meals to arrive.

"Look at them," I said to Sarah. "That was us three years ago. Do they realize how good they've got it?"

"Good?" she asked, glancing around. "We had to write a thesis, remember? And study for exams and not earn money and take a compulsory statistics course."

She was right, and I'd been as keen to finish with school as the rest of our group for just those reasons. But, perversely, I wanted to argue with her.

"Don't be so negative," I said. "Remember how we'd go to the pub after lectures, and copy each other's notes so we could sleep in, and sunbathe on the South Lawn in the summer?"

"It had its moments," Sarah replied, setting her cup down. "But you still go to the pub, as far as I can tell. And now you can afford to without worrying about the rent. Besides, from what I remember you spent at least half those nights having screaming matches with Jake, or flirting with someone else to make him jealous."

"Not half of them."

"Near enough." She shrugged. "That's not what we were talking about anyway. Tell me about Cary."

What could I say? Sarah knew him pretty well by this time, but that wasn't what she was asking. Was it serious, she wanted to know, and what about him in particular made me stay, kept me interested? It was the same thing I had asked her when it had dawned on me that she and Rick were going to last, just as Jake and I were not.

"He's sweet," I ventured. "And kind, and thoughtful."

"So's your father. Not good enough. What else?"

I thought for a while.

"He cooks me dinner and picks me up from work if it's raining."

Sarah looked unimpressed, and I was uncharacteristically stuck for words. Instead of enumerating Cary's many good points, I suddenly felt depressed. The sight of all the university students had made me feel old, had reminded me of Jake and that things fall apart no matter how much you wish they wouldn't. Ridiculously, I felt tears bite at the corners of my eyes.

"Come on," Sarah said softly, catching my mood. "What does he do that you love him for? Something your father wouldn't."

"He runs a bath for me when I'm tired." I sniffed. "And he cleans it up afterward, and he has the sense not to bother me while I'm in there."

"Good," said Sarah, nodding her head. "And . . . ?"

"He doesn't go to sleep straight after sex. He buys me lingerie, but not the slutty sort with bits cut out. He takes my side when his mother gets to be too much."

"That's important."

"He lets me keep tampons in his bathroom cupboard without getting all squeamish about it. Remember how uptight Jake was about that sort of stuff?"

"Sure do," she said, smiling. "Any more?"

I was warming to the task now. "He buys me popcorn at the movies even though he doesn't eat it himself. He apologizes when we have a fight. And if I read a book and adore it, he'll read it to find out why, even though I know he prefers those journals."

After a moment I added, "He holds my head when I drink too much and throw up. I even threw up in his birdbath once and he didn't get upset."

Sarah laughed, and I suddenly noticed that the students around us had disappeared.

"He makes me feel beautiful," I said quietly. "And kind of dazzling, as if he can't believe he has me." Then I took a deep breath for the biggest confession, one I was only just admitting to myself. "He looks after me. He strokes my hair when he thinks I'm asleep. He worries about me."

"They all sound like perfect reasons to me," Sarah said, proffering a tissue in case I was going to burst into tears again. But I didn't need it. I felt light-headed, elated, justified. Cary was different from my previous boyfriends: a lot quieter, more introspective and reserved. Though they knew he was nice enough, every so often I sensed that my friends and family wondered exactly what it was I saw in him, how his smiling steadiness could interest me after the crashing highs and lows of my relationship with Jake. Sarah hadn't asked to be convinced, but I saw that she was nonetheless, and the validation warmed me.

"He picks up after himself," I continued. "He remembers our anniversary without my nagging about it for a week in advance."

"Okay, that will do. I have to get back to work," Sarah said, pulling on her jacket.

"He rings his parents regularly. He knows that foreplay doesn't just mean undoing my bra."

"Enough!" Sarah laughed, pretending to hurry away.

"I'll e-mail you the rest," I called after her. "He's been a best man three times! He's kind to small animals!" The waitress was staring at me, but I didn't care. Her boyfriend probably expected her to wear crotchless panties.

CRESSIDA

•

I love hospitals. I'm sure that's my father's influence—how could it not be, when I remember accompanying him on ward rounds when I was only four? Still, I suppose I could have rebelled, the way children of alcoholics often turn into teetotalers, or vice versa. I didn't. I love the buzz and hum of hospitals, their pulse and throb. I suppose stock markets or large manufacturing plants have a similar level of activity and purpose, but somehow it's different when actual lives are at stake. A major teaching hospital has more energy than a theme park, and I've always found that exciting.

I realize this isn't normal. The only other person I've ever met who truly understands this is Cary. We got to talking about it once when we were meant to be discussing my research. He told me that he'd fallen off a tractor when he was eight, then been taken to the local base hospital for X-rays.

"The minute I was wheeled through the sliding glass doors, I was hooked," he told me, smiling bashfully and fiddling with his cuffs rather than meeting my eyes. "Everyone was rushing around, but they all knew exactly what they were doing and where they were going. It was so busy. Not like the farm, where you might sit on the harvester all day, or spend hours fixing the fence in the front paddock." He finally looked up. "It was kind of thrilling, you know?"

I did know, and for a moment I felt a sharp pull toward this self-effacing man. He wasn't dazzling, like Luke, but he was kind and patient, an involved and encouraging supervisor. He was gentle too. If my ideas were off track, or I hadn't thought something through properly, he'd never scold, or even correct. "Maybe," he'd say, where other supervisors might have stifled laughter or sighed to themselves, "but have you thought about it like this?" He'd guide, not push; suggest rather than tell. I knew he was married. I'd never met his wife, but I often thought she was a lucky woman.

Yet when I did finally see them together, it was Cary who acted as if he were the lucky one. Oh, Kate clearly cared for him; she was always touching him or teasing him, rumpling his hair or placing a hand on his thigh. But then she'd be off again, jumping up to call out to someone across the bar, or bent laughing with a girlfriend in a corner, never noticing the way his eyes followed her around the room. I mentioned it to Luke once.

"Did you see Kate tonight? She was everywhere." We were lying in bed, dissecting an evening out, as couples often do.

"She's certainly sociable," he mumbled against my shoulder, arms warm across my abdomen. "Particularly when she's had a few drinks."

"When hasn't she had a few drinks? But she's like that regardless. Sometimes I wonder if I should talk to Cary about putting her on Ritalin."

Luke laughed, though more in surprise at my criticism than anything else. "That's not like you, Cress," he said.

"Well, she is kind of . . . flighty, isn't she?" I tried to explain myself. "You wouldn't want her as your heart surgeon, for example. I'd be worried that if something more interesting came up she'd be straight out the door, the retractors still in your chest."

Luke laughed again. "True. She'd look good in a nurse's uniform, though."

I stiffened and he stopped. I'd seen him flirt with her and I was used to that, but there was no reason to be doing so mentally in our bed.

Yet, I did like Kate. Those days we had at Cary's house on the lake I actually got to know her a bit, we were left together so often when skiing, or while the boys fished. I'd never had the whole focus of her company before, and I enjoyed it more than I expected. She was genuinely funny, genuinely interested and interesting. I found myself opening up to her, knowing she wasn't going to suddenly abandon me midsentence; to be honest, I think she paid more attention to me, knowing I wasn't going to get paged away.

One day, while we lay on the beach, Kate asked if she could do my hair. I never usually bothered with it much—it was either down over my shoulders or up in a bun, with few variations. Not seeming to notice my hesitation, Kate rolled over and began stroking it, remarking on its color and texture. I think I flinched, but Kate can be persuasive. She went and got her brush and some gear, and for the next half hour I surprised myself by luxuriating in the experience. Her small hands were cool and sure, as deft and careful with my hair as with any artifact. While she weaved my locks into a complicated French braid she hummed and talked . . . gossip, something about the book she was reading, a few bars of a popular song: chatter that demanded nothing other than my being there. I felt totally relaxed for the first time in months. Later that day, when Luke saw my hair, he loved it, and I almost loved her for it. For an hour that afternoon she'd been the big sister I might have had if mine hadn't always been studying.

We saw even more of them after that Easter. Kate was incurably sociable, always marshaling us into catching up at the movies or a bar, or ringing to invite herself over when Cary was away and the silence of their house got too much. I missed Cary on those nights. He balanced our foursome, and I always felt easier when we were all together. Without him there the talk grew more personal, more daring, Kate and Luke trading jibes at lightning speed or leaning across me to banter with each other. I could barely get a word in, though they seemed to enjoy having me there as an audience.

Similarly, I know Luke met up with Kate and Cary when I was at work. Why not? I should have been pleased he wasn't waiting at home, watching the clock, maybe sulking a little if my shift went overtime. I bet Kate loved those nights. She craved attention; two men hanging on her every word would have been her idea of paradise.

When I found myself thinking that way I'd feel bad. I did like Kate, and it wasn't as if I didn't trust her. I was just a bit wary. She was never malicious, but she was careless. Kate is the sort of person who is always forgetting where they put their drink down at a party and wandering off to get another, so that by the end of the night they've left a trail of half-empty glasses in their wake, and don't even notice the wastage. I wondered if she misplaced friends as easily.

KATE

·

And then we got married. Actually, first we moved in together and, when this still hadn't ruined things, a year later I nagged him into marrying me. To tell you the truth I was surprised I had to ask, and a bit put out that my romantic fantasies of bended knee, sparkling gems and declarations of undying love never came true. But delayed gratification is not my thing— once I make up my mind I hate mucking around. Cary, on the other hand, prefers every possible outcome to be explored and quantified, like the genetic profiles he constructs for the expectant parents who consult him in his job. And I still got my sparkling gems and his undying love, so I can hardly complain.

We were married in October under a pewter sky, which opened as soon as we had said our vows. I'd been worrying about the weather all week, but on that day there could have been a cyclone and I wouldn't have noticed. Cary cried when I came down the aisle, and again as he made his speech. Otherwise he smiled from start to finish, seeming to forget his insistence that he couldn't possibly enjoy such a large wedding. That's the main part I remember, and that it was still pouring when we consummated the thing hours later. The wind picked up, and I think there was hail. But inside, wrapped in our marriage bed and Cary's arms, I felt warm and protected and safe.

LUKE

•

I had been married ten minutes when I first saw Kate. At the time I didn't even know her name, and wouldn't find it out till the photos came back. Still, I don't suppose I'm the first groom to encounter a surfeit of strangers at his nuptials. Weddings are for women, and I'd happily abdicated responsibility to Cress and her mother pretty much from the moment I'd proposed. Of course, Cress was too busy at work to do much more than look at a few magazines, so I suppose I should be grateful that someone was available to talk to caterers and fold napkins.

Anyway, we'd said our vows and paraded back down the aisle. I remember feeling as you do after anesthesia—everything was exceedingly bright and excessively loud and happening in slow motion and double speed at the same time. It was April, a beautiful autumn day, and as they threw open the doors at the back of the church so we could stand on the steps and greet our guests, I couldn't believe the colors outside. The blue of the late-afternoon sky, the russet of the leaves just starting to turn, the gold of Cress's hair and the unfamiliar ring on her left hand. I'd put that ring there, but I had no memory of doing so. The photographer called instructions, Tim jerked at my tie, and nothing seemed real. I was elated, triumphant, but everything unfolded as if I were an observer, not there at the center.

Cary came over to offer his congratulations, kissing Cressida and complimenting her on her dress. At the time Cress was doing her fellowship project under his supervision, and we'd met a few times when I'd come to meet her after work. He'd never said much, but seemed nice enough. Cress, anyhow, was grateful for his assistance and had insisted we invite him to the wedding.

"Really?" I'd asked when she told me. "But I don't even know him."

"That doesn't matter. He's been such a help that I just want to thank him."

"Are you sure this is the best way? Most guys would prefer a case of beer," I said—astutely, as it turned out. "Besides, after you've finished your research you'll probably never see him again, and he's hardly going to want to get all dressed up to spend the night with strangers."

"I'll see him again," said Cress, adding his name to the list we were arguing over. "I've known him since I was a student, on and off. That's longer than I've known you." She looked up and smiled, a happy smile full of excitement and plans and confetti. "And there will be plenty of people there from the hospital he knows. Plus his wife, of course."

Now the man in question was shaking my hand. We hardly knew each other, so it was a brief exchange, just time enough for me to glance at a dark-haired girl behind him and mentally process that it must be the wife Cress had mentioned. Then someone else was pushing forward to congratulate me and the church bells were ringing, notes splashing over one another like children playing in puddles. Cary and his wife had moved on, and I couldn't hear what anyone was saying.

Fortunately, as the night went on my numbness wore off, and after a few beers I was thoroughly enjoying myself. Cressida looked astounding, ethereal yet regal, the tiara that held her veil resembling a crown. If such a thing is possible she looked almost too beautiful, and I was afraid to touch her until after the photos were over for fear of disturbing the picture perfection of it all. Tim gave a mercifully bland speech, proposed the toast and then the dancing began. Five or so numbers in I was steering a bridesmaid around the floor when I spotted Cary's wife dancing with a colleague of Cressida's. She was wearing cream, which was perhaps why I noticed her. Women hardly ever wear white to a wedding—perhaps they think it's reserved for the wedding party, or they're afraid of being compared with the bride. Cary's wife obviously had no such reservations. Her dress had a slit in the back, and the colleague, quite drunk, was trying to slip his hand into it. She was laughing and shaking her head, but not removing herself from his grasp, or even wriggling away from that hand. I don't know where Cary was; I didn't see him dance with her once that night.

After the requisite five hours our reception was over, and the guests formed a circle to say their good-byes. I'd strenuously objected to this bit, but for once Cress had been adamant. She wanted to speak to everyone who had come to the wedding, she told me, and this might be her only chance to do so. I ended up doing the same thing, kissing all those maiden aunts on prickly cheeks, exchanging pleasantries with relatives and partners I would no doubt never see again. When I got around to the hospital side of the circle Cary did the right thing and thanked me for the invitation. His wife was a little less formal, regarding me quizzically when I went to shake her hand.

"So," she said, laughing, as if this were all some great big joke. "Have a nice life, I guess."

Her candor was so disarming that I had to laugh too. Then Cary joined in, and just for a second the three of us stood there, laughing together, understanding but still enjoying the artifice of it all.

Six weeks and a honeymoon later the photos came back. Cress and I had had a great time vacationing in Malaysia on a tea plantation, and already the wedding seemed to have taken place years ago. It was almost a shock to recognize Cary's wife, still laughing, in a group photo of Cressida's medical friends.

"Who's that?" I asked, sliding the photo over to Cress, who was agonizing over what should go in the album.

"Umm . . . Cary's wife. You know, my supervisor," she replied distractedly. "Kate, I think her name is."

"She seemed like fun," I ventured.

"Mmm, he's lovely too. Maybe when my project is finished I'll ask them over to dinner as a thank-you."

"I thought the wedding invitation was his thank-you?"

"That's not very personal, is it?" Cress asked. She had clearly forgotten our conversation before the big day. "And I've still got another six months or so to go, so I'll want to do something then."

I rolled my eyes, but not so Cress could see. My short experience of marriage had already taught me that sometimes it's just easier to hold your tongue.

CARY

•

As a student, Cressida was a bit of a disappointment. Not to Steve, of course, who practically started panting when I told him she'd be working with us for a while. I'd also been pleased when she'd approached me for supervision on her fellowship project, though for different reasons. I remembered Cressida as a conscientious and careful medical student, and looked forward to her bringing those qualities to our research.

It wasn't that she was no good: far from it. Her lab work was thoughtfully designed and carried out, her reports turned in on time. In the years since I'd first attended meetings with her Cressida had developed a textbook clinical manner: concerned without being overinvolved, able to mix inquiry and empathy in equal parts. She certainly had the skills for the work; it was just that her mind was elsewhere. The timing was to blame, I guess. When I agreed to her doing her project in the department she was going out with Luke. By the time she actually started at the beginning of the new academic year they were engaged. Then came the wedding and the honeymoon and weekends spent house-hunting rather than writing. In the end, what should have taken six months dragged on for over twelve, till we were both sick to death of it. I think we published the results, though I can't remember. Funny how important that seemed at the time.

Actually, it bothered Steve more than it bothered me. "What *is* she doing?" he'd moan whenever Cressida's weekly lit review was a day late on his desk, or a meeting had to be canceled so she could attend a dress fitting.

"You're too soft on that girl," he told me more than once, with an irritation that I suspected was owed to pique that she was so transparently crazy about someone else than any concern for our tenure. I don't think I even replied. For one, I enjoyed having Cressida around the place. She was smart and pretty and a welcome change after years spent hunched over microscopes with only Steve for company. And she was so darn happy that it made you smile just to see her. When we weren't discussing genetics it was Luke, Luke, Luke. "I'll leave you two to pick out your china patterns," Steve would mutter in disgust, stalking out whenever conversation veered toward the conjugal. Cressida would look momentarily abashed, then carry on with an apologetic smile.

I knew how she felt. Kate and I had been together for about six years at that stage, married for two, and listening to Cressida's chatter took me back to the early days of our own relationship. I'd remember those first few months of living together, the excitement I'd feel as my headlights picked out our house at the end of the day. How I'd find myself accelerating into the driveway in my eagerness to get inside. How I'd hurry up the path beside the lemon tree, driven by a desire that was part sexual, but mostly just a need to see Kate again. My key would fumble in the lock and then like a child playing tag I'd be home, safe, with the world shut out behind me. Inside Kate would be humming as she prepared dinner or flicked through a magazine, and she'd look up laughing at my abrupt entrance, then kiss me with lips that tasted of the apple she'd been eating or the basil she'd just added to our dinner. Cressida was now caught up in the same manic delirium, but having been such a willing victim of it myself, how could I complain? In fact, I think I enjoyed the reminder. Half a decade later I was still very much in love, but I no longer sprinted up our garden path at the end of the day. That's no failing: I defy you to show me anyone who does. In my book, familiarity breeds content; love plateaus but is none the less for that. It has to, or no one would ever get any work done.

CRESSIDA

.•

My part should have ended there, at the hospital in my wedding gown. Maybe there could have been a postscript: two healthy children, respected in her profession, a long and happy marriage. But no more, and certainly not this. What could I possibly have done to deserve it?

· LUKE

·

It just happened, I swear. That's what I told Cress and the counselor, and I mean it. I admit there were a lot of lies, but that wasn't one of them. How else can you explain such a thing? Sure, I was attracted to Kate, but I've been attracted to plenty of other women before without feeling obliged to kiss them in the middle of a dance floor in full view of their husbands. Or my wife, for that matter. Of course, there was alcohol involved, and I tried to blame it on that: a stupid, drunken gaffe. I think Cress believed me— what choice did she have? I almost believed it myself. That is, until I saw Kate again and realized that there'd been no mistake.

CARY

•

Kate sparkles; I don't. She flirts; I don't. She dances; I don't. She's an extro-vert, and I'm not. But I wouldn't say I was introverted, just that I'm neu-tral, naturally quieter, Belgium to her Brazil. Apart from that, I've always thought we were pretty well matched. Water finds its own level, my father used to say, and I believe that. I mean, we knew what we were getting into—we were together for four years before marrying, and she was the one who forced the issue then. On some basic level we must have been suited. Up until that night I thought we were perfectly happy. Maybe not per-fectly, but more than most. Then suddenly she's kissing someone who isn't me. Is sparkling and flirting and dancing worth risking a marriage over?

KATE

·

What can I possibly say in my defense? That it was dark, that I was drunk or confused or premenstrual? That I was swept away by the music and the night and had no idea how it happened? No, I have no defense, but at least I can be honest. Of course it didn't "just happen." That's not to say I expected it, but I can't say I was surprised either. I knew Luke was attracted to me, though that was no big deal; in my experience, men like Luke are always attracted to someone. I was attracted to him too. Why wouldn't I be? He was beautiful, and our both being married didn't change that. Still, I could have pulled away. The signs were there. I could have stopped dancing, gone outside for some air or to find Cary. Could have, should have, but didn't. Didn't stop, didn't think, didn't want to.

TIM

·

I wasn't there, though I heard plenty about it. It was a hospital function: a doctor that Cressida knew marrying a doctor whom Cary was friendly with. I thought that was kind of sweet, though Luke pulled a face when he told me.

"Big mistake to marry someone in your own profession," he stated firmly, as if he'd majored in psychology and not creative sciences, whatever that is.

"Why?" I asked, no doubt naively.

"They're bound to end up competing with each other. And even if they don't, imagine being in the same place as your wife twenty-four hours a day."

I reiterated that I thought it was sweet. Besides, wasn't that the whole idea of marriage—to be together?

"Not that much," he said, rolling his eyes.

Don't get me wrong. I don't think Luke ever planned to cheat on Cressida, or saw it as an inevitability. On the contrary, having made up his mind to get married, I'm convinced he took his vows seriously, and intended to honor them. Luke is basically an honorable man. Yeah, he'd cheated on women before, but he'd never made promises to any of them, never said things he didn't mean. I'm sure he told them all they were beautiful or sexy or whatever it takes to get a girl into bed, but it wouldn't have gone further than that. Cressida, he revealed to me once, was only the second girl he had told he loved. The first was when he was seventeen. "Surely that doesn't count?" he had asked me, only half joking. "I wasn't even old enough to vote." I think Luke liked the idea that Cress was his only love, his grand passion. It made good copy.

Anyway, from what I understand, Luke, Cressida, Cary and Kate had met at Cressida's thank-you dinner for Cary, then gone away together at Easter. "Luke seems to really like this couple," Cressida had told me excitedly. I was pleased for her—I knew that wasn't the case with a lot of her friends. Over the next six months their names came up quite often in conversation: "Kate and Cary met us at the restaurant"; "We played tennis with Kate and Cary." Cressida threw Luke a surprise party for his birthday, and I was introduced to them there. Cary was reserved initially, Kate far less so. I noticed how Kate flirted with Luke, but by the end of the night she was also flirting with me, at least two of Luke's brothers-in-law, and even the caterer. Cary seemed both resigned and relaxed about it. I watched him over the course of the evening, saw how he always kept a subtle eye on her as she bounced from group to group—not, it seemed to me, out of jealousy or fear, but simply because that was where his gaze was drawn. The last hour they spent together, curled up like kids in the corner of a sofa. Kate was quieter, tired; Cary, stroking her shoulder, appeared to have absorbed some of her energy, and we talked and laughed until Cress threw us out. I liked them.

I met the four of them for drinks a few times after that. Then Luke invited me to a fund-raiser for the hospital where Cress worked—it was a trivia night, and he wanted me on their team. But by the time the evening arrived the two couples were no longer speaking.

KATE

•

I used to think that there should be a rule preventing people from marrying until they were over thirty. Before then, I reasoned, you couldn't appreciate it. Part of it was that you needed to see a bit of the world, experience different lovers and ways of loving, make sure that the grass wasn't greener elsewhere. But mostly, I thought, you needed to know yourself: who you were, what you needed, the things you couldn't live without and those you could. Thirty, it seemed, was long enough to have most of that worked out. Actually, I was twenty-nine and a half when I got married, but close enough.

I was thinking all this again as we stood around at the reception after Jane and Dan's wedding. To tell the truth, I was feeling pretty smug. Chances are it was the champagne, but I remember feeling immoderately happy. As I've said, I love weddings, so there was that: the chance to drink, dance and dress up, sentimental songs, public declarations of love. Then there was Cary, looking smart and kind of sexy in black tie, squeezing my hand while the happy couple made their vows, telling me I looked great before I'd even put on any makeup. Work was going well; we had our own home and lots of lovely friends. Often at weddings I can feel a bit jealous of the bride and groom, envying them the romance and excitement of the day, that newly married rush before it all settles back into the comfort zone. Not tonight, though. Tonight the comfort zone was feeling particularly, well, comfortable. Watching the newlyweds, who looked so young, I congratulated myself. I'd married well, at the right time, and for love. I was grown-up and centered and content. Now all I needed was another glass of champagne.

My high lasted right through dinner and the speeches, then deserted me abruptly when the dancing began. I love dancing and wanted to join in. It's awkward sometimes that Cary won't. Not can't, but won't—he's funny like that. Most of the time, Cary is the sweetest, most accommodating man I know, but when he makes up his mind about something, that's it. At our own wedding he made me scrap the bridal waltz altogether. So I resigned myself to watching the dancing instead. Maybe I was jealous that I couldn't be out there, or maybe it was just that the champagne was wearing off, but I started feeling melancholy. Unbeknownst to anyone, the newlyweds had taken tango lessons, and instead of the traditional stolid waltz, Latin rhythms snaked from the dance floor. All around me people were tapping their feet, jumping up from their chairs as if bitten, placing imaginary roses between their teeth. In the center of the floor, the bridal couple moved with confidence. They'd obviously practiced, for they danced beautifully. At the slightest pressure from Dan, Jane dipped; following her lead his arms spun or steadied her. Their feet met, touched, moved as if mirrored. Fingers converged, interlocked, then were released again. Together, apart, together, apart, their bodies turning instinctively toward each other at the end of each movement. I was spellbound. So engrossed, in fact, that I did not notice Luke's approach until he was right in front of me.

"Shall we?" he asked simply, extending a hand.

I accepted without replying, hungry to dance and for who knows what else.

I'd hardly seen Luke all night; we were at different tables. Still, he'd caught my eye once, smiled and winked in the church before the ceremony started. I'd winked back, then immediately regretted it. We weren't conspiring about anything. Remembering it now I felt uncomfortable in his arms, stiff and wrong-footed. But then the music started, and so did everything else.

CRESSIDA

·

I was in the ladies' room, reapplying my lipstick, when the two girls tottered in, giggling and shrieking. Drunk, I thought to myself, glancing in the mirror while I uncapped a cinnamon lip pencil.

"I mean, did you see her?" the shorter one was saying as they took up a position at the basin next to mine. "How she has the nerve to wear something like that with her figure I'll never know."

"She probably thinks it makes her look thinner," said the other, fluffing her hair, then sniffing covertly under one armpit.

"Yeah, well, it wasn't working. That blond guy she was throwing herself at couldn't have cared less."

"God, who can blame her, though?" said the sniffer. "He was a bit of all right."

My ears pricked up. I'm always overhearing conversations like this, and they inevitably turn out to be about Luke.

"I guess his attention was elsewhere. Did you see him just now? He was in the middle of the dance floor, kissing some girl."

"Probably his wife," said her friend, dousing herself with scent while her friend picked at her nail polish. "Lucky bitch."

"Hey, from the way he was kissing her I don't think it was his wife. Maybe he's not even married."

"I bet he is. Men like that always are." They both laughed, spitefully, then left, heels clattering on the faux-marble floor.

I finished with the lip pencil, then hunted in my purse for my lipstick. My heart was hammering and my throat was dry, but I made myself complete the job. There was no reason to rush out there. Luke surely wasn't the only attractive blond man at the wedding, and besides, he certainly wouldn't be kissing anyone. I unscrewed the lipstick, then glanced distractedly at the tube. Painful Passion it was called, the bluish red of venous blood. How did they come up with these names? My hands shook as I filled in my lips.

The girls were wrong about one thing: it wasn't the middle of the dance floor, but off to the left, in the shadow of some ridiculous potted palms. Still, it was Luke. I was so shocked that it took me a minute to realize whom he was kissing. Kate, with Cary nowhere to be seen, Luke clinging to her as if he were drowning. Or maybe it was the other way around. Whatever, it was definitely mutual and more than friendly. In fact, they almost looked as if they'd done it before, her dark head fitting smoothly under his fair one with none of the graceless fumblings that usually accompany first kisses.

Stupidly, I didn't know what to do. I guess I should have raced over and torn them apart, but I hate scenes, and I didn't want to draw any more attention to the whole horrible incident. Luke was kissing Kate. Kissing her as if he meant it, as my girlfriends would say, kissing her as if he weren't married, kissing her as he'd never kissed me in public.

I think I sat down, though I can't be sure. A minute went by, then another. Where was Cary? Why wasn't he breaking this up? I should have looked for him, but somehow I couldn't look away, riveted by the car crash that was suddenly my marriage. Eventually they stopped kissing, Luke opening his eyes abruptly as if he had been dreaming, blinking in the light, then spotting me instantly. He left Kate without a word and came straight to my side, but I was already on my feet.

"Get your coat. We're going," I ordered, searching in my purse for car keys rather than meeting his eyes. We left quickly, without saying goodbye. Halfway across the room I stumbled and he reached out to grab me, but I snapped my arm away as if he were poison. Over my shoulder I noted Kate still standing alone on the dance floor, looking foolish and lost.

LUKE

•

I was bored; that's why I danced with Kate. Cress was talking medicine with her doctor friends at our table; their partners were talking golf or getting drunk. I was ripe for a diversion and I found it: Kate alone and looking wistful on the opposite side of the floor.

I don't remember what she was wearing; I'm not sentimental like that. Blue, I think, though it should have been red. What I did notice as she stepped into my arms was that there was something bright caught in her eyelashes, glinting under the disco lights like traffic signals. I actually reached to brush it off, thinking it was stray confetti or a thread from her dress, but Kate caught my hand.

"Don't. It's meant to be like that," she said, unembarrassed. "It's mascara a friend gave me, with glitter in it. We don't go to many black-tie events, so I thought I'd make an effort." We started moving together in silence.

"I didn't realize it was going to be quite so obvious, though," Kate continued after a moment. "People keep coming up and touching it."

I laughed, and spun her hard. Kate was a good dancer and kept her feet, unfurling in a graceful circle from my fingertips. Of course she had realized the mascara would sparkle and attract attention—that was exactly why she had worn it. I was tipsy and told her so. She shrugged, smiling, not at all offended, and I felt a sudden rush of affection for her. Cressida had real beauty, the sort of looks that are all about bone structure and good breeding. She had no need for anything as obvious as glittery mascara, and would have scorned it as ridiculous. Kate, by contrast, was merely pretty. But she was also daring and vivid and there was a glow coming off her that was more than just iridescent makeup. Besides, those lashes really were surprisingly long, and she was right to highlight them. She must have felt me looking and tilted her face up. Did she mean for me to kiss her? So many women have lifted their faces to mine in just such a way that my response was reflexive. I kissed her, the tango music dying in my ears. Her mouth was soft and urgent and our feet continued to move in time, at least initially. Once I remembered Cress and went to draw away, or at least thought of it. But I couldn't seem to do so, trapped by the nip of a little eyetooth and Kate's hands on the nape of my neck.

CRESSIDA

•

We hardly talked on the way home from the wedding. I drove; I always do after functions. Luke likes to drink, whereas I'm not fussed, happy to be the obliging spouse. I concentrated instead, paying strict attention to traffic signals and staying below the speed limit, refusing to allow my escalating anger to compromise our safety. The minute I'd parked, though, I felt it all flood in, and, surprising even myself, I reached across and hit Luke once hard in the chest, then again when he didn't respond.

"Hey," he said softly in the gloom of our garage, catching my wrists to prevent a third blow. "I guess I asked for that."

"Damn right you did," I spat at him, struggling to get free.

"Cress, I'm sorry," he said with a sigh in his voice, oozing remorse. "I don't know why I did such a stupid thing, or if you can ever forgive me. I didn't enjoy it."

"Well, you certainly gave a good impression of enjoying it. I thought someone was going to have to throw a bucket of water over the two of you. And in front of all my friends!" My voice cracked with fury.

"I know," he almost whispered. "I can't believe it myself. But it didn't mean anything. I'll never love anyone like I love you, Cress."

And at that, inexplicably, all my anger was gone and instead I started crying. Luke let go of my hands and held me while I sobbed on his chest, in his lap, stroking my hair while he murmured that he had been drunk, caught up by the dancing, thinking he was with me. They were not terribly good excuses but I bought them, wanting so desperately for them to be true. As my tears ebbed he carried me inside, something he'd not done in years. He laid me gently on our bed, and lit a candle on the dresser. Slowly, softly, he made love to me, saying my name over and over, telling me how he loved me, how he needed me. In bed, Luke is always passionate, fervent, but this was a side of him I'd never seen before. He was tender, controlled, far more than he'd been when he took my virginity. Afterward he held me as if I would break, kissing my fingertips and my eyelids, repeating my name again and again. For all I had been humiliated and hurt, it was a magical night.

We slept in each other's arms that night. Luke was repentant; I was forgiving. I told him that I never wanted to catch him so much as talking to Kate again, and he swore that he wouldn't, protesting anew that he would never love anyone like he did me. A year later I suddenly remembered that promise, and winced at how I'd been taken in. He hadn't vowed that he'd never love anyone else, just not love anyone in the same way. I couldn't have been listening properly at the time, or I wouldn't have missed the duplicity. Did he mean to deceive me, even back then? Or did his words just lead where his heart would follow?

CARY

·

I hardly ever get drunk, but I did that night. Usually Kate's drunk enough for both of us, though in fairness it doesn't take much, just a glass or two. But why am I being fair to Kate?

Though Steve's my friend, I think he almost enjoyed breaking the news. "Cary!" he practically shouted when he tracked me down to the veranda of the reception center, where I was talking with some people from the hospital. They'd come outside to smoke; I'd left to escape being pressured to dance. "I think you'd better come inside," he stage-whispered, tweaking at my sleeve.

"Why?" I asked, happy where I was.

"It's Kate," he urged, though now he really did drop his voice, and swallowed as if not quite sure what to say.

Immediately the tone of his voice made me panic. Had something happened? Was she hurt?

I rushed back into the reception fully expecting to see Kate unconscious in a corner or trapped under one of those implausible palm trees. But she was neither, and for a second I was so relieved that she was upright and well that I didn't take in what was happening. When I did I felt as though I had been punched in the stomach. All the air suddenly left me, and I had a mental picture of my lungs shriveling like week-old party balloons. Steve was looking uncomfortable and backing away, the scandal suddenly not quite so tasty. I started toward the pair of them, struggling for air, but as I did Luke moved away himself, his back to me. Kate stood there, the dancing continuing around her, looking dazed and still beautiful in her turquoise dress. I felt tears push at my eyes and turned away in shame.

We didn't leave, though I ached to. Instead, I carried on as if nothing had happened. I have my pride. Kate didn't dance again. We stayed at the bar, she close to my side, uncharacteristically subdued and toying with a glass of mineral water. I ordered Scotch, which I don't usually drink. The liquid burned my throat and reinflated my lungs till it seemed that I was almost breathing too much. Steve kept shooting me worried looks, but I stopped noticing after the first three glasses. I didn't see Cressida or Luke again.

I'd intended to drive, but we went home in a taxi. Kate must have said something, must have apologized, but I can't remember it. The night air sobered me up but also made things worse: clearer, sharper, altogether too large. At the front door I couldn't find my keys. I searched for them with growing anger, then shook the door handle until the small panes of glass in it rattled. Behind me, the taxi backed out of the driveway. Its headlights lit up the scene for a moment and then were gone, leaving us in the dark. Furious at being locked out of my own house I raised one fist and knocked the glass out of the door.

I don't really remember the rest. Kate had keys, of course, so we must have gotten in that way. I dimly recall us making love, or rather hammering myself into Kate while she lay unresisting in the darkness. Although I hadn't noticed it at the time, I had cut my hand on the glass, and when I came to in the morning there was blood in our bed and on Kate's body, smudged through her hair and across both breasts. She cried and I held her, apologetic in spite of myself. When she wiped her eyes she left a sodden trail of sparkles across one cheekbone, their light smudged out.

Later, I went to retrieve the car, still parked a street away from the reception hall. One of the side mirrors had been broken off, whether by accident or design I couldn't tell. My head ached. I drove home through the Sunday-morning silence, occasionally, out of habit, glancing at the place where the mirror should have been. But there was only space, a blind spot that unnerved and misled.

KATE

•

The trouble was, the kiss worked. We fitted. There was no awkward bumping of noses, no colliding chins, no glasses sliding off into my face. In heels, I didn't have to strain my neck or bend my knees: I just lifted my head and there he was.

Luke was a good kisser—I guess he'd had plenty of practice. Still, there was more there than just familiarity with the mechanics, knowing how long to go on or how much tongue was enough. Chemistry is an overused word. I prefer *fit*, that indefinable sensation when a man takes your arm as you move through a door, or leans into you to light your cigarette. (I gave up smoking for Cary and sometimes I still miss it.) Fit is an understanding between bodies: that you've been designed the same way, that you speak each other's language, and fluently. It's all about physical compatibility and has nothing to do with whether you'll last or even have anything to talk about afterward; fit is no relation to the brain, and only a distant cousin of the heart. It's something that's clearest with the lights off or your eyes closed, delineated by the way his stride matches yours or your hips meet while dancing. As he kissed me, Luke held my hand to his cheek, our fingers interlaced in a mirror of our mouths. That's fit.

CRESSIDA

•

The next morning I got up and went to work. Sometimes it seems like that's all my life consists of, but I love my job and feel lucky to do what I do. I've never said so to Luke, but occasionally I wonder how he can possibly derive any satisfaction from selling bread or cars or panty liners. At the end of the day, what difference has he made? No one's life has been changed, and someone else has gotten richer. He'd say that it's the creative side that he enjoys, that he gets paid good money to daydream and make believe, and all without getting his hands dirty. Admittedly, a lot of his stuff is pretty funny and even clever. But if the outcome is simply that a few more cartons of orange juice are sold, how can you get too worked up about that? My own results were based on a far harsher currency: lives lost or saved, children restored to their families.

I'm being hard, particularly when it's those extra cartons of juice that pay our mortgage. Public hospitals are no place to get rich, and my area of specialty doesn't lend itself to private practice. And even if I had my doubts about his work, Luke was incredibly supportive of mine. He often told me he was proud of me, and he loved boasting that his wife cured kids with cancer, even if that was only true about half of the time. He'd always put up with the long hours too, the weekends when we couldn't go away because I was on call, the bedroom sessions interrupted by my beeper. Now, as I got ready to leave, Luke was still asleep. Sunday morning, eight o'clock. I wasn't due in until nine, but there was a particular patient

I wanted to see and Luke wouldn't be up for hours. I dropped a kiss on one warm shoulder, then hurried out before he had time to stir.

Despite the events of the previous night I was in a good mood as I drove to work. I always love that time of morning: the streets empty, the traffic flowing. A fresh start. Coffee shops were setting out tables, joggers were stretching or fiddling with buttons on their watches. All was in readiness: no matter what the previous day had held, a brand-new one was about to unfold. On a sudden whim I turned off early and parked near the zoo, then walked across the surrounding gardens to the children's hospital.

It wasn't that I didn't mind that Luke had kissed Kate, and in such a public and passionate manner. If I let myself think of it the pain and anger were still fresh, adrenaline racing down my limbs to pool, hot and itchy, in fingertips and toes. But I didn't let myself think of it, concentrating instead on the way he had held me through the night. Never had I felt so close to Luke, I reflected, as some tropical bird called out from an aviary in the zoo behind me. Just remembering the lightness of his hands on my face and between my legs made me shiver, made my thighs warm and heavy once again. By the time I reached my ward I was flushed, but not from the walk.

When I stopped in to check on my patient she was sleeping quietly, and I smiled to myself as I read over her charts. At times it had looked grim, but I hadn't felt that this one was destined to die, even as her hair fell out and the white-cell count rose. I'd never been wrong before. I suppose it was bound to happen eventually, but not with this girl. Her mother, sleeping awkwardly in a chair beside her daughter's bed, woke as I put down the file.

"She's better, isn't she?" she asked me immediately, pushing tired hair out of her face.

"There's still a long way to go yet," I cautioned, "but I think she's moving in the right direction."

"I knew it," said the mother, unheeded tears suddenly incandescent at the corners of her eyes. "Around midnight the color started coming back into her face, and she asked for her teddy."

I just nodded, and together we watched the young girl in silence. Most of my patients toss and turn in pain and fever, or lie, almost comatose, in a drug-induced stupor. This one had been through both stages, but now lay sleeping the sound and rhythmic sleep of the healthy child, limbs curled around a beloved soft toy.

"Oh, God, I couldn't bear to have lost her," said the mother suddenly, her hand coming up to her mouth as if she might vomit.

"I know," I said quietly, reaching out a hand, then taking the woman in my arms, where she sobbed, shuddering, against my shoulder. As part of my training I'd worked in obstetrics, and seen some wonderful things. But for all its pain, this job was better, for how many children are reborn? There's no happier ending than a second chance.

Later that day, one of the nurses remarked in passing that there was a delivery for me in the ward clerk's office. Chocolates and gifts from grateful parents weren't an unusual occurrence, and, feeling hungry and hopeful, I went to have a look. At first I couldn't see anything for a clutch of nurses surrounding the desk, leaning over something vivid and rustling. For one ridiculous moment I panicked, thinking a patient was being resuscitated. But then one giggled and they parted, revealing an enormous bunch of deep red roses. There must have been at least four dozen, with velvety petals as large as a child's fist. The card in the center of them was addressed to me. *To my darling Cress*, it read for everyone to see, *the most beautiful woman in the world. I'll love you always, Luke.*

"You must have done something right," one of the nurses joked as I stooped to pick up the enormous bouquet. Maybe what happened wasn't so bad, I thought to myself as I smelled the flowers. Maybe it could even bring us closer, remind us of our love for each other. Maybe in the dark he did really mistake her for me. As I went to tuck the card back in my fingers brushed something soft hidden among the thorns. I pulled it out, and almost cried. It was a tiny bunch of pink daisies, incongruous amid the other regal blooms, but infinitely more precious.

KATE

·

When I first got my engagement ring I couldn't stop looking at it. It was so shiny, so vibrant, the colors rich and mesmerizing. The ring had moods, and I knew them all. Mostly it shone green and blue, peaceful, becalmed, a little planet on my finger. Sometimes, though, it darkened to violet, the color of a bruise, or red flecks appeared, flashing like beacons against the cerulean miasma. I liked to think that the changes reflected my own emotional state, as if conducted by blood to the skin beneath the band. But when I remarked on this to Cary he pointed out what I'd suspected all along: that it was probably just the light playing tricks, some alteration in the external environment, nothing more.

Yet after a while I stopped noticing the ring. I can't remember when it was, but sometime after we married. One year? Two? It had lost its sparkle and no longer clamored for my attention. The second gold band beneath it seemed to draw away some of its shine; the rest was lost to dirt and sweat, shampoo or the dusting powders I used at work. Occasionally I thought I should clean it, but then I never took it off, so I never got around to it. When I did examine the ring, mostly in boring meetings for want of something better to do, it regarded me dully, through a film of neglect.

I work with artifacts, with relics. I know in my heart that there's little that stays shiny forever, even with effort. Tarnish and rust are inevitable with age, and it's unrealistic to expect otherwise. But I did; I couldn't help it. And all of a sudden it seemed that nothing gleamed as brightly as it used to. I still loved Cary, but seven years had left a film on that too. I went for hours without thinking about him, no longer experienced the pit-of-the-stomach anticipation of going to bed together. Sex was comforting, successful, even passionate. But it wasn't new, didn't sweep across me in great waves of silver and gold light the way those fireworks had done years ago on Cup Day. How could it? I hated myself for being so shallow even as I mourned the loss. I'd insisted on that ring, picked it out and paid for it myself. Maybe it wasn't so shiny anymore, but underneath I knew it was still the same. Didn't I?

CARY

•

I didn't want to go to the trivia night. Three weeks after the wedding I was still feeling fragile, and had no desire to attend another hospital function, surrounded by many of the same faces that had witnessed Luke and Kate's clinch. Steve had started avoiding me at work, as if I'd want to cry on his shoulder or discuss the situation. The thought couldn't have been further from my mind. For more than a fortnight we circled around each other, barely speaking, until the upcoming event forced him to talk to me.

"You're still coming on Saturday, aren't you?" he asked nervously.

"I suppose so," I replied, not looking up from the DNA sequence I was examining. Each department had been allocated a table at the trivia night, which was one of the biggest fund-raising events of the year. Although our own department—genetics—consisted of only two full-time staff, we were still expected to field a team of twelve paying participants. At the time we'd agreed to split the duty, and I'd rashly promised that Kate would invite a single girlfriend to partner Steve.

"Both of you, I mean," he persisted. "Will Kate be there too?" Whether he was worried about me or about missing out on a date I couldn't tell, though I suspected the latter.

"Of course she will. Why wouldn't she be?" I answered angrily. Did he think I might have left Kate, or vice versa, that one kiss could undo seven years of loving?

"No reason," Steve almost stammered. "I'll look forward to seeing her. She's good value at these things."

I looked up at him closely, but there was no malice in the words. Kate *was* usually good value in such a situation: funny, bright, enthusiastic. The last few weeks, though, she had been subdued, quieter than usual. She hadn't gone out as much, and called every day just to chat. I guess it was her way of apologizing, of reassuring me, and I appreciated it.

"Don't worry; she's arranged a friend for you," I said to Steve, relenting.

"Oh, I'd forgotten about that. What's she like?" he asked, the rapidity of the second sentence belying the truth of the first.

"Okay." I shrugged, not wanting to get his hopes up. The only one of her unattached friends Kate had been able to talk into coming was Joan, who was apparently attending on the proviso that there might be some single doctors present. Sarah and Rick would also be there, with the six that I'd promised rounded out by an old friend of mine from university.

"Well, thanks for that," Steve said, looking pleased. "Should be a good night."

I wasn't quite so confident, though not because I was worried about Kate. We had an understanding: no drinking, no talking to Luke. He and Cressida would be at a different table anyhow, hopefully miles away on the other side of the room. Besides, I really didn't think she would be so cruel or so stupid as to do something like that again.

LUKE

·

A hospital cafeteria looks like a hospital cafeteria, no matter how many streamers and balloons you festoon the place with. Plastic tables were covered with rented linen tablecloths, their white washed out to gray, faint wine stains still evident in places. On the bulletin board the usual advertisements for roommates and announcements of flu injections had been removed, replaced for the evening by a hand-lettered team score sheet. The blackboard listing specials of the day had been left in one corner, Friday's menu still evident: corned beef, silver beet, creamed cauliflower. I lost my appetite just reading it.

"This place looks okay. They've done a good job," said Tim.

"It was kind of you to come. I hope you enjoy yourself," replied Cress distractedly, peering around the room in an attempt to identify our table.

"I don't know why they couldn't have just hired a function center like anyone else. Even that room at the Town Hall last year was better," I grumbled.

"It's meant to be a fund-raiser, Luke," said Cressida, turning to address me. "Just imagine how much money has been saved by having it at the hospital. I think it's a great idea." Her tone was dismissive and agitated at the same time. She was wearing something tight and black, and above it her creamy shoulders bobbed in indignation as she spoke.

"Can I get you a drink?" asked Tim, intervening quickly. Conflict frightens him.

"No, I'll go," said Cress. "There's some people over there I want to talk to." She indicated vaguely and disappeared into the crowd, pale blond hair splashing around her.

"Everything okay?" asked Tim.

"Just fine." I shrugged. Actually, things had been surprisingly fine in the last few weeks, the events of the wedding seemingly put behind us. It was only tonight that I'd noticed a shift in Cress: taking forever to get ready, snapping at me when I'd asked her who would be there. I scanned the gathering now as Tim and I made our way to the table.

The room was filling up. Their uniforms shed, brightly clad bodies dotted the hall like spilled confetti. The tired linoleum floor, unacquainted with stilettos, dimpled and puckered beneath the onslaught, while on the tiny stage someone was checking the sound equipment, repeating, "One, two," over and over for little apparent result. A nurse I recognized flashed me a dazzling smile, her lips redder and larger than nature intended. I pointed her out to Tim.

"There's one for you. I could give you an introduction."

"Mate, if you already know her, then it's too late for me." He laughed.

I ignored the comment and returned my gaze to the floor. In the distance Cress's fair head was nodding earnestly as she spoke with her boss. A part of my mind registered how beautiful she looked; then my eyes moved on. I guess I was searching for Kate, though not with intent. Even if she was there, what did it matter? I could hardly talk to her, wouldn't know what to say anyway. A sudden burst of feedback from the sound system momentarily silenced the throng, leaving in its wake one pure moment of silence before the babble resumed.

KATE

•

I was introducing Joan to Steve when the shriek of static made me clap my hands to my ears. Neither of them was looking particularly impressed, and I was tempted to give up there and then, melting into the crowd before anyone could protest. I hadn't wanted to come anyway, never mind broker this ridiculous blind date. Only loyalty to Cary had induced me to go through with both. That, and I owed him.

I'd spotted Luke as soon as we arrived. I hadn't meant to look for him, but my eyes were drawn to the golden corona of his hair, blazing like the sun against a sea of dark suits. He was standing with his back to me, flanked by Tim and Cressida, her own pale locks sleek against formal black. As I watched he bent his head to hear what she was saying. I felt ill and invisible, and ached for a glass of champagne.

Fifteen minutes later it was obvious that the night wasn't going well, at least at our table. I wasn't drinking, out of deference to Cary, and he in turn seemed preoccupied and disinclined to chat with Sarah and Rick. After some desultory small talk Steve and Joan appeared to have arrived at a mutual dislike, and were openly scornful of each other. Cary's school friend announced he was hungry and went off to look for some food. I was trying to concentrate on the quiz, but every time I thought of Luke I felt distracted and hot, prickles of nausea bubbling in my abdomen.

After four long rounds we were coming in second-to-last, and nobody cared. I caught Sarah looking at her watch and she smiled apologetically.

On the stage a band was setting up to play a set at the halfway point of the competition. I twisted my rings, feeling trapped, and wondered how much the music would prolong the night. The overly jovial emcee whistled to signal the start of round five, his several chins wobbling with the effort. Though I hadn't had one in years, I longed for a cigarette. Finally the questions began, then were abruptly suspended by another screech of feedback from the microphone. The emcee kept talking but could no longer be heard. Around the room, couples glanced at one another, then started to chat as the silence lengthened. I wondered hopefully if they'd call the whole thing off and we could just go home.

Ten minutes passed with no resolution, our table of strangers looking around at one another awkwardly. Then, through the still-seated crowd, I noticed a stooped man wearing an ID badge making his way toward us. Cary jumped up, obviously recognizing him, and they conferred for a moment before he returned to my side.

"That's Bill, from marketing. He's running this show but he doesn't know the first thing about electronics. I'm going to see if I can give him a hand, okay?"

I nodded my assent as he hurried away.

"I won't be long," he called back over his shoulder, and then, as an afterthought, blew me a kiss. Suddenly useful, needed, he looked happier than he had all night.

LUKE

•

The pager went off at about the same time as the sound did. It was Cress's, of course. I didn't even know that she'd brought it, though I wasn't surprised—she seemed to be eternally on call. She muttered, "Damn," under her breath and reached beneath her chair for her handbag, cleavage spilling forward as she did so. An intern on the other side of the table was watching the pale flesh with interest and I leaned forward to block his view, feeling suddenly territorial.

"I'm sorry," said Cress, studying the scratchy capitals intently. "I don't think a phone call will suffice for this one. I'm going to have to pop up to the ward."

"Does a phone call ever suffice?" I asked wearily.

"I'm sorry," she repeated, looking up and kissing me on the cheek as she rose from her chair. "You can do without me, can't you?"

I had three or four glib responses on my tongue, but Tim intervened.

"Never. Though I suppose the ward's need is greater. Just make sure you're back for the 'Movies' round."

"Yeah," I added, "and if we're to have any chance you have to be here for 'Sports.' "

We were both joking, my wife's general knowledge extending little beyond all things medical. She was a smart girl and loved her field, but it barely left her time for other interests. Cress pulled a face at us and hurried away, the sound of her heels clicking coolly after her for a second or two, then fading.

Tim, our team scribe, picked up his pen again and the quiz continued. The sound was back on, and the emcee was asking about celebrity couples.

"Number five," he droned. "Who was Tom Cruise's first wife?"

All around me heads leaned in to write or confer, but I didn't know or care. Suddenly, across a press of bent backs, I spotted Kate, sitting erect with equal indifference on the other side of the room. I tried to catch her eye, but she was too far away.

"Number six. To whom was Brad Pitt engaged before he married Jennifer Aniston?"

Tim bit the pen, wrote something down, then passed it around for confirmation. He was enjoying himself, though I was surprised he knew the answers. Maybe he didn't. I couldn't be bothered checking.

"Number seven. Where did Michael Hutchence meet Paula Yates?"

I glanced over at Kate again. The seat next to her was empty.

"Number eight. To how many men has Elizabeth Taylor been married?"

A trick question. Beneath me I felt my legs push the chair away; then I was on my feet.

"I'm going to look for Cress," I whispered to Tim. He nodded and went back to counting on his fingers as the intern reeled off names.

I left the cafeteria, crossed a small foyer and then entered it again on the far side of the room. I had been here before; I knew the layout. Kate's table was about halfway along, abutting a shadowy alcove that ran the length of the room and was littered with coats and spare seats. I moved up the alcove as far as I dared, then waited for her to see me. It took only a second. She turned her head, caught my eye, and without any signal from me unfolded from her seat like a letter being opened. I stood back to let her pass, then pretended to reach into the pocket of a coat hanging nearby as if I had come for my glasses or cigarettes. The emcee asked the last question of the round, and then I was swallowed up in the crush of bodies making a dash for the toilet or the bar.

Outside, Kate was loitering in the foyer, feigning interest in a social club announcement advertising a bowling night. Her hair was up, and her bare neck, devoid of jewelry, was vulnerable and enticing. At the touch of my hand on her shoulder she jumped.

"God," she said, spinning around. "I'm glad you came. I was starting to feel stupid."

"Where's Cary?" I asked.

"Keeping the sound system running. Shagging one of the nurses. Either/or." Her green eyes were steady, as brave as her words. Inside, the band was warming up, stray notes rising like helium balloons above the conversation. The foyer was almost empty. I took Kate's hand.

"Come on," I said. It sounds untrue, but I had no plan, no formed intent. Just an urge to be somewhere dark and oblivious and close. I steered Kate around a corner, wondering vaguely about the parkland adjacent to the hospital. But then a better solution presented itself: the day-procedures unit, sitting still and unlit outside working hours.

"In here?" asked Kate, following me through the door. Her voice was suddenly loud in the empty ward, words bouncing off shiny walls smelling of bleach and rubber and bandages. In the dim light from the corridor I could make out perhaps ten hospital beds, all neatly made and awaiting the patients that Monday would bring. The sight of so much clean, crisp linen was oddly arousing. Without answering I pulled Kate to me and kissed her, our teeth knocking with the violence of the contact. She responded with equal ferocity, and for a moment I almost felt as if I were fighting her, grappling to hang on with my mouth and hands and teeth. Then with a sigh she dissolved against me like a river flowing into the sea. Her lips became pliant; her hands reached for my shoulders and nape. I couldn't stop kissing her: mouth honey-sweet, moist and fresh as a garden at dawn. A tendril of her hair caught my lips, and I reached to release it, feeling our hips align as I did so. She was pushing herself against me, fingers agile at the buttons on my shirt, the night air cool where she'd gotten them undone. Her breasts were in my hands, round as fishbowls, small but filled to the brim. I started edging her toward one of the beds, drawing the cubicle's curtain around us. But as my hands returned to her body there was a bang. Then another. Somebody cursed and we froze; Kate's fingers stilled on the waistband of my pants.

"Bloody machine," a male voice said. "Give me my money back!"

There was another thump and Kate giggled, the sound liquid and close. Someone was attacking the vending machine just outside the clinic. Relaxing, I moved to kiss her again, but she squirmed in my grasp.

"This is too public. He might have been from the trivia night," she said, her breath warm against my ear. Disappointment consumed me like a toothache, and I started tucking in my shirt. But Kate wasn't finished.

"Let's go up to the roof," she said. "No one's ever up there."

KATE

·

Cary had first taken me up onto the roof. Once, long ago, before we were married. It had been fairly early on in our relationship, when we were still self-consciously dating, sizing each other up, committing no more than a week in advance. We'd met for lunch. I'd caught a tram across from the museum, then taken the elevator to the sixth floor, hastily applying my lipstick in the steely reflection of its double doors. As usual I was running late, and Cary was glancing at his watch as I entered his office.

"Glad you could make it," he'd said, looking up, smiling.

"I'm sorry I'm late," I began, as I had done so many times before. "The meeting ran overtime; then I got a call from a curator in Portland—"

"Forget it," he interrupted, though kindly. "There's a case conference at two I have to be at, so we don't have time to go far. We could try the staff dining room, if you're game."

"Don't bother," Steve called out from the adjoining lab, where he had been unashamedly eavesdropping. "The special today is tripe, which is all they'll have left by now anyway."

"I don't mind tripe," I volunteered untruthfully.

"Well, I do. And I've got a better idea," said Cary, steering me back toward the elevator.

The hospital was seventeen stories high, perched on the edge of the city and surrounded by gardens on three of its four flanks. The elevator went only as far as the fifteenth floor; then an internal fire escape finished the journey. Cary paused at the top, his hand on the heavy fire door leading out onto the roof.

"You ready?" he asked before opening it.

I nodded, out of breath from all those steps. He pushed on the door, and air and light rushed into the musty stairwell like bubbles up the neck of a champagne bottle. I was momentarily disoriented, intoxicated, and Cary took my hand. For the size of the building there was surprisingly little space up there, the hospital having tapered at its apex. Most of all, the roof reminded me of the pool deck on a ship, but without the pool: bare open space with a cavernous drop on either side. There was a low wall around the perimeter topped by some sort of Plexiglas that reduced the wind and discouraged suicide. Beyond that the roof was unfurnished and unoccupied, save for three empty sun lounges lugged up there by resourceful staff and a few hardy plants clinging to the concrete.

"Come and have a look at the view," said Cary, pulling me toward the edge.

I gazed through the glass and drew in my breath. Below me acres of green stretched out to the suburbs, verdant fingers seemingly pressing houses and roads back into tight lines. Out to the left a navy sea tossed and threaded its way into port, while at my back grape-purple hills sat cloaked in their afternoon shadow.

"It's incredible, isn't it?" asked Cary. "All the way from the Dandenongs to the bay. I come up here sometimes when I need to clear my head."

I said nothing, drinking in the scene, silent except for the faint hum of traffic and the throb of the autumn wind.

"See those trees?"

I laughed at the question; there were so many below us. Cary stepped behind me and pointed one arm over my shoulder.

"Down there. Where the leaves are falling."

I followed the line of his finger to a knot of bare limbs and bright colors, orange canopies like small bonfires against the surrounding green.

"Most of the gardens are native now," he said, arms warm around me. "That's all that's left of the original planting, when the city was first settled."

"What are they?" I asked.

"Plane trees, oaks, maybe an elm or two. Descendants of those brought over here by homesick settlers. Maybe some of them are even the originals themselves."

"Really?"

I felt him shrug. "Certain species can live for hundreds of years. It's not inconceivable." He paused. "Just imagine that. All the way from London or Liverpool or Dartmoor. Acorns tied into handkerchiefs in Cornwall, damp and dusty from months at sea, still shooting now on the other side of the world."

I shivered in Cary's arms. I had felt this before in my own work: all that time, all that distance, the lives that had elapsed while some trinket lay buried. The continuity of objects—jewelry, pots, seeds—never failed to move me, to give me hope. My new boyfriend kissed the top of my head and spoke into my hair.

"And aren't they beautiful now? It's amazing how things can endure."

I'd been up to the roof since then, but never at night. And never, of course, with Luke. We barely looked at each other in the elevator, moving to opposite walls, afraid perhaps to break the spell or to have to think about what we were doing. On the fifth floor the elevator stopped and a trolley was wheeled between us. A small figure lay upon it under a starched sheet, immobile and with eyes closed. I couldn't tell the sex, or even if it was breathing. The child was accompanied by a theater technician anonymous as an astronaut, only his eyes visible under the surgical garb. He stared at the floor for eight levels; then the elevator jerked to a halt and he soundlessly wheeled the body out again into a dim and silent corridor.

Luke kissed me on every stair of the fire escape. As soon as the elevator doors closed behind us his mouth found mine, and we stumbled to the staircase locked in the embrace. By one flight up my blouse was undone, his shirt pulled open, my lips bruised and starting to swell. We held each other, panting, on the landing while he removed my stockings, still kissing me and without even looking. For a moment I felt we might just slide to the floor and climb no higher. My hair came undone and Luke muttered into it, "How much farther?"

"One floor." I gasped as his hands moved back to my breasts, lifting them up and together before he bent to kiss the cleft he'd created. His hair felt like silk against my throat, his body still steering me upward as he touched and tasted.   ·

I suppose the night air must have been cool, as it was still only spring. But I can't say I noticed it, can't say I noticed anything except the stars peeping in and out in the sky above and the static spark from the Plexiglas as Luke slid me against it. All I was aware of was heat: heat from his skin, heat in his eyes, heat rising inexorably through my system, my belly, my thighs. "Kate," Luke murmured against my forehead, his mouth leaving mine for the first time in minutes. Later I wondered if he'd been giving me a chance to escape, a moment to cry *no* or push away. If so, I didn't take it. When I stayed where I was he whispered my name again, this time slowly, with promise. I felt the weight of his body move against mine, felt my own body soften and sigh and accommodate him, opening up against the length of his thigh, the pressure of his chest. With one strong hand he was holding both of mine, pinioning them lightly at my side; with the other he slowly, deliberately traced his forefinger down the curve of my face. I felt his breath on my cheek, heard my own breath coming in gasps. His finger outlined the contour of my mouth: up, down, up, over the bow, sliding slowly over my shaky bottom lip. For a moment I felt dizzy, thought I could hear the band playing all that way below us. In one small corner of my mind there was Cary; there was shame. But everything else was here, caught like a fly in amber in the fullness of the moment. Finally, irrevocably, his lips were again on mine, my mouth open before they even met, his tongue sliding inside me like a serpent. Lower, I felt the same thing happening between our bodies, easily, fluidly, without force or strain or resistance. For a second I was shocked by the speed with which he had taken me. But then there was only pleasure, the hiss of the jungle, the undergrowth, and I was kissing him back, moving against and in time with him, hands, now released, in his hair, everything concentrated on the warmth and the want between us.

Afterward, opening my eyes, I saw the lights of Melbourne flickering beneath us like a thousand tiny candles, like a church on Christmas morning.

LUKE

·

Afterward, what struck me most was how easy it had been. I was thirty-four, with probably more than my fair share of conquests, but none of them had transpired as effortlessly as that. In my experience, there's a degree of bargaining, of contract making, that goes into any sexual encounter, usually unvoiced. Everybody knows the rules, but no one articulates them. People don't just meet and sleep together, even if the attraction is mutual. Something has to happen in between, usually instigated by the male: a meal, maybe, a drink or a dance, a pledge of marriage or the promise of a phone call. Even the most tawdry of my one-night stands didn't just happen without a string of compliments or cocktails, something to pave the way. It's almost as if sex is too vast, too frightening or too wicked to exist by itself, and purely for its own sake.

And that was what was so unique about Kate. There was no game playing, no pretense. I didn't have to tell her she was beautiful; I didn't tell her anything at all. Or take her out, or buy her flowers, or scheme to get her alone. The attraction was there from the moment we first danced together at the wedding. I'm sure we would have made love then if circumstances had allowed. But they didn't, and I didn't spend the following weeks plotting or phoning or promising. Don't get me wrong—it's not as if I don't enjoy those things; in fact, I often found pursuit more satisfactory than plunder. It's just that for once it was so refreshing, so simple. She wanted me; I wanted her; we had sex. Easy.

Easy, too, even in the most practical details. For one, no one saw us. Early on I was careful to be circumspect, but once we made it to the stairwell I don't think I would have noticed if the fire brigade had turned up. Really, either Cary or Cress could have finished what they were doing and come looking for us, but they didn't. The day hospital was empty, and so was the roof. It wasn't raining, and Tim wasn't following me around the way he normally does. Even the architecture was on our side. It gives me chills now to think of how I trusted our combined weight to a single sheet of Plexiglas seventeen stories up, suicide repellent or not. But it held, as did our luck.

Then there were the actual mechanics. Without wishing to sound too technical, I hardly ever make love standing up. Quite frankly, it's too difficult. Your partner has to be just the right height, and light enough to lift if necessary. There's all that maneuvering for the angle, trying to ensure you stay coupled when gravity and pretty much everything else is working against you. It wasn't what I would have planned for a first time with someone new. It wasn't even something I'd attempted with Cress, who preferred sex lying down and by candlelight. But somehow it just worked. When I leaned against Kate her body clicked into mine like a joint in a socket and I couldn't bear to move away, couldn't bear even to lose the time it would take to lower her to the concrete. Thank God she was wearing a skirt.

We made it back to the trivia night by the middle of round nine, and before we were even missed. Kate giggled all the way down the fire escape, pulling her hair back up with practiced hands, smoothing out stockings and buttoning her blouse. She smiled when I caught her eye, looking flushed and soft, like a child not long woken up. The elevator was empty and I kissed her again, surprised at how much I still wanted to. As we drew apart it occurred to me that I hadn't even seen her naked.

Outside the dining room Kate paused and indicated the ladies' room.

"I'm just going in here. You go ahead."

Then she disappeared and I was left loitering uncomfortably, as I'd done not an hour ago. I wondered if I should wait, until it dawned on me that she was being cautious and trying to avoid our being seen together. It felt almost sneaky to be slipping away like that—no good-bye kiss, no words exchanged, sincere or otherwise. Another first.

On the way back to our table I scanned the crowd for Cress's familiar face. I needn't have worried, as she still wasn't back. Tim was deep in conversation with a sharp-eyed brunette, and barely looked up as I resumed my seat.

"I couldn't find Cress," I whispered to him as casually as I could. "She didn't turn up while I was gone, did she?" He shook his head, no longer even bothering with the trivia questions. Glancing to the stage I could faintly make out Cary in the background, fiddling with some piece of equipment. It appeared that no one had cared about my absence, that I'd gotten away scot-free. I was tempted to go back and find Kate again.

CARY

•

Despite myself I enjoyed the trivia night. I'll admit I didn't expect to, and it certainly didn't begin well, but by the time I returned from helping with the sound system the table had finally clicked, people were laughing and Kate welcomed me back with huge and glowing eyes. I guess, too, I was feeling better: useful, successful. I enjoy using my hands, working things out. I think I would have liked to have been a surgeon, if I'd had the grades.

The competition was essentially over when I did get back, though, and I felt a little guilty for missing it all. Still, it wasn't as if the team had been winning, or I could have done much to change that. Kate didn't seem to have suffered either. After our seven years together she knew quite a few of the hospital staff and must have moved around to speak with them, because she wasn't at our table when I'd glanced out from the stage wings once or twice. Besides, she also had Sarah, Rick and Joan, though when I looked Joan wasn't at the table either. I suppose the two of them were off somewhere together, doing whatever it is girls do two by two in bathrooms. Anyway, the main thing was that I knew Kate wouldn't be upset by my absence, that she could more than look after herself socially. It's one of the things I've always admired about her.

Considering our loss, she was in high spirits when I returned to my seat. Kate has a competitive streak, and I remember her anger all the way home after the first hospital trivia night she'd attended, when Steve fluffed the capital of Panama and blew our chance of coming in second. The funny thing was that she hadn't known the answer either.

Tonight, though, it appeared that she couldn't care less, her mood so good that I risked a gentle jibe.

"Thirteenth out of fifteen teams? What happened? I've obviously been propping you up all those other years."

Sarah started to reply but Kate quickly interjected. "They were silly questions," she replied airily, jumping out of her seat to kiss me. "Let's go out and console ourselves with a drink."

I looked around at the others, who'd been silently preparing to leave: pulling on coats, fishing car keys from their bags. None seemed as if they were particularly keen to prolong the evening.

"Come on," urged Kate, sensing the reluctance. "I've hardly had a chance to talk to you all night, Steve." She flashed him a smile so intense that I almost felt it make contact. "Or you, Sarah," she continued, gathering her friends around her. "And Rick! You must tell me how that lovely daughter of yours is. Does she like school?"

One by one she was winning them over. I saw Sarah peek down at her watch, then exchange glances with Rick.

"Well, I suppose one wouldn't hurt," he conceded. "The babysitter's booked till twelve thirty."

"Fantastic!" Kate bubbled. "You're coming too, aren't you, Mark?" she entreated my defenseless friend. "The Redback's not far from here; we can easily walk. Steve, you'll bring your friends as well, won't you? Cary, see if there's anyone from orthopedics who wants to join us. Now, where's Joan?"

But despite Kate's organizational frenzy Joan could not be found, and we left without her. Others had had the same idea, and by the time we got to the pub it was packed, hospital staff and their partners crowding doorways and spilling drinks on one another in the crush. I volunteered to buy the first round, though it took nearly twenty minutes. Finally successful, I spotted Kate in a corner and headed toward her. She was talking with Sarah, or rather to her, the other girl simply nodding now and then as Kate's lips moved on and on. So absorbed was Kate in the conversation that she didn't notice my approach, and jumped when I held her cold drink to the small of her back.

"God, you scared the life out of me," she scolded, momentarily angry. I handed her a glass in reply.

"What were you two discussing so intently?" I asked, curious. Sarah colored. Maybe she and Rick were having problems.

"This and that. Girl stuff," Kate said breezily, then took the drink with glee. "I thought I wasn't allowed to have any of this?"

"After the team's performance tonight I figured you'd need cheering up." She smiled, delighted, opal eyes ablaze. On impulse I leaned down and kissed her.

"Cut that out," said a familiar voice, though one I hadn't heard in a while. I straightened up to find Tim smiling and extending his hand. The other one, I couldn't help but notice, was holding fast to Joan, who lurked like a smirking pixie at his shoulder.

"You're here!" exclaimed Kate, rather obviously. "We couldn't find you, so we left. I'm so glad you've turned up. And with Tim," she added, her surprise almost comical. "Have you two been introduced?"

They laughed, and Tim's clasp on Joan tightened. "Not by you, thanks very much. No, I bumped into her at the hospital; we got to talking and then realized we both knew the two of you."

I rapidly surveyed the crowd around us but couldn't see Luke or Cressida. Hopefully Tim had come without them. Kate wound her own arm around my waist, distracting me.

"Well, that's great, isn't it, Cary? Now, Tim, this is Sarah and Rick, and Cary's friend Mark. Joan, you've already met Steve, haven't you?"

One drink turned into two, and it was four or five by the time the pub closed. Sarah and Rick had long gone, but the rest of our group had stayed on, as had most of the evening's participants. Even as we left some of them were suggesting moving on to a club, determined to drag every possibility out of the night.

"Are you interested?" I asked Kate, feeling surprisingly wide-awake.

"Uh-uh." She shook her head and slipped a hand inside my jacket for warmth. "It's been a big night. Let's just go home to bed."

It was cold inside the car, but the roads were empty and we didn't have far to go. Kate was quiet, tired, staring out the passenger window. As the heater came to life and we crept through the sleeping suburbs I had the distinct sensation that we were the only two people in the world, a unique partnership protected and enclosed in our warm metal capsule. It was a pleasant thought. Kate yawned and stretched, her thin arms brushing the roof of the car, and I felt a sudden rush of love and gratitude. Gratitude that she was here, with me, unbelievably my wife. And with the gratitude the first sharp stirrings of desire, familiar but rare in this intensity. More than desire. Something I'd been thinking about for a long time, perhaps without even realizing it.

We were stopped at a traffic light, though there were no other cars to be seen. Outside a discarded can was being blown around in the gutter, jangling like a tambourine. Kate was looking out the window again, the lights of the opposite signals reflecting green in her hair. I reached over and tucked a strand behind her still-cold ear.

"Kate, I've been thinking," I started, suddenly nervous. If I'd planned my proposal this was how it would have felt. "I know it's been a bit tough between us lately, but that's all over. I love you madly; I always will. You know that, don't you? I hate it when things aren't right." She nodded, still looking away. I felt tears thickening at the back of my throat and hurried on. "Let's have a baby. A little girl who looks just like you. Or a boy. Twins, I don't care, three or four or five. What do you say?"

She finally turned toward me, eyes deep green and wet. With joy, I supposed, or hope, or love. Wordlessly she held out her arms. As we embraced she cried into my hair, and we kissed and held each other as the lights cycled from green to red and back again.

SARAH

•

Kate can be flighty, but she's not dishonest. Or so I'd thought. I'd assumed even the flightiness had gone by the time she'd been married to Cary for a year or two. I remember commenting on it to Rick, when they'd been over for one of Alice's birthdays, how she seemed so relaxed, settled, as if she'd finally grown into her skin. Kate's my closest friend and one of the most generous people you could ever meet, but for years she lived her life as if she were learning to windsurf: overbalancing, overcorrecting, swept off course by the slightest current. But then again, maybe that was just youth; maybe we were all like that in college.

I knew about that first kiss, but I hadn't thought it was serious. She dropped around for coffee about a week after it happened, acting as if the whole thing were a big joke while scrutinizing my face for any hint of disapproval. It sounded innocent enough, though I doubt I got the whole story. The baby was distracting me anyway, and I was trying to shoo Alice out of the room in case she heard something she shouldn't.

"I can't believe I kissed him." She giggled. "I must have had too much to drink."

"What about Cary?" I asked, gently breaking Patrick's suction on my right breast and raising him to my shoulder to be burped. Warm milk seeped slowly from the nipple he'd vacated, like an old tap that can't be fully turned off. The light in Kate's face was dimmed, and in contrast to her breathless confession five minutes earlier the words were careful and flat.

"Cary's okay with it. He knows it didn't mean anything."

"And did it?"

"Of course not! I told you, it was just for fun. Maybe you had to be there."

I think she expected me to see it as she did, a great big joke, an adventure, the sort of thing we had shrieked over in our student days. Except we weren't students anymore, and all I could think of was how silly she'd been, how selfish, how I might even have felt ashamed of her had I been there. Kate changed the subject. I'd disappointed her with my worries about Cary and my moral high ground and my tired leaking breasts.

Now this. I'd seen the blond man sidling toward our table at the trivia night, lurking in the shadows as if his impossible looks weren't sucking attention from every female eye in the room like iron filings to a magnet. I saw him follow Kate out and guessed who he was. The situation almost gave me heart failure, but by a stroke of luck Cary stayed backstage and seemed none the wiser when he finally returned.

In a hushed half minute while Cary got the drinks at the pub Kate admitted that she had been with Luke during her lengthy absence. I could only begin to imagine in what sense.

"Do you think she slept with him?" asked Rick, as we undressed for bed later that night.

"I wouldn't think so. She was only gone for half an hour."

"Heck, they could have done it twice in that time!" He laughed, making a grab for my uncovered body. The speculation was turning him on.

"But where? In the gardens, or one of their cars? How uncomfortable! Plus just getting out to the parking lot and back would have taken ten minutes alone, never mind undressing and . . . the rest."

"Undressing and having sex, you prude," Rick teased, his hands on my bra. "Not everyone restricts it solely to bed."

He kissed my neck and I started relaxing against him, glad that I at least would be confining any congress to between my own sheets. Then Patrick began howling and the moment was lost.

Now Kate was on the other end of the phone evading my questions.

"We just went outside for a cigarette, nothing more. I didn't want you to tell Cary because you know how much he hates me smoking."

"I thought you'd given it up?" I didn't believe her anyway—why would she kiss this guy in full view of an entire wedding reception, then when she was alone with him somewhere dark do nothing more than light up?

"I have, except occasionally," she replied. "I could stop if I wanted to."

"What are we talking about again?" I asked.

"Very funny," Kate said, in a tone that implied it was anything but.

I tried another tack. "Look, you don't have to tell me anything. Just be careful. These things have a way of getting out of control."

"Nothing's going to get out of control," she said, finally dropping her guard. "It's just fun, you know?"

I couldn't help myself. "But what about Cary?" I asked, repeating my question of a month or so before.

"Cary's fine. I love Cary. I'll always be married to him. This is just a side dish or something, a trip down memory lane."

"A what? Did you used to go out with this guy?"

"No, of course not. I just meant the excitement, that feeling you get when you realize you're connecting with someone."

"Doesn't Cary excite you anymore?"

"I knew you'd think that. Yes, he does, and the sex is still good, to save you from asking. It's just not really . . . new." She sighed, stuck for words. "Doesn't the grass ever look greener to you? Don't you wonder what it would be like to be with someone else, to start again?"

"I'm too tired to even notice the grass most days," I replied truthfully. "Anyway, who'd want me, with two children and stretch marks? Rick sees me in my tracksuit every day and still loves me. That's what those vows we made are all about."

"I know, I know." Kate sighed. "It's just that sometimes it isn't . . ."

"Enough?"

"No!" she protested. "I was going to say *spectacular*."

"Well, nothing is. Get used to it. I would have thought you got all the spectacular you wanted with Jake, but you didn't marry him."

"You're right; I'm wrong." She sounded contrite, but I knew she didn't mean it. If we'd been talking face-to-face we would have looked at each other and burst into laughter, or tears. Instead there was silence on the phone, awkward and strained.

"Just be careful, won't you?" I pleaded, longing to hug her or shake her, or both. "Use condoms. Don't get pregnant."

"Oh, God," she groaned. "That's something else I have to tell you."

CRESSIDA

•

On the Monday morning after the trivia night Emma was readmitted. She'd been my first patient after I started the pediatric oncology fellowship, and I remembered her well—a quiet child who had blond hair like mine, missing front teeth and ALL, or acute lymphoblastic leukemia, a type of cancer where for some reason the body makes too many of the infection-fighting white blood cells. These don't mature properly, but collect and crowd out the other cells. Emma's mother had first become worried when her daughter fell half a foot from the monkey bars and was bruised for weeks. Then other bruises started appearing with no apparent cause, lingering on the girl's pale skin like tattoos. The night Emma had a bloody nose that would not stop, her parents finally brought her to the hospital. They hadn't wanted to make a fuss or sound paranoid, they said. Maybe she was just accident-prone. Children were always hurting themselves, weren't they?

It was the first time I'd had to give a diagnosis like that. I was . . . what? Twenty-five? Twenty-six? Too young to be reassuring, or even empathetic. I'd told anxious mothers that their sons had fractured an arm or leg, had tonsils that had to come out or an ear infection that needed treatment. But this was something else altogether, the major league of bad-news breaking.

"Just be as natural as you can," my supervisor advised me. "They won't be able to take much in, so have some information sheets ready to hand out, the phone number for the Leukemia Foundation. Don't linger on the prognosis—talk about treatment, remission rates, survival after five years. Be sympathetic. Do it somewhere quiet. And take tissues."

So I told Emma's parents what I knew, watching their faces collapse, their postures deflate, clenching my nails into my palm every time I felt tears threaten. "ALL is treatable," I informed them. "Chemotherapy to send it into remission, then later maybe a bone-marrow transplant, if it's necessary and if we can find a matching donor." Throughout the fraught half hour Emma lay in her father's arms, listless, too quiet. Her red blood cells had been overrun by the lymphocytes, trampled like hapless spectators at a soccer match. She was only six. She should have been tearing around the ward, making the nurses frown and shush, not this limp puddle in her father's lap.

About half the children who develop ALL survive it, at least for the following few years. Eighty percent if you believe some studies, though I don't. Chemotherapy puts almost all in remission; radiotherapy comes next to prevent any remaining rogue cells from starting the process over. Nonetheless, I had a bad feeling about Emma. It was the first time I'd experienced such a thing and I didn't recognize the sensation, but the minute I'd first reviewed her history I'd felt something lodge in my throat, as if I'd swallowed a moth. I coughed and it was gone, but an unnerving furred sensation remained. I know that taste now.

Emma stayed with us for almost six months, going home once or twice but always needing to be readmitted within the week. As predicted, the chemotherapy worked, but at a cost. It devastated her little system, weakening her defenses to all the other bugs that thrive in hospitals . . . first a chest infection, then blood in her urine. One morning we heard a scream from Emma's room and rushed in to find her mother shaking and sobbing. The girl's hair had literally fallen out overnight, lying in golden clots like spilled coins all over her pillow. I gathered it up and tried to give it to the woman, but she wouldn't touch it. "She's dying, isn't she?" she hissed at me as she pushed the locks away. *Yes,* I thought, glancing at my patient. She was barely conscious, nothing but bone wrapped loosely in a tent of skin, eyes sunken and rarely open. "No," I said, slipping into doctor-speak. "Hair loss is a side effect of radiotherapy. She's doing fine."

I didn't think of it as lying; it was what we had been taught to say. And as it turned out, Emma didn't die. She crashed once while I was off duty but was revived, the wasted frame forced back into life by a massive jolt of electricity. After that, to our great surprise, she made slow but steady progress, the white-cell count dropping as her hair grew back. I plaited the strands I'd salvaged into a skimpy ponytail, which a staff nurse suggested I attach to a cap for Emma to wear until her own head sported more than pale fuzz. She smiled broadly when I gave it to her and I could suddenly see that her new front teeth were coming in. That surprised me—I don't know why. She'd been so sick, and yet through it all her body had kept making these teeth, relentlessly preparing for her adult life. Where had the energy come from, when she'd needed all of her resources just to get well? The sheer persistence of those teeth staggered me. Was it just physiology, I wondered, or can cells hope like the rest of us?

I hadn't yet met Luke at the time, though I told him about Emma later. I don't think he understood, and I couldn't fully explain. He just saw biology and luck; I saw a little girl whose body had never given up, who was eventually declared cured and discharged for good. A success, when there were so many failures.

LUKE

•

Kate makes love with her eyes open, blue-green orbs like miniature globes swimming before me as I touch her and hear her call out. Only when we kiss, I think, does she close them, and then only because there is nothing to see. The rest of the time she is alert, aware, unwilling to miss a thing. Her whole body hums, alive in the moment. She watches me reach for her, watches the effect her own caresses have on me. When I enter her, her pupils dilate, swelling and spilling over the irises like an eclipse, a shout louder, more joyful than any that might leave her lips.

Cress closes her eyes; she sighs and murmurs. *Look,* I want to plead when we lie together, *show me that you want me; make me want you. Just look!* There is nothing more erotic, I want to tell her, than watching your partner respond, her eyes clouded by desire or surrender, yet never leaving yours. But how would I suddenly know this? And would I want to replicate it anyway?

CRESSIDA

·

I'd headed to the ward round that morning hoping it would be quick, that there'd be some chat about the trivia night, a few case reviews and we'd all be on our way. A short round would give me a chance to catch up on the discharge summaries threatening to engulf my desk. Instead, I found that Emma was back. One of the nurses filled me in. She'd been admitted late the previous night, once again covered in bruises, so sick she could barely open her eyes. It seemed the leukemia had returned.

"Damn," muttered the consultant, flicking through the thick file. "It doesn't look good. And she was doing so well too. Anyone remember her from her last admission?"

"I do," I called out.

"Your caseload's already heavy enough, Cressida," he replied without even looking up. "Someone else had better take this one. Gabrielle? Grant?"

The two doctors in question studied the floor, neither keen to volunteer. We were all too busy.

"I can do it," I pleaded across their hesitation. "She was my first patient in the unit. I know the family. I want to help."

The consultant finally lifted his eyes from the history, weary behind smudged glasses. "It's not going to be pretty. Are you sure you want the case?"

I nodded and he handed me the file. "The WBC count is twenty-one thousand. We'll do chemotherapy, then think about a bone-marrow transplant. Better talk to the parents and get them tested. Any siblings?"

I'd answered in the negative, though I turned out to be wrong. When I went to reintroduce myself to Emma's parents they were cradling a small blond child, unmistakably Emma's sister. The likeness was so uncanny that for a moment I was confused, thinking it was the girl herself, only three years younger rather than older. The father recognized me, and held out his hand.

"I was hoping never to see you again," he said bluntly. "What are her chances?"

"Good," I reassured them. "When relapse occurs over a year after discontinuing the initial therapy there's a thirty to forty percent chance of long-term survival."

"That's good?" asked Emma's father. "Less than fifty-fifty?"

"It's less than ten percent with relapse in the first year," I replied. Emma's mother began crying soundlessly as I outlined the treatment plan.

Over the next two months chemotherapy brought Emma into a second remission. Her best chance now was via a bone-marrow transplant, provided a suitable donor could be found. We took blood from her parents to test their compatibility; then I placed the tourniquet around Emma's little sister Shura's chubby arm. Veins swelled beneath the skin like fat pink worms.

"It seems cruel, doesn't it?" I said conversationally, preparing the tubes I would need to catch Shura's blood. "It's going to hurt, and she has no idea why."

"She doesn't need to know," replied her mother, lips set. "Besides, it's nothing compared to what Emma's gone through, and to the benefit it might bring."

She was right, of course, but her tone made me uneasy as I slid the needle in.

"You know that siblings don't always match, don't you?" I asked, slowly drawing up the plunger. Shura flinched as the red liquid rose in the cylinder.

"Yes, but Emma and Shura will. They have to," the woman responded with determination. It suddenly occurred to me that for a two-and-a-half-year-old Shura didn't speak much.

"Good girl," I told the toddler, withdrawing the needle and hunting in my pockets for a toy. "You were very brave. Would you like to play with this monkey?"

The child reached for the animal, but her mother pushed her hands away. "It might have germs, and we need you to be healthy for Emma," she said, heedless of her daughter's disappointment. "When will we get the results?"

The day the results were due I felt nervous, scared. Trying to hurry breakfast that morning I dropped my coffee cup, then cut a finger as I picked up the pieces. Luke heard me yelp and rushed in from the bathroom, where he had been shaving. As he helped me to my feet I burst into tears.

"Does it hurt that much? What's the matter?" he asked, turning the injured digit over for inspection.

"It's not that," I sobbed. "I'm worried about a patient—Emma, the one I told you about. We'll find out today if we can do her bone-marrow transplant. It's been worrying me all night—I hardly slept."

It was true. I'd tossed and turned while Luke slumbered on beside me. These days he was sleeping more deeply than ever. What a luxury to have nothing to keep you awake, no issues more bothersome than the latest sales figures for toilet paper.

"Oh, Cress," said Luke, kissing my finger and drawing me into his arms. "You care too much about those people. About everything. You've got to let go, my love. I know it's sad, but you can't let it consume you."

He was right, of course, but how do you stop caring? Emotions can't be turned on and off like tap water.

KATE

•

The second time we made love it was at the museum. First Cary's workplace, then mine. Cressida's too, I guess—that first time, I mean—though I thought about her as little as I could.

We hadn't seen Luke and Cressida since the trivia night, and it bothered me. When I parted from Luke after our tryst on the roof I had felt elated, euphoric and supremely confident that that wasn't the end of it. How could it be? We had been too natural, too good together, the fit just right. There had been too much desire for it to have all been spent. So I left him outside the ladies' room without a backward glance or a second thought, sure I'd be seeing him again soon.

Only I hadn't. Three weeks had passed with no word, just Cary following me around, wanting to talk about children. I snapped at him once, then immediately felt guilty. He loved me enough to be asking this, yet all I felt was irritation. I didn't even dare analyze why. Six months ago the idea of kids had been quite an attractive one. I was thirty-two and happily married; it was time to get on with such things. Cary would be a good father, and a break from work appealed. But now I'd gone cold, and the reason was Luke. I wanted what had happened on that roof to happen again—the sex and the starlight and the subterfuge. Pregnancy and children didn't fit the equation.

Still, maybe it wasn't going to happen again anyway. I cursed myself as the days stretched by without a phone call, an e-mail, a sighting. Luke was undeniably attractive to women—maybe he did this sort of thing all the time. Heaven knows he was a flirt; I had seen him in action at too many parties or pubs to mention. But I was a flirt too, and I'd been so sure it was more than that. Something, I'd thought, had been simmering between us for a while. Was it so easily appeased?

Midway through Friday afternoon at the end of the third week the phone in my office rang. Foolishly my heart leaped, but it was only Cary. I wondered again why Luke hadn't called as Cary explained that he needed to go through some slides for a conference with Steve, and wouldn't be home until late. That was fine, I told Cary. I might go out with my colleagues for a drink after work, or even just head home for an early night. I was tired; it had been a long week.

"I'll see you later then," said Cary. Then he paused, and added, "Maybe we can even get started on that project?"

He meant the baby, of course. "Maybe," I'd replied noncommittally. Weeks ago I'd said something to him about going off the pill, but had done no such thing. After I hung up I stared at the phone for a long minute, feeling confused and unsettled. It didn't ring.

Two hours later I was leaving work when something caught my eye. It was a beautiful evening, spring easing into summer, a November night unable to make up its mind. At first I thought the flash of gold was the sun going down in the west, or reflecting off the windows of the tram trundling down Nicholson Street past the museum. For a second I was even annoyed that I'd missed that tram; then I turned my head and recognized the source of light. Luke. He smiled when he saw me, a warm, natural smile that pulled like the moon. I felt my own face come alive with pleasure and barely managed to stop myself from kissing him.

"What are you doing here?" I asked, awkwardly banging my briefcase against my legs in clumsy delight.

"Hoping to see you. Is there somewhere we can talk? Would you like a drink?"

"Yes and yes," I replied recklessly. "Yes to everything."

We went to the Pumphouse across the road. Luke had a beer, and bought me champagne without asking.

"So, how have you been?" he asked, sitting opposite me. The bubbles in my glass jumped and popped, heedlessly racing up through the liquid to explode on the surface.

"Good," I replied simply, still smiling.

"I'm sorry I haven't called," he said, pushing his beer around on the table. "God knows I wanted to. But every time I picked up the phone I thought maybe I shouldn't, maybe it was all too complicated. You know."

And I did; I understood perfectly. Three weeks of second-guessing myself dissolved like those bubbles.

"Where's Cressida?" I asked.

"At work. She's on all night. Till eleven, anyway. Cary?"

"He's working too. A conference presentation or something. He'll probably be home around nine."

Simultaneously we looked at our watches, then laughed as we caught ourselves doing so.

"Is there somewhere we can go?" asked Luke. His words were low and heavy with intent, his blue eyes suddenly darker. My hands felt shaky, and I set the glass down unfinished.

"Uh-huh," I muttered, not trusting myself to speak. We stood up from the table together.

I've always loved being in the museum after closing time. On the evenings I worked late it was a treat to wander out through galleries suddenly free from crowds and the shrill voices and smeary hands of school groups. In the quiet, I'd stop and look at some of my favorite exhibits: the Clunes goldfield diorama that I was first shown as a child at the old Russell Street site; the cross-sectioned rocks and minerals, their impossible colors glinting even brighter in the encroaching darkness; the blue whale skeleton, its jaw a perfect horseshoe of bone. My heels would tap on echoing floors, the soaring glass vault of the foyer as still as a cathedral.

Now I was making the journey in reverse. I swiped my ID pass, nodded guiltily to a security guard, and hurried Luke to my office as if he were just any visiting colleague with whom I had work to discuss. Luke trailed behind me, looking around, obviously interested.

"I've never been here before," he said.

"Never?" I was astonished. I assumed everyone in Melbourne had.

"Not this one," he corrected himself. "I was taken to see Phar Lap at the old museum when I was about eight. I think it's a compulsory childhood experience, isn't it?" He smiled, then looked around again. "But this building is something else. It's beautiful."

He couldn't have touched me more if he'd said the same about me.

My office wasn't actually just mine, but an area I shared with three other anthropologists. Each of our desks squatted in a corner of the third-floor room, which was lit by a long rectangular window overlooking the Science and Life Gallery below. I brought Luke over to it. For a moment we stood there in silence, the blue whale skeleton seeming to swim away beneath us into the gloom. In the aftermath of leave-taking, computers hummed on deserted desks, their screen savers glowing with stars or fish or family photos. Some desks, like mine, were strewn with paper; others had been cleared with more care, the list of next week's tasks already placed precisely for Monday morning.

"No one's coming back?" asked Luke.

"No one ever comes back," I told him, only just getting the words out before his mouth met mine.

We lay down this time, on the rug between the desks, beneath the fading light. Luke removed my clothes slowly, almost tenderly, scrutinizing each inch of flesh as it came into view. First he would look, then lightly touch, and finally kiss the exposed skin, moving slowly and deliberately down the length of my body. Once I reached for him, but he gently moved my hands away.

"Not yet," he murmured against a rib, tracing its curve with his lips. "I want to know you first."

So I waited until I felt I would explode with my need to touch him, then, naked in his arms, began my own survey. His chest was warm and steady, his navel a perfect O. The hair below it, I was surprised to see, was only slightly darker than that on his head, a burnished gold the color of doubloons or buried treasure. When I took him in my mouth I tasted salt and soap and heard his cry.

Later we held each other as the sky outside grew dark. Luke cradled me closely, occasionally moving to kiss an ear, a finger, my forehead, our heartbeats gradually returning to normal. In the half-light the past loomed all around: dusty files, old bones, the smell of formalin and the earth. And us, the smell of us, the present, the future, the new.

CARY

•

I knew almost immediately that Kate wasn't keen, but thought that if I kept talking about it she'd come around. Children, that is. To be fair, we'd never actually discussed the issue, but she had been so eager for me to propose that I assumed she felt as I did. What's the point of even getting married if you don't want to have kids?

I thought we were of one mind when I first raised the subject after the trivia night. She'd seemed to agree, had said she'd go off the pill and have her rubella immunity checked. Some days later I noticed that the shiny pack of Nordette had disappeared from the bathroom, and my spirits soared. But as the weeks went by and no announcement came, I couldn't help but wonder if Kate had simply shifted the pills to her purse or her bedside drawer and continued to take them.

I didn't like distrusting Kate. I'd never done so before, but it was her own fault for giving me reason to doubt her in the first place. It sounds crazy, but before she'd kissed Luke at that wedding I hadn't even conceived of the possibility of her being unfaithful. What's that old saying? *It doesn't matter where you get your appetite, as long as you dine at home.* Kate might tease and charm and trifle, but I thought we both knew what we had in each other, and were more than happy to eat in.

Initially everything appeared to have been smoothed over. It was just a drunken indiscretion, one tango too far. We'd talked; she'd apologized; I'd forgiven her. I'd put it out of my mind, started looking forward to the prospect of fatherhood. After a week or two, however, it became apparent that Kate wasn't rushing to join the mothers' club. She changed the topic when I brought up babies, shrugged her shoulders when I asked about those rubella results. In bed she was as accessible and desirable as ever, but something wasn't right. I'd imagined us curled together postcoitally debating the merits of potential names, or where we'd send the kids to school. She was happy to make love but fell asleep almost immediately afterward, the silky arch of her spine curved toward me like a question mark.

I didn't know what to do. Was she in this or not? I started thinking about the kiss again. And the more I did the more I began to feel that she owed me: a child to prove her love, to re-cement our vows. To be completely honest, I guess a part of me also wanted to secure her, to tie her to my side with blood. I didn't feel like this all the time—when we cooked a meal together or shared a laugh at the end of the day I'd forget about such mad mental arithmetic. But by myself, stuck in traffic or waiting in line at the hospital cafeteria, I'd suddenly recall the way her shoulders had tilted toward Luke or wonder about the absent contraception, and my hands would go rigid around the steering wheel or tray. It wasn't like me at all.

Of course, I'd wanted children long before this. That kiss might have intensified the drive or changed its impetus, but it didn't provoke the desire. I'm an only child and I'd long ago determined that I'd have a big family of my own. Three children, preferably, two at the least. That seemed big to me.

CRESSIDA

·

The results weren't good. The most likely source of a bone-marrow donor is always a sibling, but Shura didn't match. She wasn't even close. Only thirty-five percent of siblings do match, so the odds were never on Emma's side, but still the news was devastating. I sat in the tiny doctors' area reading the slip over and over before crumpling it in my hand. Then I reconsidered and smoothed it out. I'd have to show her parents, explain what it all meant and where we went from here. I longed to tell Luke and have his comfort alleviate some of the pain, but something stopped me from reaching for the phone.

Luke seemed preoccupied lately, and busier at work than he'd ever been. I assumed that the two were related. At first I was glad to see him as immersed in his job as I was in mine, not always asking me when I'd be off or phoning my cell if I was still at the hospital an hour past the end of my shift. But then I started to miss those calls. I missed knowing he was at home waiting for me, preparing our dinner and listening for the sound of my car in the drive. It was childish, really—most of the time he *was* at home waiting, eager to talk and share the few hours before pediatrics claimed me once more. But on a few occasions I arrived home before him to a dark and empty house, dinner unprepared, the ingredients not even purchased. Invariably he'd turn up not much later, the glow of outdoors still in his cheeks, full of talk and excitement for the campaign he'd been busy with or the deal he'd clinched. For years I'd been wishing that he'd like his job more, resent mine less, but when it finally happened it irked me. I don't know why.

I ushered Emma's parents into an interview room devoid of windows or any ornamentation save a struggling African violet perched precariously on the light box. I carefully lifted it onto the desk before turning to shatter their hopes.

"The news isn't good, I'm afraid," I said, my palms sweaty on Emma's thick file. "As you know, neither of you was a perfect match. Shura wasn't either."

I heard Emma's mother swallow hard. "You can still do the transplant, though, can't you?" asked her husband.

"I'm afraid not. The HLA typing wasn't nearly close enough. Giving Emma Shura's bone marrow would do more harm than good."

"But how can that be?" cried the mother. "They look so alike I was sure they'd match. They're sisters, for God's sake!"

I said nothing, letting the news sink in.

"So you can't use her at all?" asked the father, gesturing toward his younger daughter. Oblivious, Shura played on the floor with some cars I'd thought to snatch up from the ward on the way to this meeting.

"We can look elsewhere for a match. Try the bone-marrow registry, maybe test Emma's cousins, if she has any." Out of the corner of my eye I saw Emma's mother shake her head.

"We need to tell Emma," said the father, rising to his feet. "We promised her that it would all be okay."

"It still may well be," I called after him as he left the room. I turned to the mother, but she was also collecting her things, tears streaming down her face.

"My poor baby," she keened. "My lovely girl."

Neither had thought to pick up Shura, and she toddled after them crying.

Over the next week I saw the family again a number of times. We needed their permission to start a registry search and eventually obtained it, but only after they'd insisted on having Shura retested. The match was no different, and it saddened me. After the second failure the child appeared to have been dismissed from her parents' notice. Not unwanted, but disregarded—as far as I could see her basic needs were met, but little else. Though Emma was sure to die if a matching donor couldn't be found, Shura's fate worried me more. Her sickly sister had her parents' full attention and love, while healthy Shura was left to wander out into the corridor or the nurses' station searching for company. One day I found her crying outside the bedpan-cleaning room, obviously lost and frightened.

"Mama," she shrieked, "Mama," holding out her arms to my familiar face. When I tracked down her real mother I could barely contain my anger.

"She was screaming for you. Didn't you hear her crying?"

"Oh," said the woman, barely looking up from her vigil at Emma's bedside. "I thought that was somebody else's child."

The same afternoon I bumped into Cary in the corridor. I was late for a meeting; he was heading who knows where. We were both embarrassed and hurried away without much more than mumbled greetings, but I realized after he'd gone how much I missed him. Not just him, but the foursome that we'd made. For over a year he and Kate, Luke and I had been so close, had seen one another so often. It had almost been like family, or what I imagined a family would feel like if they stopped being doctors long enough to actually talk. Now as I sat in that meeting, not hearing a word that was said, I felt angry at Luke and Kate all over again. Not just for that wedding kiss or their fecklessness, but for ruining something worth so much more than any momentary pleasure they might have gained. I'd liked and respected Cary—he'd been a good supervisor and a steady friend. I'd liked Kate too, been drawn to her vivacity, won over by her generous spirit and love of laughter. But even more I'd liked who I was when Luke and I were with them: part of a team, a clique, where I belonged and was welcomed. Now all that was gone, and for a moment I felt as bereft as Shura.

LUKE

·

Soon it was all I could think about: Kate, and when I could see her next. Or talk to her, spend a minute with her voice in my ear and the phone cradled damply against my skin. We both had direct lines, though only I had my own office. At first we'd talk once a week, then every few days, until it got to the point that I couldn't let the morning go past without speaking to her. My work suffered and I started to bargain with myself, to use those phone calls as rewards: once I got through that budget I could call her; if I finished the presentation I would let myself phone again. Of course, she wasn't always there and then I'd have to set some other goal before dialing once more, hanging up if the shrilling wasn't answered in the first three rings. If she was there, she always picked up.

Kate rarely called me. But then, she couldn't, not with those other three desks lurking so close, those colleagues who would be sure to wonder at so much time spent talking to a man not her husband. When I called she would have to act as if it were business, restricting herself to yes-or-no answers, throwing in the occasional reference to relics or techniques I'd never heard of. Somehow she maintained this throughout even our raunchiest conversations. Or monologues rather, me at one end describing how I'd touch her the next time we met or the way she'd tasted when I kissed her, she at the other primly saying, "Yes," or, "Maybe," or, "Sorry, could you repeat that?" It drove me wild—her covert encouragement, the chance to verbalize everything I felt and wanted, being met with nothing but the faintest intake of breath and a cautiously officious, "Go on."

I'd never tried talking dirty with Cress. It just hadn't seemed right—not because she was my wife, but because she was a doctor. I wondered if maybe the words would sound crude to her anatomically correct ears or, worse still, silly. Of course, her being a virgin when we met had meant that I'd initially avoided the blue language for fear of shocking her. Then after a while it was just habit, I guess—most couples stick within the same sort of sexual routine, give or take the odd anniversary experiment. That was certainly true of me and Cress, and I don't mind admitting it. It wasn't broken, so why fix it? I'd tried pretty much everything before I'd gotten married. It was fun at the time, but after the frantic maneuverings of unattached sex, with all its posturing and trying to impress, there was something to be said for the comfort and tranquillity of the marital bed.

Or so I'd thought. Why, then, was I grappling with Kate on her office floor at every opportunity we had? Or making love to her in the backseat of my car, or the shadow of a Moreton Bay fig in the Royal Botanic Gardens, or against the wall in Tim's apartment once when he was away on vacation and I was meant to be watering the plants? I began to long for a bed, to feel that there would be nothing more erotic than to lie with Kate between white sheets, all our clothes removed rather than hastily pulled up, down or aside. We never used our houses. Cary's hours were unpredictable, and I couldn't relax at my place. Tim was always dropping in, or the hospital would ring looking for Cress, and I worried she'd notice anyway. I couldn't be sure she wouldn't detect marks on the sheets, a strand of Kate's dark hair in the bathroom.

There is nothing better than sex: anyone who says otherwise simply isn't doing it right. In college one time some guys I had gotten friendly with invited me on a surfing trip. I'd never tried the sport, but their enthusiasm was infectious. "You'll love it," said one. "It's better than sex!" Surfing was fun, but better than sex? Since then I've heard the expression used in many contexts, describing chocolate, football, even in one of our own advertising campaigns—for beer, if I remember correctly. Yet I'm still not sure if people actually mean it. How could they? There are lots of things that are enjoyable, but sex is a world apart. Sex, in fact, is the key. What else distinguishes, defines the relationship between a man and a woman?

Isn't that what marriage is all about? Legalized sex, recognizing that it is the carnal act that binds the two of you together, identifies you as husband and wife. For better or worse, sleeping with someone shifts the relationship from mere friendship or desire into a whole other dimension.

Kate and I rarely spoke when we were together. Sentences, that is—logical phrases with a beginning and end, the time for a reply. As soon as I saw her I was erect, aroused, the clock already ticking at my back. Who can converse in such circumstances? Instead our conversations were limited to moans and sighs, her whispered *yes* as my tongue probed between her thighs, my own half sob as I spent myself inside her. Afterward, we'd be too dazed to chat, communicating with smiles and kisses until forced to part or the passion rose again, muting us. That's not to say we never talked. Between those one-sided exchanges during work hours and the wordless trysts outside them we found a way. Every few days Kate would work late, ostensibly sweating over a grant or categorizing the museum's latest acquisitions. Her colleagues, government employees every one, would be out of the building on the dot of five, leaving us thirty, forty minutes to laugh and chat on the phone before Cary called to pick her up. After a while, and to my surprise, I came to enjoy the talking as much as the touching, stopped regarding one as a poor substitute for the other. I'd been infatuated before and had assumed that this was just another instance of it. But I had never really wanted to talk to those girls, never wanted to know what they thought or tease a smile out of their voice. Now, with Kate, I did. And I realized it was getting serious.

KATE

·

And then it was Christmas. For five weeks I'd been sleeping with Luke, going to work, dating artifacts, yet somehow completely missing the decorations that had sprouted like a tropical fungus across the museum's foyer and the carols spilling out of every store in town. Distracted, I guess. Intoxicated, overwhelmed by Luke, caught up in something that I didn't understand, but had no desire to get out of. Sex, sure, but more than that. Just being with him made me happy, as banal and trite as a teenage crush. I didn't know what to make of it. Cary had won my love steadily and sweetly. This, though, was an abduction, a takeover, the violence of my emotions both thrilling and fearsome. I shook when Luke made love to me.

Sarah brought me back to reality by calling me at work to ask if I could fit in drinks and dinner before Christmas.

"Christmas?" I'd asked stupidly, flicking through my diary, looking for the date. To my surprise it was December 15.

"Yeah—ho, ho, ho and all that," she replied while her brood shrieked in the background. "You'll know all about Christmas soon enough, when you have kids."

"Um, yeah," I mumbled. "How about next week, the twenty-first? After work? We could go to that pub you used to like."

"The Lemon Tree? Too noisy. I want somewhere we can talk. I feel like we haven't caught up properly in months. And you didn't rise to my bait."

I heard the chime of an e-mail arriving. "What?" I asked, nonplussed. Everything was confusing me.

"Kids. Anything happening there? You told me Cary was keen."

"God, no. Who'd be pregnant at Christmas, with so much drinking to be done?"

"Hmmm," she responded. "I don't think I'm getting the whole story. But I will next week. *In vino veritas*, or whatever it is."

I hung up the phone feeling vaguely uneasy, then opened the e-mail. It was from Cary.

Kate, I've been meaning to talk to you about Christmas, it read. *Mom and Dad have asked us up to their place for a few days. We didn't go last year, so I thought maybe we should. Is that okay with you? How about we leave after work on Christmas Eve and come back on the thirtieth—we don't have any other plans, do we? Love you, Cary.*

Six days, almost a week. My immediate reaction was to e-mail him straight back and say no. Or that he could go, but I wouldn't. The thought of being away from Luke for so long alarmed me. We'd been seeing each other every three days, two when we could manage it, and talking at least twice in each twenty-four-hour period. But six whole days? Yet I had no excuse. Cary knew that the museum offices closed between Christmas and New Year, that I always had leave at that time. I hadn't suggested alternative plans, and his parents were owed a visit. My fingers hovered over the keyboard. Damn. Why was I even hesitating? Luke would no doubt be spending the time with Cressida anyway. For some reason, the thought almost made me weep.

•

Sarah was already waiting at the restaurant when I got there, a bottle of champagne chilling on the table.

"What are we celebrating?" I asked, sliding into my seat.

"Nothing in particular. I just thought that seeing as it was the festive season . . . Why—is there anything we should be celebrating?"

"Not as far as I'm concerned. Maybe making it through another year."

"Don't be like that. There must be something you want to toast. Your job? Cary? Having children? Not having children?"

I smiled, feeling my defenses wane. "Why are you so upbeat?" I asked.

"Rick's home with the kids and I can stay out as long as I want. Plus I finished all the shopping today."

"More Barbies?"

"More Barbies." She nodded. "More designer outfits, more little shoes to get sucked up by the vacuum or caught between Tyson's paws. But if that's what she wants . . ."

We raised our glasses, briefly touching them together.

"To Barbie," I said facetiously.

"To us," Sarah responded firmly. "To friendships that last through everything. To you and me."

So I told her. I hadn't planned to, knew she wouldn't approve, but after her toast I felt compelled to reveal all. Maybe I was testing her words. I knew how highly Sarah regarded Cary and valued fidelity. Would she still be my friend when she found out I'd betrayed both? Maybe, too, I just wanted to talk. To say my lover's name, acknowledge his role in my life, make him as real to Sarah as her own children.

Predictably she was shocked, but surprisingly nonjudgmental.

"Oh," she said after I'd finished, the champagne going flat on the table between us. "I guess it's too late for warnings then?"

I nodded. She sighed.

"God, Kate, I just want you to be happy; you know that. And if he's what makes you happy, well, I can live with that. But what are you going to do about Cary? Where's it all heading?"

I shook my head. The future wasn't something I'd even thought about, as unanticipated as ill health. Why should I, when the present was so delicious?

"I love Cary. I really do. I've told you that before, and I mean it. I'd never want to hurt him."

"Well, you're going to, whether you like it or not. Don't you think he'll find out? Or do you imagine you can just keep on switching between the two of them, flitting from one to the other with everyone being happy?"

Actually, the idea had some appeal. Already I couldn't imagine giving

Luke up, but the same was true for Cary. Luke was fireworks and flattery, desire, intrigue and elation. Cary was my past and my home and the warm body next to mine as I slept. I was having no difficulty moving between the two of them sexually, and saw no reason why I couldn't do so emotionally either. They were poles apart, opposite but complementary.

I tried to explain this to Sarah, but she wasn't convinced.

"Do you think about Luke when you're with Cary?" she asked.

"Not in bed, if that's what you mean. But sometimes, I suppose. When I'm cooking dinner or we're watching TV."

"Uh-huh. And do you think about Cary when you're with Luke?"

I blushed, the color admitting the answer.

"There you go," she said quietly. "And you think no one's going to get hurt."

"Cary won't find out!" I protested. "He's away a lot at conferences lately. We're careful."

"Is that the point?" she mused. "At first it was just flirting. Then it was just a kiss; now you're just sleeping with him. Where's it all going to end? Are you going to move in with Luke? Have *his* children?"

"You're being ridiculous!" I almost shouted. "Nothing's going to change! It's just an affair."

"Yeah, but you always said you'd never have one of those. Swore, in fact, before a church full of friends and relatives and God. And?"

I couldn't answer. Something hot pushed at my eyelids.

"Look, Kate," Sarah said, reaching across the table to take my hand. "Whatever you do is okay by me; it really is. I'll always be your friend, and vice versa, I hope. I just want you to think about where it's going. Can you do that?"

I nodded as a waiter set down our meals. Steam curled from a plate of pasta I'd ordered hungrily twenty minutes ago, but my appetite had fled. Where was this going? I couldn't even begin to guess.

TIM

·

For the first time I understood why they called it the festive season. It wasn't that I'd ever disliked Christmas, but I hadn't experienced it like this. With a partner, that is: someone who made it personal, made it matter. I did my shopping well ahead of time, tapped my feet to carols in elevators, found the lunchtime crowds exciting and colorful rather than a nuisance. For weeks I deliberated over Joan's present, trying to decide what would best provoke her sharp smile as she unwrapped it, imagining the scene and enjoying the indecision. Jewelry? We'd been going out for only a month, yet I wanted her to know I was serious. Or if that was too much, maybe perfume? Lingerie? I ventured into one such store, all lace and static cling, but the range overwhelmed me. Camisoles, teddies, basques. Who knew what was appropriate? Such things were Luke's territory, and I hadn't brought him with me.

Actually, I hadn't seen much of Luke lately. There'd been the night I met Joan at the hospital trivia competition, then dinner a few weeks later. I'd wanted to introduce her properly to Cressida and Luke, to revel in the novelty of a double date instead of always being the spare tire to their cozy twosome. But the evening wasn't a success. Cressida appeared distracted, fatigued, her mind elsewhere. She later apologized, claiming worry over a patient with leukemia, but I wondered if it was something else. Joan was Kate's friend, at least originally, though they didn't seem close now. Was Cress made uncomfortable by this reminder of her husband's indiscretion?

I hoped not—that kiss was months ago, the incident surely blown over by now. Nonetheless, I never suggested to Joan that we go out with Kate and Cary. I missed their company, but I knew where my loyalties lay.

Afterward, I asked Joan if she'd enjoyed the evening.

"They're a striking couple, aren't they?" she said. "I'm amazed you've stayed friends with them."

"What do you mean?" I inquired, gazing in the rearview mirror as I negotiated the ubiquitous pillars in the multistory parking deck.

"Well, it's just that people who look like that are out of my experience. And league."

"But they were nice enough, weren't they?" I replied, nonplussed. Luke's looks had ceased being an issue for me long ago.

"I guess," she conceded, then was quiet. Experience told me that she was thinking, and not to interrupt.

"I suppose I'm surprised," she confessed after a minute. "Quite frankly, we're average, and they're not. Didn't that ever bother you? Didn't you ever hate him for it at school?"

"Hate him?" I was surprised. It all seemed so long ago. "I don't think so. Not once we were friends, anyway."

"*Once* you were friends?" she emphasized triumphantly. Before us a line of cars waited their turn to pay, brake lights tapping on and off impatiently as tickets were located, change was counted. "So before that you didn't like him?"

"We met on our first day of school when we were made to sit together. There wasn't really time to feel anything except hope that I wasn't going to get beaten up."

Joan persisted. "And even when he was your friend, did you think it would last? Didn't you assume he'd just move on to someone else once he didn't have to sit next to you anymore?"

I sighed. Maybe I had once thought that about Luke, but it felt like a betrayal to say that to Joan.

"What's your point? Did you like them or not?" The words were sharper than I intended, though that seemed to work with her.

"I did. I thought they were nice. And they obviously care about you, which is the main thing."

"But?" I prompted, knowing one was coming.

"I don't know. I'm being silly. But I guess I just couldn't trust a man who looked like him—so attractive to women that he's bound to exploit it occasionally. I'm glad you're not like that," she finished without guile.

"Thanks a lot. But what about Cressida? You thought she was beautiful too. Does that mean she's also under suspicion?"

"How would I know?" Joan smiled as we finally made our way out of the building, into the clean night air. "She's a woman. What do I know about them?"

In the end I chose jewelry. A small gold cross on a necklace so fine it was almost invisible. Joan wasn't religious as far as I knew, but still I was sure it would appeal to her: meaningful, discreet, tasteful without being trendy. In return she bought me a novel and appeared unconcerned by the discrepancy. That was fine by me—I had worried she'd chastise me for spending so much. Instead her keen eyes simply widened as she opened the gift, saw the sky-blue box, caught the glint of the object inside.

"Put it on me," she instructed, sweeping aside her heavy hair and presenting me with her pale and freckled nape. The small dots seemed to blink in the unaccustomed sunlight. On a whim I bent to kiss the marbled skin, surprisingly warm beneath my lips. Joan giggled, an unfamiliar sound.

"Hey, do as you're told!" she protested, yet didn't move away. I drew her around to face me, then not for the first time kissed her self-sufficient mouth, feeling it relax into surrender, the gold cross still winking in its box. Joy to the world! Goodwill to all men!

CRESSIDA

·

Emma went downhill all through December, withdrawing a little further from us each day. We tested each of her relatives but none matched; none even came close. Next we tried the bone-marrow registry, but there was no joy there either, at least within Australia. I completed the paperwork for the larger international registries and sent it off with Emma's condition listed as critical. After that all we could do was wait. Such a search usually takes between six and twelve months, but Emma didn't have that kind of time. What sort of God makes us so unique it can kill us? Couldn't there have been more margin for error?

A third round of chemotherapy brought a temporary remission, though only a short one. As Emma faded so did her parents, their faces growing more pallid with each passing day. The nurses moved her into a bigger room and placed a mattress on the floor so her mother could remain with the girl around the clock. But I never saw her sleep, no matter what the shift. Instead, she was invariably bending over her daughter, whispering to her or smoothing her hair, Shura clinging to her legs or tangled in a fitful doze beneath the bed. The father visited whenever he could, his workdays growing shorter as Emma declined. Toward the end he gave it up altogether and moved into the ward with the rest of his family. Each day, as soon as I got to the hospital, I'd open letters and check my e-mail, praying that a donor had been found. Then I'd make my way to Emma's room, where their waiting faces would turn to me like plants following the sunshine, desperate for the news that never came. Hope slowly leached out of their eyes and was replaced by fear.

When I was little I looked forward to Christmas all year long. It wasn't even the presents, but the novelty of my father being home for a full day, not just popping in for an hour or two between rounds and his own private practice. Since becoming a doctor myself, though, I've found the occasion depressing. I've worked too many shifts on Christmas Day, where the only thing that distinguishes it from any other is cold turkey and a paper hat in the hospital cafeteria. I've witnessed too much grief exacerbated by the supposed joy of the season, seen too many children lying inert and stuffed with tubes when they should have been unwrapping gifts or tying tea towels around their heads for the end-of-year nativity play.

My premonition was right, though it took three years to come true. Emma passed away in the early hours of Christmas Eve, not even having the strength to hold on for the visit from Santa she'd been so anticipating. I wasn't there at the time, though the staff nurse called me at home. For the first time ever I'd been granted leave, five whole days to spend with Luke and our families. I'd planned to sleep in, but when I glanced at the clock it wasn't even six.

"That was the hospital," I told Luke, returning briefly to our bed for warmth after taking the call.

"I figured," he grumbled, turning over as I tried to burrow into his arms.

"Emma died. The one I told you about, with ALL." My voice cracked as I spoke, tears spilling down my face, seeping into my ears like slugs. "I'll have to go in."

"God, Cress, you're meant to be on leave," said Luke, extending an arm in a belligerent approximation of comfort.

"I know, but she was my patient. I should be there for the parents, at least." The bed felt chilly, and I shrugged off the covers and got up.

Luke settled back to sleep, with one final comment: "Well, at least it happened today. There's no way I would have let you leave on Christmas morning."

I slammed the door on my way out of the house.

The words irritated me for the rest of the day. *Forget it*, a part of me said; *he was half-asleep, disoriented; he didn't know what he was saying. And if he did he was just worried about you working too much, wanting you to be able to enjoy a rare holiday without something like this.* Such reasoning worked for a while, but then I'd get angry again. He didn't give a damn that she died, only that it was inconvenient. He didn't understand how deeply I was feeling this grief.

But why *was* it affecting me so much? I'd had patients die before, scores of them, children just as appealing and brave and deserving of life. I'd shed tears for some, but never like this. All that Christmas Eve whenever I wasn't angry I was crying. I cried with Emma's parents and with poor dazed Shura and with the nurses who had cared for the girl. I cried as I made my last entry in her history and completed the death certificate, then cried some more in a locked toilet in the staff bathroom. Emma had been my first patient in the oncology unit, the first time I'd experienced my strange second sight, the first child whom I had admitted already knowing whether she'd live or die. Even so, my reaction felt out of proportion. Was it because I'd dared to hope, discharged her three years ago with everything pointing to a full recovery? Or was I just worn-out after becoming entangled in her long, slow fall toward death?

I bumped into a consultant as I emerged from the bathroom, red-eyed and sniffing. It was Dr. Whyte, the one who had agreed to let me take Emma on when she'd relapsed and returned to the unit only three short months ago.

"Oh, Cressida," he said, ignoring my disheveled state, "I've been meaning to speak to you. Do you have a minute?"

He must have heard about Emma, though that wasn't what he wanted to discuss. I was ushered into his tiny office, textbooks concealing three of the four walls, diplomas papering the last.

"I've got something I thought you might be interested in," he said, scrabbling among a drift of papers on his desk, then transferring the search to an adjacent filing cabinet. Finally the document was located.

"Here we go. The Stevenson Fellowships." He read from a dog-eared brochure. " 'For research and study in the United States. Funded for two years in the applicant's choice of field. Recognizing clinical excellence,' et cetera, et cetera, and so on." He looked up to make sure I was listening. "The department thought we might nominate you, if you were interested. We'd hold your post here, of course."

I didn't respond. I'd thought about working overseas before—anyone who was serious about her career did. The best jobs, the longest tenures, inevitably went to those who had proved their worth in the wider world, far from the academic bell jar of Australia. But I'd always put off such a decision, comfortable where I was, unwilling to disturb my life. Dr. Whyte took my silence for reluctance.

"They're very prestigious, you know," he advised. "Something like that on your résumé would take you a long way. Of course, there's no guarantee you'd be successful, but we thought you were our best shot."

He smiled and I felt my own mouth lift for the first time that day. Suddenly the idea appealed. What was I so afraid of leaving? Luke and I were married. He'd come with me, find it easy enough to get a job in the country that practically invented advertising. Maybe his own firm could relocate him? I was sure they had offices somewhere in the States. My mind raced. It might do us good to start afresh with just each other.

"Anyway, have a think about it," Dr. Whyte was saying. "Applications close in May, so there's plenty of time yet. But you do need to come up with a proposal, some sort of research project that will convince them to spend the money on you. We can meet again in January and talk about it."

I took the brochure and shook his hand, then left the hospital. Outside it was nearly Christmas.

CARY

·

Kate insisted on staying for drinks at her work on Christmas Eve, so we didn't get away until late. I don't really know why she was so keen. It was a long drive to where my parents lived and we'd already attended her department's Christmas dinner only a few days before, but I figured the extra time would give me a chance to pack the car, water the plants, install the timer switches—tasks that were unlikely to have even crossed Kate's mind.

When I got to the museum at our prearranged meeting time of eight o'clock Kate was waiting on the steps, more than a few sheets to the wind. The former surprised me; the latter didn't. I'd half suspected I'd have to go in there myself and coax her out, but she climbed into the car readily enough. I leaned across to kiss her, her lips still tasting of wine.

"Did you have a good time? Do you want anything to eat? I made some sandwiches; they're on the backseat. Just Vegemite—I didn't want to leave anything in the fridge that might go off."

"Cary, we're only going away for a week," she replied with mild exasperation, eyes closing as she settled back into the seat. "And I'm not hungry. Not for sandwiches. How about some McDonald's? A hamburger, or some french fries, just cooked and dripping with oil."

I grimaced. "Not in my car. We'll smell it for days. And we're already late enough. I'll stop in Ballarat if you're still craving junk food then."

Kate didn't answer. She'd fallen asleep.

Years ago, the drive from home to town had seemed to take forever, a daylong odyssey of golden paddocks and solitary gum trees cycling endlessly like the background in a TV cartoon. We lived just outside Horsham in the Wimmera, a wheat-growing district three or four hours north of the city. Age and new highways had condensed the journey. I'd learned there were more distant places, though it never seemed so when I was growing up. Back then, Melbourne was another country, as foreign and exotic as Paris.

Now I was going back for perhaps only the fifth or sixth time in the two decades since I'd left. There had never really been much of a need. Mom and Dad visited Melbourne frequently, and there was no one from school whom I'd stayed in contact with. Usually, when I thought of the area it was with a wash of ennui, of hours just aching to be filled, long, hot afternoons with no company save the heat waves crackling over the endless fields of wheat.

But as the car moved beyond the suburbs, then through the bigger country towns, I felt the stirrings of excitement. We slipped through Ballarat, then tiny Beaufort, the halfway point, and on past Stawell. The Grampians flickered briefly to my left, bulky as a liner against the undulating oceans of grain. Bogong moths as big as finches fluttered against the windshield, and every so often my headlights picked out the eyes of some night creature crouching amid the stringy trees on the edge of the road. Kate slumbered on, her head against the window, face flushed and childlike. Seeing her like that I felt protective, almost paternal, and very much in love. Things had shifted subtly between us in the last month, but there were lots of reasons for that: the time of year, my being away at conferences, her own increased workload. Then, too, there had been the question of children. To be honest, I had dreamed about crowning Christmas Day by telling my parents that Kate was expecting, knowing that they were anticipating such an event almost as keenly as I was. It hadn't happened yet, but I had reason to hope. Just last week I had arrived home early and come across Kate in the bathroom, sobbing her eyes out. When I asked her what the matter was she had hesitated, then hidden her face in her hands and hiccuped that it was that time of the month. I'd consoled her, of course, but secretly I was elated. If she cared that much she must want it too.

Kate finally stirred as we inched through Horsham, deserted by all except the most determined revelers. It was five to twelve; we'd made good time.

"Hey," she said stretching. "You never stopped at McDonald's."

The smile that followed was provocative and cheeky and mine. I felt my heart contract in gratitude, and suddenly realized what I'd been looking forward to through all the miles behind us. Not going home so much as going there with Kate. Time just for us, with no distractions—time we'd been sorely lacking in the last six months. Time to spend with Kate and Mom and Dad, the only people in the world I loved. I felt my foot go down on the accelerator. Beside me, Kate hummed a carol and threw an arm around my shoulders even though I was driving.

LUKE

•

Though it was only a week I thought it would never pass. Christmas took care of one day; then we spent another couple at home bumping uneasily against each other in the unfamiliar togetherness. The days were long and hot and quiet, our friends away on holiday, the suburbs deserted. It was almost a relief when Cress went back to work.

For years I'd nagged her to take some leave, and when she finally did what happened? All I could think about was Kate. Cress may have been my wife but she was suddenly a distraction, a nuisance, something I had to attend to when all I wanted was space to fantasize. Everything Cress and I had previously enjoyed together—walking a neighbor's dog in the local park, going out for breakfast—became a trial, tedious and inconsequential. I snapped at her once or twice and I know she felt the change in me. There were tears late one night and I ended up making love to her apologetically, relieved that I still found her desirable enough to at least get some pleasure from that.

I didn't like the person I'd become; nor was I proud of what I was doing. I tried to talk about it to Tim on a rare occasion when he wasn't trotting at Joan's heels, but that was no use.

"Don't worry about it," he'd advised, suddenly the expert on relationships. "You're just readjusting to each other. When was the last time you spent more than a day together?"

I had to think. Cress usually ended up working at least one shift each weekend, and half the time when she was home I had arrangements for golf or to go to a football game. When it came, the answer wasn't reassuring.

"Easter last year," I'd told him. "But we weren't alone—we went away with Cary and Kate."

"Ah, yes. You haven't seen them for a while, have you?" Tim was almost smirking. Since going out with Joan he'd become far too confident.

"Well, thanks for your help, mate," I'd said, turning as if to go.

"Hang on, Luke. I was only kidding. Sorry—I thought that was long forgotten."

"It is, but that wasn't what we were talking about." I'd toyed with the idea of telling Tim—to unburden myself, and for the rich guilty pleasure of Kate's name on my lips. But now as we spoke I realized just what a pipe dream that was. Tim would never recover from the shock, the defilement of his moral boundaries.

"You're just out of practice with the whole togetherness thing. Go on a vacation. Take up a hobby that you both enjoy."

I guessed that the advice was sensible, though I didn't see how any amount of ballroom dancing or wine tasting was going to put things right. Still Tim trickled on.

"Join a gym together, or buy a beach house—something that gives you a focus. How long have you been married?"

"Coming up to two years."

"There you go then. Plan some romantic getaway; fly her to King Island or Uluru; take a balloon trip over the Barossa. Make it something memorable, just for the two of you."

Despite everything I had to laugh.

"Balloons? King Island? This from the man who thought Lorne was the height of vacation excitement only a few short months ago."

Tim flushed and conceded my point.

"Yeah, you're right, but things change. You meet someone and everything's new. Nothing's ever the same again."

I couldn't have agreed more, though I kept the thought to myself.

Two weeks before I'd agonized over what to get Cress and Kate for Christmas. There's an old joke about a man who buys a cookbook for his wife and a negligee for his mistress. Somehow, though, the two parcels get mixed up and he fears that all will be lost. But on the contrary, both women are delighted: the wife thrilled to be viewed in a sexual manner after years of domestic tedium, the mistress overjoyed that her lover considers her as more than just a body. I imagined the scenario as I trudged my way through Myer and David Jones. Should I look for lingerie for Cress, reassure her that despite all the hiccups of the past few months I still loved and wanted her? I thought I did, but a leopard-print G-string didn't seem the right way to express that.

As I left the department store I had a sudden nauseating vision of Cary presenting Kate with the same thing. I assumed that they must have sex. They were married; there was no reason not to. And if she didn't he'd no doubt become suspicious, so it was in my interests that she kept him happy as well. But why should I even imagine that she didn't? Kate was a sexual woman; she'd have no trouble sleeping with both of us. Stupidly I found myself trying to remember her underwear. There was a purple set I'd seen her in once or twice, albeit briefly. The color was remarkable, regal and whorish all at once. Not something Cress would wear, though it would suit her too. Was it a gift from Cary? Had he gone into a shop, knowing her measurements, familiar with the weight of her breasts in his palms and anticipating exactly how she would look when she tried them on? I found myself suddenly sweating and angry and with no justification for either.

Cress solved one problem by suggesting we buy a barbecue as a joint gift to each other. She'd already picked out the model. I was grateful to be let off so easily and in my relief bought a tiny bottle of her favorite scent so she had something to unwrap on Christmas morning. Kate's gift was proving more difficult. She never wore perfume, claiming that clean skin was a more appealing fragrance. She barely wore jewelry either, or makeup, and I could hardly buy her clothes. Maybe it would have to be a cookbook after all.

I gave her the present on Christmas Eve. We had just two short hours together, having skipped out of our respective office parties to meet under the Moreton Bay fig in the botanic gardens. Dusk was falling, a humid twilight with the sun hanging heavy and crimson above the horizon. There was the prediction of a scorcher for Christmas Day.

"What's this?" Kate asked, looking delighted and abashed all at once as I handed her the package.

"Open it and find out," I replied rather predictably, enjoying her excitement.

She tugged at the wrapping, shredding tissue paper and tape. Inside was an unlabeled CD, the silver disk blinking up like the eye of some great landed fish.

"I made it," I explained. "It's all the songs I hear you humming, plus the ones that remind me of you." I hurried on, suddenly scared she would think I was cheap or presumptuous. "I've left it anonymous, just for us to know about. Play it in your car or put it on your iPod for when we're apart."

Kate was quiet for a moment, turning it over in her hands, not meeting my gaze. When she did look up her eyes were wet.

"Thank you," she said simply. "That's the most beautiful thing that anyone's ever done for me."

She moved into my arms and we kissed, deeply and at length, passion joined for the first time by something stronger. When we broke apart Kate was smiling.

"I didn't bring anything for you, but I've just had an idea. Close your eyes."

I did as I was told, leaning forward with my head in my hands. Kate busied herself behind me, quietly crooning the melody from one of the songs I had recorded. After five minutes she announced she was ready.

"Turn around," she commanded, lifting my fingers away from my eyes. Carved into the trunk of the Moreton Bay fig in front of me was a small heart, its outline sharp in the desecrated wood. Inside it were our initials, stacked neatly one above the other like a child's blocks.

KH
LS

The gesture was pure Kate: impulsive, heartfelt and probably illegal. Instinctively I glanced around to make sure we hadn't been spotted. The tree was well over a hundred years old. I'd read somewhere that it was thought to have been planted by a descendant of the First Fleet, yet Kate had defaced it without a second's thought. The gesture moved and awed me.

"Do you like it?" asked Kate, sitting back on her heels and reattaching a tiny Swiss army knife to her keys. Its red casing winked once between her fingers like blood.

"Like it? I'm overwhelmed," I replied truthfully, flattered but a little uneasy.

"Don't worry. It will grow over in time. Soon no one will know it was there." She regarded me coolly, as if daring me to express relief. I felt it, but kept my counsel and kissed her insouciant mouth instead. What the hell. There was more at stake than a tree.

KATE

·

Five more months it went on. Good months, that is, the ones before the tears and the ultimatums and the all-encompassing pain. Summer months composed entirely of stolen hours and phone conversations, months when we must have made love a thousand times. Months of getting behind in my work, of frowns followed by warnings followed by reprimands. Months when I laughed and glowed and didn't care about anything in the whole damn world except Luke and when I would see him next. Months, in short, when I lived.

I played the CD the first time I was alone after Cary and I returned from our Christmas visit to his parents. As I lifted it from its case a tiny scrap of tissue paper floated to the ground. I picked it up, assuming it had come from the wrapping, but there was something written in Luke's hand on the opposite side. *I love you, Kate.* The fragment leaped and quivered in my fingers, as fragile as a bedroom promise. So he loved me, enough to put it in writing. To plan and consider, to set down the words free from pressure or desire, without hope of any immediate gain. I tucked the scrap in my underwear drawer, then, reconsidering, fished it out and placed it in my wallet instead, sandwiched anonymously between two business cards. I wanted the words close to me, where I could read them at will, warm my hands at their blaze.

Of course I loved him. Had for a while, maybe even since that night on the roof. Is it possible to fall in love with someone so quickly? I imagine

Sarah would say no, that any such emotion was the product of lust and likely to be as fleeting. Cary, too, would say that love grew out of trust and time, a slow revealing of yourselves to each other. Maybe so, but then, I'd known Luke for a year or two before he requested that tango. It wasn't as if he were a complete stranger. We'd been friends before we were lovers, and the latter was enhanced by the former.

Well, mostly. I loved him, but I didn't want to know about his life. His real life that is, the part where Cressida shared his bed, sat opposite him at dinner, assumed his surname. The part where I no longer existed, banished since that kiss at the wedding. Once, in January, he mentioned going away with Cressida for the weekend to her family's beach house, how for some reason she'd been all over him for sex, walking in on him in the shower, grabbing his thigh under the table at mealtimes. I think he was complaining, but I didn't care. The words seared; the images lodged in my brain like fishhooks. Out of pique, I needled him back. Yes, Cary could be like that too. Wanting to try things we'd never do at home—it must be something about a novel environment. "What things?" Luke had asked, and I'd shrugged my shoulders nonchalantly. "Oh, you know. Role playing, a bit of bondage—nothing too heavy, though. Wanting me to pretend to be the nurse to his patient, or some girl he'd picked up in the street." Luke blanched at the last one, but he never called Cressida by name with me again. I returned the favor: whenever we conferred about when or how we'd meet, our spouses were only ever *he* or *she*, not even mentioned unless absolutely necessary. As if neglecting to name them could somehow nullify their very existence.

For a while I thought about Sarah's question: *Where's it all heading?* Doubts and worries would surface like sharks whenever I left Luke, hurrying home or back to work with my thighs damp and hair disheveled, or waking up the next morning and realizing it wasn't his arms around me. But I never found an answer, so after a while I stopped wondering. I had enough on my mind. There was the whole juggling act to plan, and Cary to mollify. Every so often I'd realize guiltily that I wasn't giving him as much as I should: as much time, or attention, or affection, or sex. I was still his wife and I was around most nights, but as Sarah had predicted my thoughts were elsewhere. I stopped making an effort over our meals, lost track of how his research was progressing, missed three departmental functions in a row. When he finally confronted me about the lapses I burst into tears and sobbed that I was depressed about our inability to conceive. As I'd envisaged, he was immediately all concern, forgiving me everything and sharing my sorrow. He suggested we look into IVF, but I shook my head no; I wanted to have a baby naturally. Besides, I'd never stopped taking the pill, and couldn't risk that secret being discovered.

I'm not proud of any of this; truly I'm not. Looking back I can't believe how I acted, how each deceit flowed so seamlessly from another. My only excuse is that I was addicted, and like any addict all I could think about was my next hit. Hurting Cary didn't seem of any consequence; neglecting Sarah or my work was unimportant. All that mattered was Luke and the singing in my veins whenever we were together.

CRESSIDA

·

As summer faded into autumn I began to prepare my application for the fellowship. Over the previous months I'd hugged the secret to myself like an unplanned pregnancy, unwilling to talk about it even with Luke lest he scoff at my chances and destroy the dream. Late nights and sunny weekends were spent chasing references at the university medical library, or investigating possible research centers using the Internet. Every other week I'd meet with Dr. Whyte, nervously handing over my latest ideas or proposals. I wasn't home much, but Luke never complained. Actually, he wasn't home all that often himself.

I wanted to study leukemia—in memory, I suppose, of Emma. More specifically, I hoped to trial methods of reducing infection rates in unrelated allogeneic bone-marrow transplants, where the donor comes from outside the patient's family. Dr. Whyte appeared excited about the work and, more important, my chances.

"It's just the sort of thing they'll go for," he declared in early March as he read through my latest draft. "Children, technology and fatal illness—great stuff."

I blushed, praise unnerving me more than criticism.

"The application doesn't need much more work," he continued, "but have you thought about which hospitals you might try?"

I had, actually. Originally I'd found myself daydreaming about the East and West Coasts, New York or Los Angeles. Isn't that where everyone aspires to succeed? My searches, however, had revealed that my best chance lay with the less glamorous but funding-rich specialty centers of the interior: Chicago, Pittsburgh, Minneapolis. I mentioned them all to Dr. Whyte and he sat back in his chair, tapping his teeth with a pen.

"Maybe even Michigan," he said. "There's a very impressive pediatric oncology center that recently opened there. Let's see if I can find their number. . . ."

He began burrowing through the papers on his desk, mumbling to himself, but I wasn't listening. Michigan or the moon, it didn't really matter. I just wanted to go.

CARY

·

Another six months passed with no baby and growing panic, at least on my side. I was thirty-six and in possession of possibly the only male biological clock known to mankind. Every month I found myself anxiously wondering if maybe this time we'd cracked it; every evening I was alone with Kate I scanned her for signs of fatigue, nausea, even weight gain. She was moody, not sleeping, but there was still no announcement.

I'd always liked children, but this was different. Before, I'd simply enjoyed having my friends' offspring around at picnics or dinner parties; now my eyes followed every baby carriage that passed on the street, watched covetously as the gestational bump of a departmental secretary inflated beneath her clothes. Without telling Kate I went off and had my sperm count checked in case the problem lay with me. One hundred million, with excellent motility. I should have been proud, but it wasn't getting us anywhere.

I dearly wanted Kate to undergo some tests of her own. I'd waited long enough and now it was time to get serious, but I didn't know how to approach her. Kate had become withdrawn, unpredictable. Weeks went by when I felt as if there were a fine mesh between us, distancing and distorting every communication. I'd call in the evening when I knew she should be home, yet the phone would go unanswered. She'd appear distracted, and I'd no longer hear her singing to herself as she went about the house. Then, just as I'd start to panic, the mood would shift and the old Kate would resurface, complete with bursts of affection, sex and laughter. I wondered if it was hormones, or some form of depression. Every time we hit a trough I resolved to speak to her about it, though such a course was fraught with danger and liable to end in denial and tears. Weeks would pass while I screwed up my courage for a confrontation; then the pendulum would swing back and I would relax and think everything was okay. Maybe it was her reaction to stress, and what was more stressful than trying—and failing—to conceive? I knew that pain only too well and resolved to be more understanding of Kate's moods. Whatever happened, we were married. I was sure we could ride it out.

LUKE

•

Everything was wonderful, but at times I felt guilty. Not because I was cheating on Cress or deceiving her per se, but because I had so much for so little. An embarrassment of riches, like the millionaire who wins the lottery. Before Kate I would have said that my life was close to perfect: a beautiful wife whom I loved, a good job I enjoyed, an income that allowed us everything we wanted. Cress's hours were a pain, but in all honesty I didn't always mind them, even if I said I did. I liked being free to do my own thing, be that playing golf, meeting friends for drinks or just watching TV without interruption. I loved that I'd retained most of my independence within marriage and had the best of both worlds. Everything was pretty well settled.

Then there was Kate, and life got better still. She restored perhaps the only things I'd been missing from my bachelor days: the thrill of the chase, the excitement of sexual hunting and gathering. And at first, as I said, I felt almost guilty. Also a little apprehensive—I had it all; I wasn't just tempting fate: I was taunting it. But you know what? After a while guilt fades, fear evaporates, and you start believing in the status quo. Initially I wondered how long it could last, but soon I forgot to do even that. Kate exhilarated; Cressida soothed. One stirred me; the other needed me. One for private, one for public. Between them they were everything a man could want. This was my life, and I had no desire to change it.

KATE

•

Early May. We were now meeting every day, making any excuse for half an hour and the chance to talk or kiss or make increasingly frantic love. Every weekday, that is, weekends being off-limits. Cressida's shifts meant that Luke was available at least every second weekend, though I didn't have such a ready-made excuse with Cary. Where he'd once popped into work on the occasional Saturday, now he'd spend the days puttering about, never far from my side, suggesting we go for a walk or to the movies or out to dinner. Keeping an eye on me. That's what it felt like, though I had no real reason to be paranoid. I could still get away if I had to. I saw a lot of Sarah that summer, even spending two memorable weekends together down on the coast. Not that she knew anything about it, of course, but I figured she'd cover for me in a pinch. I bought a second cell phone and left it turned off. Only one person had the number, and it meant I could check his messages and movements without worrying about the call showing up on my real phone or relying on e-mail. Not even Cary knew I owned it—I paid cash so it didn't show up on any of our credit card statements. The little deceptions.

For all that, it wasn't easy. I felt like I spent half my life looking at my watch, or driving furiously from one man to the other. Fatigue shadowed me, but I found it difficult to sleep. I'd never had so much sex in my life—not just with Luke, but with Cary too. I'm not a fool. I knew that we'd drifted apart, though not a terminal distance; I saw the hurt in his face when I was late coming home again or disinclined to chat after dinner. Naively, I thought I could make up for it with sex—that by maintaining one variety of intimacy I'd sustain the illusion that we'd preserved it all. Cary went along with it for his own reasons: reassurance, maybe, or to try to conceive the child he thought we were striving for. But gradually the passion went, and then the enjoyment. Cary and I had always laughed and talked during sex. Now we performed in silence, as if locked in combat. I hadn't wanted anything to change, but it appeared that something would have to.

LUKE

·

It was Cressida who brought things to a head.

"Here, read this," she said one night after dinner, a rare meal that we'd prepared and eaten together, her pager obligingly quiet on one hip. I took the document she handed me, photocopied and crumpled, obviously much perused. *The Stevenson Fellowships*.

"What is it?" I asked, not much interested. "A conference or something? Is it expensive?"

"Just read it," she replied, a little insistently. I glanced up and was surprised to see her looking flushed and nervous, her hands threaded together in front of her as if they might otherwise begin to tremble.

Research . . . Scholarships . . . Applicant's choice of destination. I was about halfway through before it dawned on me just what she was after.

"Do you mean you're interested in this?" The words came out with more force than I'd intended, but Cress didn't appear perturbed.

"Yes, I am. Dr. Whyte thinks I have an excellent chance." When I didn't reply she quickly went on, pressing her case. "It's two years overseas, full funding for my research. I can go anywhere in America I choose, provided, of course, that the hospital or university accepts me. But the fellowships are so generous that no institution is going to decline."

"I didn't know you were so keen on research," I said, my head swimming. "You haven't done any since that paper with Cary." It felt strange saying his name out loud.

"I know," she conceded, "but I quite liked that. And it's not as if I get the time—I hardly have the chance to eat lunch at work, never mind conduct studies as well. This would give me the opportunity to try something different. Even if I hate it, it would look great on my résumé, so I could apply for more senior positions when we return."

Cress has always been ambitious, so I shouldn't have been surprised. Those senior positions were important to her, the same positions that her father and sisters held. She'd spoken before of how difficult advancement was within the hospital system, how you had to move outside it if you were to get ahead. I'd never really paid much attention, to be honest. She'd always achieved everything else she'd set her sights on, so I'd figured that if a consultancy was what she wanted, then in time she'd get that too. Still, I should have seen this coming.

"What about me? Do I take it I'm part of the deal?"

"Don't be stupid," she replied, color in her cheeks. "We're married. Of course you'd come. A fellowship would cover both our airfares, plus something for accommodation. We could even rent this place out, make some extra money while we're gone."

"But I'd still have to give up my job."

"Yes, you'd have to give up your job," she snapped, voice angry and rising. "But why is that such a big deal? America must have thousands of jobs in advertising. Your company could probably even transfer you, if you asked. Or you could go back to studying, try something different while we have the luxury of doing so."

"You've got it all worked out, haven't you?" I asked, not bothering to keep the sarcasm out of my voice. To tell you the truth, her proposal had knocked me sideways. "I suppose you've already decided where we're going?"

"I've looked into it, yes, but only so I could tailor my research project to facilities with the appropriate equipment and personnel."

"And?"

"And I thought maybe Michigan. Actually, it was Dale's suggestion. There's a brand-new pediatric hospital there he tells me is state-of-the-art."

"Dale?" I asked. Jealousy lunged at me before I had a chance to reflect on how ridiculous that was.

"Dr. Whyte. Don't look like that. He's about fifty-five, with grand-children. And he's my principal reference, so I need his support."

"Michigan? God, could you have chosen anywhere less glamorous?"

"It's not about glamour, Luke; it's about my career. Why are you being so negative?" She pushed back her chair and stood up. "I thought you'd be excited. The timing's perfect: we're both young, with no commitments. We can add in some travel, see something of the world before we're tied down to school vacations or my private practice or whatever. And there will be more time just for us! I'll be doing a research job: regular hours, no shifts, no pagers." She leaned across the table, eyes bright, breasts rising and falling in agitation. "You could at least be pleased about that, but all you're concerned about is being somewhere glitzy. I bet you don't even know the first thing about Michigan anyway!"

And with those words I fell in love with her again. I don't think I ever stopped loving her, really, but I had stopped feeling it, as if a dimmer switch had been used on the emotion. Apart from her looks, one of the things that originally attracted me to Cress was her drive, her ambition. At times now her dedication to her profession annoyed the hell out of me, but in the beginning I was impressed by her single-mindedness, perhaps because I wanted to be single-minded too. Maybe it's me, maybe it's the job, but I've never gotten into my career the way she has hers. I enjoy it, but what I enjoy is not so much the work but the ease of that work, the idea of it—getting paid for making things up, for saying things you don't mean. Work without feelings or accountability or even much effort. Now here was Cress, passionate and focused. It was a long time since I'd seen her like that, and it sparked something in me. Or reignited.

We talked some more after that. Actually, we sat up half the night and talked, something we hadn't done since before we were married. Despite myself, I was intrigued. My job wasn't going anywhere in particular, and while it paid well the figures weren't so staggering as to tie me to it for life. Anyway, America probably paid even better. We moved into the lounge and Cress insisted on making up a fire, the first for the season. In the light of the flames she looked young and excited, happier than I'd seen her for a while, animation accentuating the beauty of her features. For a second I felt content, an emotion so unfamiliar it took me a moment to identify it.

"Here it is," said Cress, looking up Michigan in the atlas, then passing it across for me to see. The state nestled in the top right-hand corner of the country, spread across two peninsulas jutting into the Great Lakes.

"Imagine how lovely it would be in the summer," Cress was saying. "We could go camping or sailing or waterskiing."

And with that my reverie ended. Waterskiing. God, what was I thinking? Just the word brought Kate so sharply into focus I could almost taste her, feeling again the way her quicksilver thighs had moved through my hands, her breath warm on my neck as she shuddered beneath me. I glanced at the map once more. Michigan looked trapped, caught between Canada and the USA, surrounded by water.

"When do we have to make a decision?" I asked Cress.

"Applications close at the end of this month. I'm ready to submit mine if you're okay with that. Then I'd hear if I was successful in another few months, and we'd leave for the start of the academic year in September."

"Do you think you've got much of a chance?" I asked, palms suddenly damp.

"Dr. Whyte does," she replied modestly. "He's supervised other successful applicants." Then her face broke into a huge smile, and she wrapped her arms around her legs like a girl of five. "Won't it be wonderful if I get one?"

Wonderful indeed. What the hell was I going to do?

KATE

•

Things came to a head the night Cary arrived home clutching a crumpled brochure. Without saying anything he placed it between us on the kitchen table, the action both deliberate and defiant, like a man in debt playing his final ace. Only Cary has never been a gambler.

"Read it," he instructed, hands clutched to bloodlessness around the top of a chair. His behavior was so out of character that I could only stare at him, but he didn't look away. Eventually I picked up the pamphlet. *Melbourne IVF*, it read in tasteful letters, and my heart sank.

"I've arranged an appointment for us on Friday," Cary said. "At lunch-time. I'll pick you up. It's just to talk, maybe do some preliminary tests." When I still didn't respond he exploded. "God, Kate, I know you're not keen but it's been over six months. We're not getting any younger. I've tried it your way; now how about for once you try mine?"

The outburst was so unexpected that I almost burst into tears. Still, that wasn't saying much—lately the smallest thing would have me damp around the edges. Immediately, though, Cary relented.

"I'm sorry—I didn't mean to upset you. It's just that I want this so much." He ran a hand through his ash-blond hair distractedly, and for a second I felt a rush of love and compassion sweep over me. I hadn't been thinking much about his feelings.

"Okay," I replied, fighting to keep the panic out of my voice. "Do you mean this Friday?" It was Tuesday. Even if I stopped taking the pill now, wouldn't it still show up on a blood test?

Cary nodded. "Kate, we don't have to agree to anything; I promise. I know you'd rather do this naturally, but we might not have the option. Doesn't it make sense to at least be prepared? I want this so much."

His eyes were so fervent, his hope so raw that there was no point arguing with him. But I couldn't risk keeping the appointment either, having to explain why I was still using contraception when we were supposedly trying to get pregnant. Maybe I'd have to invent an urgent meeting or feign illness. Or confess everything, an idea I'd been toying with anyway.

•

I saw Luke the next day, during my lunch hour. As usual we met across town at the botanic gardens, where we wouldn't bump into anyone from our offices, though the days were getting shorter and I wasn't quite sure where we would go once winter set in. He was waiting under our tree, scanning passersby and scuffing at the grass around his feet. Usually when Luke spotted me his face would light up and he'd hurry over, grinning, brushing off his pants and embracing me all at once. This time, although he smiled, he rose slowly, as if suddenly old, and waited for me to reach him. Without speaking he took my face in his hands and kissed me, thumbs taut on my cheekbones, mouth intense and seemingly reluctant to ever leave mine. The want between us flared as easily and naturally as ever. . . . Seven months since we first kissed, and it moved me as much as the first time. When we finally broke apart I rested my head on his chest and wrapped my arms around his waist. Luke's heart was racing and I waited for it to slow down before I told him about Cary and the appointment he'd made.

Only I never got the chance. Before I could speak Luke was talking about Cressida, naming some fellowship and muttering into my hair how they might be moving overseas for two years. We stayed locked as we were, not looking at each other, my gaze fixed on a family feeding the swans on the other side of the lake. A small boy was gleefully hurling whole slices at one bird while his mother tried to stop him. Luke talked on, explaining and appending, his words scattering like leaves in the autumn wind. I felt suddenly very weary.

Half an hour later I left the gardens without even mentioning my own concerns. Left feeling scared and sick, my head full of words I hadn't wanted to hear. This was Cress's dream, I'd been informed, something she'd been working toward for months. It was all she wanted; how could he say no?

"And what do *you* want?" I'd asked him, numb and still afraid to meet his eyes. The family at the lake had gone home.

"I want you," he'd said, and in a tone that almost made me believe it. Then he lifted my chin so I had to look at him and repeated the words. "I want you, but I don't know how to handle this. I'm so scared, Kate."

Well, so was I. Scared and sick and never more in love with him. Loving and losing. They're such similar words.

LUKE

·

I sweated over the situation for two nights, then realized I should just wait it out. Really, it occurred to me, what was the point of making a decision? If Cress didn't get a fellowship there wouldn't be a problem; things could go on as they were. What were the odds? From what I could make out, the fellowships were highly sought after, and she was still only a junior doctor with no track record in research to her name. Cress might be bright, but so were her competitors, no doubt. Once I realized that I felt much better, and cursed myself for having panicked. Kate would still have had to know, but I could have downplayed it, dropped the thing into conversation as if it were of no consequence. Would that have been taking the easy way out? Maybe, but such strategies had worked in the past.

I just couldn't imagine life without Kate. I'd tried, but it felt empty, stunted. In the weeks since Cress had told me about the fellowship everything between Kate and me had intensified: the sex, our phone conversations, even the weather. There was a sudden last burst of sunshine, unheard-of at this time of year—nine or ten days where the city was flooded with light and you could almost kid yourself summer was beginning all over again. We met every lunch hour we could, making love once in the gardens for what was probably the final time before it got too cold to meet there, Kate pressed up against the trunk of the Moreton Bay fig while I kept an eye out for tourists and held a hand over her mouth to stifle the giggling. Before walking back to work afterward I pulled a leaf from the tree and tucked it in my wallet. Who knew if I'd be coming back next year?

At home life went on as usual. Meals were prepared and eaten, bills were paid, sex, when it happened, was confined to the bed. Cress submitted her application and, after some initial excitement, slipped back into the grind, working long shifts, appearing tired and distracted. She refused to talk about her chances or speculate on where we might live if she was successful, superstitious for the first time in her resolutely scientific life. I'd watch her napping, exhausted, on the couch after dinner and feel both tender and annoyed, torn between the urge to cover her with a blanket or wake her up so I had someone to talk to. On occasion I daydreamed about living with Kate, but the contingencies were too vast to fully envisage. Separating from Cress, the explanations and tears, informing our parents, selling the house—I just couldn't imagine going through with anything so chaotic. So instead I'd try to picture Cress and me together somewhere foreign: her coming home at a reasonable hour, me watching the Super Bowl and drinking strange beer. Neither alternative seemed possible or indeed likely. But were there any other options? My imagination was my paycheck, but it was failing me now.

KATE

·

Fortunately, I didn't have to take the blood test. For an hour and a half I sat in dread in the muted surrounds of Melbourne IVF, Cary clutching my hand as if I might run away. The temptation was strong, yet what would be the point? Over the last few days I'd wearily realized that there was no way out. Cary would only reschedule if I canceled; would become suspicious if I refused. As it was, he'd insisted on picking me up from work rather than just meeting me there, as if I couldn't be trusted to show up otherwise.

During our interview, Cary answered most of the questions while I dully regarded the babies beaming down from the walls around us. Newborns, babes in arms, carefully cradled by parents with proud smiles stretched so wide you feared for their lips. The success stories of the clinic. I suppose they were there as motivation, but I felt nothing. When Cary and I married I had assumed we would have children, but in a distant and detached fashion, the same way you accept that one day you will die. I hadn't been ready for a baby then, and it occurred to me that I still wasn't now. Was that because of Luke, or would I have felt this way regardless? Hard to remember what I even wanted before Luke.

A too-calm voice interrupted my ruminations.

"Now, Kate, let's find out some things about you. Are your periods regular?"

I flushed, but out of guilt rather than embarrassment. Of course they were regular. I was on the bloody pill.

"Seem to be. Regular as clockwork, every twenty-eight days," Cary volunteered when my silence extended for a beat too long. I wanted to reach across and pinch him, to temper all that enthusiasm with some pain. The nurse conducting the interview was taken in, though, smiling at him as she made her notes.

"That's very impressive, Mr. Hunter. Most men have no idea at all about their wives' cycles."

And how lucky those women were, I thought to myself. Cary had probably set up a spreadsheet on mine once we started trying to conceive.

"So then," said the nurse, reluctantly turning again to me, "do you experience any symptoms of ovulation that we can work with? Spotting, cramping, maybe some increased discharge?"

Now I did feel embarrassed. I didn't want to talk about this stuff, and the idea that "we" would be working together was the most unappealing yet. A vision of the woman flashed into my mind, perched on our bedstead with clipboard and stopwatch while Cary made love to me beneath, glancing up every so often to see how he was doing. Mutely I shook my head. She glanced across at Cary, but I dug my nails into his palm in a caution against answering.

"No previous pregnancies? Abortions? No diagnoses of endometriosis or polycystic ovaries, nothing like that?"

I shook my head so often I began to feel dizzy.

"Then there's just one other thing. We need to check your hormone levels, make sure that you are in fact ovulating normally and that your body could sustain a pregnancy."

Here it comes, I thought. The request to roll up my sleeve, clench my fist until veins stood out beneath my skin. Should I fake a faint? Run screaming for the door? Sweat oozed suddenly beneath my arms and behind my knees, warm as blood against my skin. My heart raced, but the nurse had her head down, writing out a referral. She handed me a folded piece of paper.

"There you are. Make an appointment to see your GP ten to fourteen days after you first start your next period. He'll send the results to us and we'll take it from there." Having finished with me she gratefully returned her full attention to Cary. "You should have your test around the same time, though hopefully it will be a little more enjoyable." She handed him a small plastic cup, practically winking in case he hadn't caught her meaning. Cary took it uncomfortably, trying to fit it into his shirt pocket before handing it to me instead. I was so relieved that I accepted the squat receptacle with grace, tucking it into my bag as Cary scheduled our next appointment. Late June. I had five more weeks, surely long enough to work out what the hell I was doing. Or wanted.

But my relief lasted for all of about thirty minutes. Despite the reprieve, things were getting far too complicated. I spent the days staring at the computer screen when I should have been working, then spent the evenings catching up on work when I should have been with Cary. Throughout it all my mind cycled incessantly. Should I come off the pill for the blood test and risk getting pregnant to Cary, or own up to the fact that I wasn't yet ready for a family after all? And what about Luke? If I went off the pill we'd have to use something else. Maybe that was irrelevant, though, if he was moving away. Whenever I remembered this possibility I'd panic and have to see him. We'd meet and he'd reassure me, so unrelentingly calm about the whole thing that I'd be appeased, comforted, at least until we parted and the doubts started up again.

Everything began to slide: my work, my weight, my concentration. It was the not knowing that killed me, and at times I yearned to fast-forward my life a year or so simply to see what happened. Would Luke leave, and how would I cope if he did? Or would he stay, and if so could we possibly maintain things the way they were? I didn't want to have to make a decision, but I couldn't bear waiting for one to be made either. I felt as if I were treading water, marking time, and I began to resent it. More and more it seemed to be my life that was being decided by the board of the Stevenson Fellowships, not Cressida's, not Luke's. What were a few years overseas compared to a whole relocation of the heart? As I waited for their verdict I became increasingly angry. Angry that after all our passion, all our love, a neutral party would decide our fate. Angry at Luke for allowing this to happen, for letting others make a decision for which he should have taken responsibility. I wasn't prepared for my life to be determined by the whim of a committee. I loved Luke, and deserved more. If he was going to leave me he had to do just that: choose and be damned, not turn some chance event into an alibi. Besides, I was sick of lying to Cary, sick of hurting him and feeling our own marriage crumble around us without having the energy or will to do anything about it. Someone had to decide.

SARAH

·

Kate called one evening around six o'clock, the worst time for those with young children.

"I need to talk to you," she said as soon as I picked up.

"Hello to you too," I replied, jiggling Patrick on one hip as his dinner heated in the microwave. The abrupt greeting was not out of character—when Kate was focused little else was allowed to intrude.

"Are you free now? Or can you get away once the kids are in bed?"

I looked around the bomb site that was my kitchen. Was I free now? I almost laughed. I hadn't been free for a long time, not since Alice was born. There was always something that needed doing, someone to be fed or bathed or satisfied.

"Uh, no," I replied, testing the temperature of Patrick's dinner as I balanced the phone between my chin and the downy head of my son. He smelled of milk and apples. "Alice needs to be bathed, Patrick and the cat need to be fed, then after that there'll be stories to read, teeth to brush and Rick to be catered to." I didn't intend for the words to come out as waspishly as they did, but honestly, didn't she have any idea?

Apparently not. "What about I come over then?" Kate asked. "I'll bring a bottle of wine and some chocolate."

"I'm not up for wine right now and I don't know when Rick will be home. Can this wait till the weekend?"

"I guess so," said Kate, then sniffed. For the first time I detected a note of desperation in her voice. Despite myself, I softened.

"Look, make it around nine then. By that time the kids will be asleep, we'll have had dinner and I can tuck Rick away in his study. I can't promise I'll be scintillating company, though." Then, as an afterthought, I added, "Is anything wrong?"

"Not really," she said, sounding strangely subdued and very un-Kate-like. "There's just something I have to tell you. I guess I want to ask your opinion. Maybe even advice, if you're lucky."

That was more like it, and I found myself looking forward to the chance to chat. Besides, I thought, my glance dropping to my stomach, I had something to tell her too.

Of course I was curious as to what Kate wanted to tell me, but after I hung up Patrick pushed his food off the high chair and Alice stepped in it and . . . well, I didn't have the time, never mind the energy, to think beyond getting them cleaned up and into bed. That's not a complaint, just the way life is. My life, anyway.

On top of that, since Kate had told me about her affair with Luke things between us had cooled a little. Not on my side—as far as I was concerned I just wanted her to be happy, and I hoped she believed me when I told her that. No, the distance was from her. Partly as a result of spending all her free time with Luke, and partly, I suspected, out of shame. I never meant to make her feel guilty, but under the circumstances I imagine that simply our differing situations would do that. There I was—married with kids, bogged down in the life of my family, defined by them. What could I possibly understand about obsession or attraction, about desire so strong it kept you awake?

Kate gave me a hug as soon as I opened the door to her ring, then bolted inside and flopped down on the couch. I hadn't seen her in over a month and the change was marked. She'd lost weight when she'd had no need to do such a thing, and the fine lines around her eyes had deepened and spread. As she opened the bottle of wine I noticed her wedding rings hanging loosely on her left hand, catching against the corkscrew and getting in the way. Neither of us spoke until the stopper was out.

"Just half a glass," I said, and she complied without inquiring why.

"So how's Alice?" Kate asked, and I smiled, touched that she'd thought of her goddaughter in the midst of whatever it was that had driven her here.

"She's fine," I replied. "Though that's not what you came to talk about." We were circling each other, suddenly awkward and abashed, searching for a way into the conversation.

Kate swallowed hard and opened her mouth to speak, then suddenly lost her nerve. "No, you first. Tell me about you. I know I've been dreadful about keeping in touch."

"You have, but I guess you've had other things on your mind." She grimaced where I'd expected a smile.

"Well . . ." I continued when the pause grew too long, "Rick's really busy at work, though he could be in line for a promotion. Patrick's cut two more teeth, and Alice is finally out of night diapers. The gutters should be replaced and the cat needs worming. What else? Oh, yeah, I'm pregnant again."

Kate shrieked in genuine excitement, throwing her arms around me. I laughed at her response—by number three everyone else I'd told had been pretty blasé, including Rick.

"That's fantastic!" bubbled Kate. "When is it due? Have you been sick yet? Do you know what you're having?"

"Too soon for that. I'm due in November. And before you ask, it *was* planned, God help us."

"Well, naturally—everything you do is planned." Kate smiled.

"Used to be," I conceded. "And you'd be surprised how many people assume that a third child must be a mistake, particularly when you have one of each sex."

"Forget about them. What would they know? It's your family—you should have ten if that's what you want."

I was moved by her loyalty. "No, I think three is it. Just pray it's not twins."

"A toast," said Kate, lifting her glass, then bumping it against my stomach. "You hear that?" she addressed my abdomen. "Keep it down in there."

I started giggling and all of a sudden it felt as if we were back in school, gossiping in the cafeteria with nothing more pressing than haircuts or weekend plans to worry about. Kate joined in and we fell against the couch, laughing inanely in ridiculous whoops and snorts. Finally I sat back up and dried my eyes.

"You know," I said, "I always hoped that we'd be pregnant together, that our kids would be forever at each other's houses, going off to school hand in hand. Do you think it's going to happen?"

As the words left my lips Kate's face shifted from mirth, crumpling as if she'd had a stroke. She began to cry.

"I don't even know if I'm going to have children," she sobbed. "And what's worse, I don't know who I'd want to be the father."

"So it's still on with Luke?" I asked softly.

"I guess so, though he might be moving overseas. Cressida's in the running for some fellowship."

"Well, that might be an easy way to end it," I mused. Then, regarding the stricken figure on my sofa, I added, "But I take it that's not what you want?"

"I don't know what I want," she wailed, rocking slightly.

"Do you love him?" I asked.

"Yes," she replied.

"Does he love you?"

She almost shrugged. "I think so. He says he does. But how could he just walk away if that were the case?"

"Are you sure that's what he's doing? Has Luke told you it's over?"

Kate began to cry again. "He says we shouldn't worry about it until we know the facts. But that's letting a bunch of total strangers make the decision. I think he should know by now who he wants to be with. God, it's like waiting for the results of an AIDS test."

I wondered briefly if she'd ever been through such a thing. If so, I hadn't heard about it.

"So I take it then that you've made your decision?" I felt almost teary myself. This was far more serious than I'd anticipated.

"No, I haven't." Kate sighed, tugging at the fringe of a cushion on her lap. Then she looked up, her eyes blue-green and awash. "But I can't bear to leave it to the toss of a coin. That's the whole point. This is about *us*, Luke and me, not some chance verdict that doesn't take into account the first thing of what we have."

"And what's that?" I probed, as gently as I could.

"I told you, I love him. But I've been in love before, and this is nothing like that. Every time I see him it's like the first time. Every time he touches me it's like he's never touched me before. I want him more and more, not less as time goes on. Six months now and it's better than it was when we started. Do you know how rare that is? Everything is still fresh, still electrifying. That's never happened before."

She flushed as she finished, no doubt realizing how very monotonous that must make my own life. I ignored her embarrassment. This wasn't about me.

"Don't you think, though, that that might just be because of how things are between you? You can never know when you're going to see him next, and it's all subterfuge when you do. Of course it's going to be exciting, but you can't carry on like that for the rest of your life."

"I've thought about that, I really have. But I think you're wrong. We talk on the phone every day, and my heart still races when I hear his voice. It's not just sex."

I sighed to myself. How could I tell her that it, whatever it was, wasn't about tachycardia or sweaty palms or even about sexual compatibility? She'd been married three years. Surely she knew the gratification of coming home to a man you trusted, of laughing together late in bed with the lights off and his body warm next to yours? Luke was her lover, but was he her friend? Desire ebbs and flows, but friendship—or the lack of it—is what defines a marriage.

I found myself voicing my perennial query. "What about Cary?"

"I don't know," she said hopelessly, eyes filling again. "He's done nothing wrong, but it can't compare."

"Would you leave him?"

The question hung in the air while Kate plucked at the cushion. Fat tears rolled down her face and fell onto the velvet fabric, spreading like ink stains. Finally she answered, "I can't bear the thought of hurting him. But if Luke chose me, I think I would."

"But what about you? What do you want? Before there was Luke did you want to leave Cary?"

"No, of course not," she said, sounding genuinely shocked. "And I do still love him, despite everything else."

"But your choice now is Luke?"

"I haven't made a choice. I can't. It's not in my hands anyway, but I'll be damned if I leave it up to chance. That's what I came to tell you." She sat up, pushing the sodden cushion aside, suddenly determined. "I've given Luke an ultimatum. Three weeks to decide who he wants and how it's going to be. Cressida won't know if she's been successful until the end of June—that's about four weeks away. If he chooses me, with any luck she'll be leaving anyway, and we can make a fresh start. If he chooses her . . ." Her words trailed off. When she spoke again there was a tremor in her voice. "Then I still hope she gets it, and they can both go. I couldn't bear to ever see him again."

I took a deep breath. Comfort or challenge? What did Kate need more from me: my support or a reality check?

When I finally responded I surprised even myself. "It's not really fair to put it all on Luke."

"Well, it isn't fair to leave it to the vote of some academics either. I just wanted you to know in case you have to pick up the pieces." She smiled at me wryly, a sad, lopsided smile, and my heart broke for her. "I can't imagine leaving Cary, but I can't afford just to let this slip either. The last six months have been like another world. I have to give it a shot. If he wants me, I'm his."

"But he has to choose?"

She nodded. "He has to choose. It can't be fate or luck or the fall of the cards. He has to want me as much as I want him. No half measures, no waiting to see how things turn out."

It was a typical Kate decision, and I admired her for it even as I grieved at the turn things had taken. No good could come of this. Even if Luke did choose Kate, how could any union be built on the foundations of so much destruction? I sighed for all of them: my distraught friend Kate; Luke, who I hoped was just as torn; Cressida, whom I'd never met; and Cary, unknowing, blameless Cary. But there was no point arguing with her. Once she made up her mind Kate saw things through.

"Are you still going to see Luke until then?"

"I thought about that," she replied, "but why not? He'll still be seeing Cressida, so why should I just step aside? Besides, I can't imagine giving him up."

Words so raw and vulnerable and sincere I felt scared. I think we talked more, but not long afterward I made some excuse, then fled to the study, where I buried my head in Rick's familiar neck.

LUKE

·

Sometime over that summer Kate had mentioned that Cary wanted to start a family. At the time I didn't pay much attention.

"Well, he's older than me, I guess," I told her. "And you're past thirty. I suppose he thinks you ought to get going."

We were in bed, a borrowed beach house somewhere on one of those stolen weekends. Even now if I try all I can remember is that room: an old iron bedstead, bare boards, blue-and-white curtains. We must have gotten up at some stage, maybe even ventured outside, but if we did I have no recollection of it. Just Kate in bed, her body dark against the white sheets.

She pulled a face. "You saw thirty longer ago than I did, and I don't notice you rushing to procreate."

I rolled over, burying my face in her hair.

"No need. I can still fire one off in my dotage."

Children were such a foreign concept that I wondered vaguely if I would even have done so by then. Kate sighed and I pulled her to me. My mouth sought her throat and I felt her words before hearing them.

"But he's serious, Luke. He wants me knocked up tomorrow, a baby before next year." When I continued to kiss her she went on sarcastically, "You needn't panic. I'm still on the pill."

"Good," I'd said, or something like that. "Let's put it to some use then." I pulled down the sheet that separated us. Her nipples glanced up at me like dark eyes, alert and inquisitive, and I felt my breath catch at the back of my throat. She reached for me as if we hadn't made love in years, and I responded as though it had been longer.

It was only later, driving home alone, that I reflected on her words. Leaving Kate was always a wrench, and the longer we'd spent together, the worse it felt. After an entire weekend to ourselves I was depressed and negative. Why had she brought that up? Should I have questioned her more? Maybe she was trying to tell me that she wanted children. Even as I thought it I rejected the idea. Kate didn't play games; it was one of the things that had first attracted me to her. If there was something on her mind she'd have made sure I knew.

Still, though, a baby. The idea was terrifying, but more than that, abhorrent. I had no paternal urges of my own, but the thought of another man's child growing inside her made me want to retch. I'd loved her for a long time, maybe even from that day at the lake. At first I'd assumed it was just lust—there had been plenty of other women I couldn't stop thinking about, at least until I'd slept with them. Usually, desire waned with conquest, a little more erased on each occasion. Even with Cress, I had to admit, though that was different because she was my wife. Now, for the first time in my life, the inverse was taking place. The more I saw of Kate, the more I wanted her. And not just wanted: loved, even needed. What else could explain the emptiness I now felt? If anyone was going to impregnate Kate it should be me.

As the miles slid by I had a vision of how things would be. If you'd asked me previously I would have argued that Kate was too vibrant to be tied down by motherhood, yet suddenly I saw us all some years hence. Or rather I saw them: Kate sitting on the top step of a porch, a baby in her lap and a toddler standing beside them, his arms flung around her neck. Instinctively I knew the children were mine: they were blond, and the older was calling out to me to hurry up and take the photo. I basked in the image for the remainder of the journey, so clear I couldn't believe I hadn't already lived it. The high-pitched voice calling out, "Daddy!"; Kate smiling and calm as she talked to our son; the flaxen down covering the baby's head. And me just out of the shot, focusing a fictitious camera on the fictitious scene, proud and happy as I captured a moment that had never occurred.

·

The vision returned to me as I considered Kate's ultimatum.

A week or so before she'd called me at work, something she never did.

"I have to speak to you. Today."

Her voice was taut and brittle, like freshly set ice.

"Now?" I asked. I'd seen her only the evening before, when I'd offered her a lift home from the museum. We managed such a thing once or twice a week, always careful to take backstreets and for Kate to get out at least two blocks shy of her house. She'd said something about wanting to talk then, but we'd ended up making love instead under cover of the early dusk, our bodies craning toward each other before she'd even unfastened her seat belt.

"No. The others will be back from lunch any moment. Plus I need to see your face."

Her words worried me as I waited for a tram to the museum two hours later. What could be so urgent that it demanded such precipitate attention? Scenarios flashed through my mind, each more frightening than the last. She'd gotten cold feet, was tired of the whole thing. Cary had found out and was threatening to kill us both. Or—and this in a rush of horror as I boarded the overdue tram—she was pregnant. By me or him, it didn't really matter. Melbourne slouched by unnoticed outside my window as the tram crept along Nicholson Street, past the Carlton Gardens and toward the museum. Fuck. She was on the pill, wasn't she? But if she was pregnant what the hell were we going to do? If it was mine things would be complicated enough, though not without some compensations. But if it was Cary's . . . I shuddered. Would she even want to keep it? Surely not, though I didn't know the first thing about arranging an abortion.

I'd suggested we meet at a pub near Kate's office, the same one she had taken me to the first time I'd approached her after the trivia night. I'd hoped the nostalgia might work in my favor, but when I arrived alone the place felt alien, part of somebody else's life. Three o'clock: an unusual hour for us to be convening. I had to be back at four for a meeting.

Kate showed up a few minutes later. From my seat in the corner, I watched her scanning the half-empty room until she found what she was looking for. Cressida's gaze would have moved methodically from one table to the next; Kate's roamed randomly until alighting on me in delight. Despite my fears I couldn't help but smile. There would never be a time when I wasn't pleased to see her.

"So," she said, sitting down without kissing me. That was usual in public, but when I reached for her hand she drew away. That wasn't.

"Do you want a drink?" I asked.

"I have to go back to work, and so do you. Besides, I'm so nervous that I'd probably spill it."

"Nervous?" I inquired encouragingly, as if I weren't scared half out of my wits myself.

She stared down at her hands spread out on the table, dusting powder trapped under the nails.

"Luke," she said finally, looking up. "You have to choose. Me or her. You've got three weeks."

•

Is it a terrible thing to admit that my initial reaction was elation—that she wasn't pregnant, that Cary hadn't found out? No outside variables intruded; the situation as far as I saw it hadn't really altered. It was only later, despairing of the trams and walking back to work, that I began to realize that she was serious. I hadn't responded at the time. Kate had started crying and I was too worried that someone might see us to take in the full impact of her words.

"Three weeks," she'd repeated between sobs. "I can't do this anymore. I want to be with you . . . or even him . . . but not both. I'm sick of creeping around to see you and I'm sick of deceiving Cary."

Three weeks. As I trudged back through the darkening afternoon the two words repeated themselves over and over, like a jingle I couldn't get out of my mind. Things were perfect the way they were—why did she want to change them? Three weeks. It dawned on me that we wouldn't yet know the outcome of Cressida's application by then, something Kate had no doubt taken into account.

The next days were dreadful. At home, I'd find myself studying Cress, evaluating her faults and weaknesses, trying to assess which way to jump. Once or twice I found myself in front of our wedding photos, ranged across the mantelpiece like trophies, hung above our bed as a talisman. I looked content and confident, as if I'd passed some complicated examination. Cress was damp-eyed and pale, made somber by her joy. My pride still swelled at what an attractive couple we made. And if I'm honest, part of my reluctance to make a decision had to do with not wanting to appear to have failed; a marriage breakup, no matter the reason, is always a failure. I didn't want to be the guilty party either—I'd never been the bad guy before. But then, turning away, I'd catch that glimpse of Kate cradling our children on an imaginary veranda. I had to give up one picture, and I couldn't decide which.

I didn't make up my mind straightaway. Three weeks I had, and it took me almost all of them. Give me credit for that, at least.

KATE

·

I didn't think it could happen. Stupidly, I thought he'd choose me. I was *sure* he'd choose me, or else I don't imagine I would have given him the ultimatum. I suppose I always knew that there was a chance it might backfire, but the odds seemed so remote, the payoff so great. Every time we slept together Luke would hold me and whisper that he never wanted to leave; once we talked about marriage and he vowed that he'd propose in a heartbeat if the situation ever arose. *If.* What did he think was going to happen? That Cressida would be struck down by typhoid? That Cary would gallantly step aside, conveniently leaving us free to wed? Situations don't arise; you create them. Luke must have told me he loved me a thousand times in our six months together, must have risked his marriage at least half as many times to meet me or call or make contact somehow. Why then choose that marriage? Everything he'd said and done—the risks, the vows, the meetings—implied that *I* was the one. Evidently not.

The news came by e-mail. An innocuous-looking one at that, materializing in my in-box with a chime, the subject line blank so as not to arouse suspicion. I opened it almost absentmindedly, concentrating instead on the spreadsheet in front of me. For almost three empty weeks I had thought of little but Luke and the ultimatum I'd given him: sleepless at night, anxious by day. Once or twice I had even allowed myself to daydream about how he'd break the good news: arriving with champagne at work, maybe presenting me with a ring at one of our trysts. I didn't think of Cary. I'd deal with that later. Then this, when I was least expecting it, turning later into now.

> Dearest Kate,
>
> I'm sorry but I just can't do this. Too many people are going to get hurt, ourselves included. Cress doesn't deserve it and neither does Cary. Can we make ourselves a life by destroying theirs?
>
> I still want to see you. I don't want anything to change. At least let me talk to you.
>
> I love you more than ever.
> Luke

Someone at a nearby desk must have seen my face.

"Are you okay, Kate?" I heard them ask. "You've gone all pale."

"I think I'll go home," I replied, my voice automatic, the rest of me numb. "I'm feeling a bit sick." I'd barely stood up from my desk when the nausea hit, vomit splashing to the carpet where we'd once made love.

CRESSIDA

•

I didn't think it could happen. I never even suspected. Sure, we'd been distant, but I blamed myself for that, always at work or in front of the computer doing research. Still, I thought Luke understood. Whenever things felt particularly strained I'd reassure myself that it was only temporary—once the fellowship came through I could relax, and we could begin planning a whole new life together. Admittedly, Luke didn't seem as excited about the idea of moving overseas as he'd been when I first brought it up, but I figured he was trying to prevent me from getting my hopes up. Too late for that. For the last month or two all I'd thought about was Michigan. I hadn't told Luke, but I'd been in regular contact with the hospital where I hoped to do my research. They seemed as excited about it as I was, and had even started sending me practical information: how to apply for a U.S. driver's license, a guide to the neighborhoods around the hospital. Late at night, when Luke was asleep or out with friends, I'd begun to haunt the local real estate Web sites. The houses intrigued me. Shaker style, nestled close to the lake, all clean, straight lines and minimal trimmings. Our own home in Melbourne seemed suddenly fussy, full of overstuffed furniture and outdated accoutrements. I yearned to start afresh with my life pared down to its basics: just Luke, my work, and a square white house as fresh and simple as a child's drawing.

So when the news came, a few days earlier than expected, I wasn't so much excited as relieved. Oh, I was pleased and happy enough, but mostly

I just felt vindicated. I'd planned to be successful, and hadn't allowed myself to consider the alternatives. Now I didn't have to. This was a dream that was going to come true. Impulsively, I decided to tell Luke in person, start our new life off on the right foot. No more late nights or early starts. No more pager or weekend shifts, plus the excitement of all the travel we'd be able to do! He was bound to be thrilled.

I'd hoped to duck out in my hypothetical lunch hour, but as usual a ward round ran late and then a parent needed to speak to me urgently. By the time I could carve out a quick half hour it was late afternoon. I thought of calling Luke before I left for his office, but then decided to make it a surprise. Given the time of day, he was sure to be in—and if he was in a meeting, well, he could always pop out for five minutes, couldn't he? I wanted to see him anyway to make sure he was all right. The evening before he had had a migraine and had resorted to tablets to sleep. All through dinner I had watched it coming on, like a thundercloud rolling across the horizon. He'd barely talked, couldn't eat, was almost teary with the pain. At times he'd buried his head in his hands and groaned until I could stand it no more and had put him to bed, then returned to my Internet meanderings. As I tucked him in I had vaguely wondered what had triggered this attack. Maybe he was as nervous as I was about the fellowship results. The thought made me tender and I kissed him lightly on the forehead before leaving the room. Hours later when I joined him in bed he was lying in the same position, deeply asleep and as lost to me as if he were dead.

Surprisingly, Luke wasn't in. His secretary had no more idea of his whereabouts than I did, but knew who I was and invited me to wait in his office. I seated myself opposite the desk, then, feeling self-conscious, rose again and wandered aimlessly around the room. It was a largely impersonal area. Two awards he had won for some forgotten campaign hung on one wall; a small copy of my graduation photograph lurked discreetly in a corner of the bookcase. On the desk was the pen I'd given him for his thirtieth birthday, still shiny four years on, the cap tight with disuse. A yellowing peace lily perched on the windowsill, slowly dying of dehydration. I moved toward the flaccid plant, intending to take it out for some water, when a flash in the street two floors below caught my eye. Luke, of course, his hair radiant as a halo, four or five doors down from the entrance to the building. I raised my hand to knock on the glass, then realized he wasn't alone. Kate was walking beside him, their steps reluctant as they came into view. No sooner had I spotted them than they stopped, disturbing the flow of pedestrians. Luke steered Kate to the side of the walkway, then reached out to tuck a strand of her hair behind one ear. I saw him take her hands. Saw him glance furtively around, then lean in and kiss her. But not the kiss of friends or even the sort I'd witnessed at that wedding—this was the embrace of people who have been intimate many times and who know what they are doing. A kiss with history. I shrank back against the desk, afraid to see any more. Later I realized that Kate had been crying, but by then it didn't matter.

LUKE

·

I went over it all again as I waited for the elevator. Kate hadn't been convinced, and though I wasn't really surprised, the decision hurt. Ached in
fact, resonated throughout my chest as if I had just been hit. Surely she'd
change her mind. For a moment I experienced a surge of hope; then I
remembered her walking away. Shoulders set as the distance between us
lengthened, the taste of her mouth fading on mine, dark head disappearing
into the crowd. As I relived the scene I felt my eyes become damp and to
my horror thought I might weep. The elevator finally arrived but it was
bound to be full of my colleagues. As the doors opened I turned in panic
and fled into a nearby bathroom.

Two flights of stairs later I was out of breath but back in control. As I
passed her desk Anna was busy on the phone, so I didn't stop for messages.
She motioned for me to wait, covering the mouthpiece with one hand, but
I headed straight to my office instead. I'd speak to her later, when I had
recovered my composure.

"Where the hell have you been?"

The voice broke behind me as I turned to close the door, familiar but
angrier than I'd ever heard it before. It was Cressida, so pale she was almost
as transparent as the window she was silhouetted against, eyes like huge
pools of ink, their color smudged all over her face. In one hand dangled a
defeated-looking plant. For a second I thought she was going to throw it at
me, but as I watched it slipped from her grasp and fell silently to the floor.
Potting mix stained the beige carpet.

"Cress," I stammered in surprise. "Were we meant to be meeting? You said you were on until ten tonight."

"I am, but I thought I'd surprise you," she shot back, her words clipped and furious. "Turns out I was the one who was surprised."

"How long have you been here?" I asked as calmly as I could, still attempting to read the situation.

"Long enough to watch you kissing Kate in the street below. Quite the performance. Is infidelity so trivial a matter to you that you don't even care who witnesses it?"

"Infidelity? What are you talking about?" I retorted, thinking quickly. When in doubt, deny.

"You looked as if you wanted to fuck her then and there, you bastard. I'm surprised you didn't. What stopped you—not enough room to lie down?"

I had a sudden flashback to the night on the hospital roof, and in my guilt and grief felt a simultaneous urge to hurt Cress as much as possible. *There was never any need to lie down*, I wanted to tell her, *not now, not then.* Instead I took a deep breath and cautiously approached her as one would a hissing cat.

"Look, I'll admit I kissed her, but the rest is in your head. It didn't mean anything—if I really was having an affair, do you think I'd be stupid enough to conduct it in public like that?"

Cress wavered, wanting to be convinced. "But you promised you wouldn't see her at all!" she wailed.

"I know, and I'm sorry. I should have told you. I've hardly seen her at all—she just called once or twice, then asked that we meet today. What could I do? She's going through a rough patch and needed someone to talk to. It looks as if she can't have kids and her marriage to Cary is on the rocks." I was ad-libbing furiously, casting around for something to grab on to as desperately as a man sinking in quicksand.

"Why you?" Cress asked, her skepticism evident. "Kate has lots of friends. And why did you have to kiss her?"

"I felt sorry for her, that's all. Plus I was telling her that it wouldn't be right for us to meet again, because of you. And I guess she confided in me because she wanted somebody neutral. No point setting all her friends against Cary; then they end up staying together after all."

I thought I was doing well, but Cress suddenly burst into tears.

"You lying bastard," she screamed, loud enough that I feared Anna would hear. "You don't comfort someone by sticking your tongue in their mouth, then leaving it there for five minutes. You've been fucking her, haven't you?"

"You're obviously in no state to talk about this rationally," I replied as calmly as I could. "Come on; I'm taking you home." She protested but let me maneuver her out of the office, veiling her face behind a drape of pale hair.

We drove home in silence, Cress staring out of the window and occasionally sobbing. She spoke once, but only to request I call the hospital to tell them she was sick and had had to leave work.

As I set my key in the door the house felt suddenly alien, as if I had been away for a long time. Cress followed me in, sniffling and surly, while I wandered from room to room as though I were in a museum. I hadn't realized there were so many photos of the two of us, grinning out from frames of wood and gold and glass, the eyes trailing me accusingly as soon as I moved away. I had the urge to turn them all facedown, as if we were dead. Instead I tried to talk, but got no further than I had at the office. Cress flung accusations; I retorted that I hadn't done anything but comfort a friend. She claimed she despised me; I reiterated that I loved her. It had worked after I'd kissed Kate at that wedding. Anyway, it was true—wasn't that why I had made the damn decision in the first place? Somehow, though, the words had less effect on this occasion. Cry, deny, cry, deny—we scrapped back and forth until after midnight, neither having budged an inch. When we finally went to bed I tried to make love to her but Cress rolled into a tight ball at the farthest reaches of the mattress. When I woke up she wasn't in the house.

KATE

·

I saw him once more. The day after I received his e-mail Luke called me at work, claiming that he couldn't bear to end it that way, that we had to meet and talk things over. It was lucky I was even there to take his call. I hadn't slept the night before and couldn't stomach the idea of facing colleagues, of cataloging relics and dusting bones as if my world hadn't just imploded. Studying my ashen face as I dragged myself out of bed, Cary wondered aloud if I wasn't coming down with something, then volunteered to stay home and look after me. That was all the push I needed. Somehow his concern was even more unbearable than having to hold myself together through a workday, and I feared that if he were any kinder I would break down and tell him the whole sorry tale.

Really, though, I reflected as I walked from the tram stop to work, a confession wouldn't achieve a thing. Actually it might, but only to the negative: I'd be left with no mate instead of two. Did I want to stay with Cary? I supposed so, though it was almost impossible to think of anything but Luke. Still, I'd been happy with Cary before Luke showed up and presumably could be again—if things with Luke really were finished, that is. I'll admit I was hoping they weren't. So when his call came through a few hours later, how could I say no? I was sure that once he saw me again he'd change his mind.

As it turned out he was after the same: that I'd see him and reconsider, come around to his point of view. We met at a café in the city. Luke sat me down at a table scarred with cigarette burns, kissed each eyelid, red with tears, then launched into his proposal with a fervor I imagine he usually reserved for winning campaigns. "Let's leave things as they are," he'd entreated. We'd work something out—what we had was too good to throw away. Mutely I shook my head. Luke persevered. It was just that the timing was wrong—couldn't I see that? Cress had worked so hard for the fellowship, but she'd never accept were he to leave her now. She deserved to be able to realize her dream. Just one year away, two maximum; then we could talk about marriage when he returned to Australia. There would be no children, no complications; he could guarantee that. And if Cress's application wasn't successful, how could he add to her grief by asking for a divorce? "A year," he repeated. "I owe her that. She's done nothing wrong."

At first I listened; I really did. I tried to understand his point of view, but there wasn't one, just a desire not to rock the boat. A year away—then we could talk? I couldn't give in. I loved him too much to have only half of him, and not even the best half. Besides, he'd as good as admitted that if he stayed with Cress he'd be moving overseas. "E-mail," he'd said, shrugging, "the phone. It's only for a year—we can pick up where we left off when I get back." I didn't like the sound of that: that I could be put on layaway, kept for a rainy day. How could I trust him not to do the same with some American girl? How could I wait for a year when right now two days without him seemed an eternity? And how long could we keep it up? Sneaking around at thirty-two may have had some shabby sort of cachet; sneaking around at fifty was decidedly pathetic.

And by now I was angry with him. He hadn't chosen me, hadn't wanted me as much as I'd wanted him. My pride stung almost as much as my eyes. Without thinking about what I was doing I picked up my bag and got to my feet. Luke was beside me in an instant.

"Where are you going?" he asked, cut off in midsentence.

"This isn't achieving anything," I replied. "I have to get back to work." I felt strong, resolved and clinically dead. The whole scene unfolded as if it were being played out somewhere far away, as if I were at the movies or watching from a distance, disconnected from my body, my heart. The only way I could bear to leave.

"Wait!" Luke was calling. Despite myself my steps faltered in hope. He pulled on his jacket and caught up to me. "I'll walk you back to the museum."

So there wasn't going to be a happy ending after all. For a moment pain flared; then it all shut down. Amputees must experience the same sensation.

Really, we should have just gone our separate ways, left the grubby little café and never seen each other again. But my route took me past his building anyway, and a tiny part was reluctant to finish it there, amid dirty coffee cups and the paper napkins I'd shredded while he was talking. So we struggled the block to his office, like sleepwalkers or shipwreck victims coming ashore. A discreet doorway or two away Luke pulled me to him and we kissed good-bye. It was a kiss as sweet as every other time, comforting and poisonous. I felt tears rolling down my cheeks and turned my back, walking away without saying good-bye.

CRESSIDA

•

Where else would I go? I went to work. I wasn't due until later that day but there didn't seem any other option. I couldn't stay at home, not with Luke sleeping so soundly in our marital bed when I'd done little but doze and fret and cry all night. I couldn't go to my parents' home, and didn't want to tell any of my friends. Most of them would have been working anyway—given my schedule, the only friendships I'd really maintained were with others in the same profession. They understood the long hours, lack of social life and six-month pauses between phone calls, but were always on duty when I was off. As for my parents . . . my hunch was that they wouldn't be home anyway, my father hard at work at some hospital, my mother heading a committee or attending a benefit. And if they were there, what would I tell them? That I'd left Luke? That he'd had an affair? Maybe a room would be grudgingly found for me, but I knew what they'd be thinking. That I should be at home, with my husband, that it was bound to be a misunderstanding.

Besides, had I left Luke? I didn't believe his denials, though part of me ached to. If he were attracted to Kate, and history told me he was, he wouldn't have been content just to be her friend. The idea of him holding her hand through her marital difficulties without trying to take something for himself was laughable. And if it was all so innocuous, why hadn't he told me? I knew our own marriage wasn't perfect—that Luke was a flirt and I was away too often—but deep down I believed in it. He'd proposed to me, after all.

So what now? The more I thought about it, the more panicked I became. I couldn't live with him if he'd had an affair; would never be able to trust him again. But I didn't want to end my marriage, particularly if there was a chance I could be wrong. A slim one, but a chance . . . I held on to that. And what about the fellowship? I had a week to accept, to make my own requests. Airfares, but for how many? A house, or simply an apartment? Could I even go without him, set off alone to the other side of the world, to a place where no one knew my name? I needed the truth before I could think about anything else.

Did Tim know? I called him on my way to work, fingers clumsy on the tiny buttons of my cell phone. He would still be asleep—it was barely six, after all—but I didn't even consider waiting until a more respectable hour. Anyway, he could go back to sleep easily enough. Who knew if I'd ever have that luxury again? His voice on the line was disoriented, cautious.

"Hello?"

"It's Cressida. Do you know anything about Luke and Kate?" No point beating around the bush.

"Luke and Kate? Do you mean the wedding?" he replied sleepily. "That was ages ago—I thought you guys had sorted things out."

"Not the wedding. Since then. Are they having an affair?"

In the background I heard a mumbled query and realized he wasn't alone. It annoyed me somehow. I still couldn't get used to the idea of his having a partner.

"Hang on. I'm going to take this in the kitchen."

Good old Tim, ever the gentleman. I waited impatiently for the line to click back to life. When it did he sounded wide-awake.

"An affair? What are you talking about?"

"Luke hasn't told you about this?"

"I've barely even seen Luke the last few months. Just figured you two were busy."

"He didn't tell you he was seeing Kate, supposedly helping her through some marriage crisis?"

"No. To be honest, I thought you'd banned him from seeing her after that wedding. And fair enough too," he added hastily.

"So did I," I replied. In the silence that followed I heard the faint buzz of another conversation on the line. What on earth could people be talking about at this hour?

"Look, Cressida," Tim said finally, sounding upset, "Luke's never been a saint, but he's no hypocrite. I don't know what's happened, but I'm sure he hasn't been messing around with Kate. It's you he loves."

The tears started up again then, slipping silently down my face. I swallowed hard, staring at the receiver until it came back into focus.

"I got the fellowship, by the way."

It had suddenly occurred to me that I had yet to share the news with anyone, even Luke. But there was no joy in speaking the words, just the absence of anything else to say.

"Good for you!" said Tim, genuinely pleased. "Work all this out with Luke; then we'll celebrate in fine style. Really, Cress, I'm sure it's nothing."

I hung up unconvinced. He might be sure but I wasn't. Whom else could I ask?

CARY

•

Cressida phoned me at work. I recognized her voice on the line immediately, though it had been months since we'd last spoken. Even so, the memory of our shared humiliation made me anxious. This couldn't be a social call.

It wasn't.

"Kate and Luke have been seeing each other," she informed me in a voice gone dull with pain. "I had to find out if you knew. I think they're having an affair."

I didn't know, of course, and strenuously denied the possibility. Yet even as I spoke I realized that what she was saying might be true. It would explain so much: Kate's distraction, her weight loss, our unconceived children.

The voice on the line continued, escalating in panic.

"He denies it, but I don't believe him. What do you think?"

My mind was racing. I couldn't answer, just shook my head instead. Cressida went on, in tears now, and I could almost hear the receiver shaking in her grip.

"Can you find out for me, Cary? I have to know. So do you. What are they doing? Is it over? Please."

I don't remember answering her; don't remember hanging up. Instead I went back to my microscope and my slides, forcing myself to finish the job I'd started, squinting down the barrel until my eyes ached and my head pounded. Somewhere, somebody else was also waiting for news, for a verdict that could change his or her life. I concentrated on determining that fate before I allowed myself to think about my own.

KATE

•

The day after I'd said good-bye to Luke, Cary came home from work early. I'd done the same, unable to concentrate on the shards of a clay pot I was trying to date, worried that my trembling hands would drop the artifact or give me away. How was I ever going to work again? I couldn't concentrate, could barely draw breath without thinking of Luke, going over it all just one more time. Even being at the museum made me ache. There was the phone that didn't ring, the rug where we'd once lain together, even the blue whale skeleton we'd kissed under on our way out of the building that long-ago night. Relics of our own short history, unclassified, uncataloged. How long till time buried these too?

Cary's car was in the drive, its hood still warm. I felt a stab of annoyance. I'd wanted to have a bath and a good long cry, maybe call Sarah and tell her what had happened. Now I'd have to continue to act as if nothing were wrong, maintain the facade that was giving me a migraine. For a second I thought about running, but where would I go? The decision had been made, and this was still my home.

I braced myself, then pushed open the door, calling Cary's name. Maybe he'd want to have a drink—God knew I could use one. I expected him to be at his desk or maybe already busy in the kitchen, but when I finally found him he was sitting in our living room in darkness.

"Are you okay?" I asked, suddenly wary. Something was wrong. The house was cold. Cary hadn't even turned the heat on.

"I had a call from Cressida today. You remember her. You kissed her husband once at a wedding."

I stopped breathing, my hand frozen as it reached for the light switch.

"She told me everything. She saw the two of you kissing again yesterday, outside Luke's office. When she confronted him he confessed it all."

"All?" The word was little more than a whisper, ash blown on a faint puff of air.

"All of it—that the two of you have been having an affair, sneaking around, deceiving us both."

Apart from in the earliest days, I had never seriously considered that Cary might find out what I was up to. The possibility had concerned Sarah, but never me. Maybe that's a common delusion of the adulterer, or perhaps it was because he was just so trusting—always willing to accept every excuse or deception I might offer. I'd grown careless with his faith in me. Now all of a sudden I realized I'd squandered it like change.

"Well?" he prompted as I continued to stand there. The body is an amazing thing, perpetually optimistic in its functioning: though I felt as if my heart had stopped, my eyes were adjusting to the late-afternoon gloom. Cary looked grim and defeated. I cleared my throat but no sound came out. A perilous silence stretched between us. Only words could be more dangerous.

"Talk to me, Kate!" Cary shouted, halfway between a demand and a plea. I thought furiously, trying to come up with a plausible story, a defense of sorts. But it was no use, and suddenly I was too tired for any more deceit.

"I wish I'd told you first," I said, meaning it. "I was going to, once I got it together in my own head."

"Told me what? That you slept with him?"

I nodded, ashamed for the first time. The color drained from his face, almost as if someone had pulled out a plug.

"So it's true?" he cried.

"It's over now," I hedged.

"When did you last see him?"

It was dawning on me that perhaps Cary hadn't really been sure, that he'd called my bluff. Yet he must know something to have made the accusation. Either way I lacked the energy to lie.

"Yesterday," I whispered, and he buried his head in his hands.

For a long time we stayed like that—me immobile in the doorway by the light switch, Cary slumped in the chair with his face covered. He was so still that I almost feared he was becoming catatonic, but after about half an hour he suddenly rose and walked past me without once looking my way. I heard him leave the house, shutting the door quietly behind him, then start the car and reverse carefully out of the drive. His control scared me more than any show of anger. I began to shake, at first with cold and shock, then with rage. Before I knew it I was dialing Luke's number. I needed to find out how much had been said and what I could salvage. But more than that, I was furious he had revealed anything at all—that he wouldn't have me, but wouldn't let me have my marriage either. I didn't stop to consider that it wasn't in his interest to have told Cressida anything himself. She answered the phone anyway, and I hung up without speaking, suddenly terrified.

CRESSIDA

·

I'd moved out within the hour after Cary called back. Had me paged, actually, at the hospital, where I was still going through the motions. Fortunately my shift was almost finished. I cut it short, abandoned the charts I had yet to write up and broke every speed limit to get home. Luke wasn't there. Still at work, I presumed, though after what Cary had told me anything was possible. Despite everything I was disappointed not to see him. I felt jagged and edgy, off center somehow. I needed to fight and scream, to rid myself of some of the adrenaline. Instead I packed. Clothes for work, pajamas, my cosmetics. Underwear, ten pairs. Who knew when I'd be back?

The phone rang once as I moved about the bedroom. I swooped on it, hoping it was Luke, still feeling strangely high. But the line went dead and no one called back. Not his style. Maybe Cary? I doubted it. He'd been so devastated when we spoke the second time that he couldn't end the call fast enough. No details, just the facts. That they had slept together, probably more than once. That Kate had said it was over. That he didn't know what to do. Those were his last words. Just a statement, articulated as precisely as any theorem. He wasn't looking for advice, and I couldn't have given him any. But I knew what *I* had to do. Get out, leave Luke. Put as much distance between us as I could.

The house was quiet as I locked the door behind me. I wasn't sure where I was going, but probably the hospital. The residents' quarters, or one of the rooms they kept for parents. Of course the house was quiet. It was always quiet. We were rarely home, either together or apart. I was out of control, less myself than I'd ever been. Like Eve must have felt after the fall, I reflected as I drove away. Leaving Eden for a land unknown.

CARY

•

Can I bear to recount the weeks that followed? A year later I could still taste the pain, rising to the back of my throat like bile: wretched, sour and indigestible. I literally felt gutted, as if someone had hollowed me out, removed my core. Patients in the final stage of dementia revert to an almost neonatal state, their brains so atrophied they can only breathe and digest, suck and pout. That was how I felt. I continued to function, but only at the most basic level, my existence little more than a collection of primitive reflexes. If I ate I'd need to defecate straightaway, stomach cramps tying me to the toilet for an hour at a time. If I slept it was only through the work of my reticular activating system, craving some respite from the constant ache. That I breathed at all was a miracle.

For almost two weeks I remained dry-eyed. Then one day Kate came into work, still trying to talk to me. As soon as I saw her I cried. Maybe it was the setting—the only place up until then that didn't remind me of what had happened or how much I'd lost. I cried in front of Steve and a new lab assistant, tears coursing down my face to smudge notes and contaminate petri dishes. Kate looked as though she wanted to comfort me, then turned and fled instead. Later I blamed the incident on hay fever, and my colleagues were kind enough to appear convinced.

I hadn't told Steve, of course. I hadn't told anyone. Partly I suppose it was pride, though that wasn't the whole reason. Somehow it seemed that talking about it would make the whole thing more real. Thinking about it was bad enough and something I avoided at all costs, attempting to simply live through the pain as if it were a toothache. But to actually articulate the words, to admit out loud that Kate had slept with someone else, been unfaithful, undressed for him when she'd promised me . . . I couldn't even continue the thought. There were deeper implications too. I need to care for someone before I slept with them, be involved emotionally as well as physically. I knew that for Kate that hadn't always been the case, but her track record was small comfort on the long nights that I lay without sleep.

I suppose I could have asked her. Technically we were continuing to live together, though only because neither one of us could work up the momentum to move out. It was never discussed. I had no intention of doing so—it was originally my house, after all—and Kate continued to turn up each night regardless. Instead, I shifted into the spare room. I couldn't bear to lie beside her every night, angry when she slept, torn when she tossed and sighed as I did. Once or twice she had reached out, tentatively, to touch me, as if testing the heat of an iron. "Cary," I'd hear her whisper, "I'm so very sorry." I couldn't bring myself to respond.

The spare room was comfortable enough. We'd left a double bed in there—ironically, it was Kate's from before our marriage. Six months ago I had begun referring to the room as "the nursery" and collecting the paraphernalia I was sure we would soon be needing. Stuffed toys, a changing table that somebody at work was getting rid of, a wooden mobile made up of bright black-and-yellow bees. Kate had indulged me, though I realized now that she'd never contributed anything herself. Most nights I'd barely see the room, hiding out at work and often eating there too, staying away until it was so late I could be sure that fatigue would allow me to sleep. But not always. Some nights, no matter how exhausted I felt when I put my key in the door, just being at home rendered rest impossible. Instead, I'd find myself lying in bed staring up at those bees, their incessant and unproductive circles paralleling my own dark thoughts, the red-painted smiles seeming to mock and jeer as they sailed through the air above me.

LUKE

·

I didn't think Cress would move out for long, and I was right. Trouble was, I hadn't anticipated what she would do next. One afternoon, about ten days after I had first come home to an empty house, I arrived at one that I couldn't get into at all. An envelope was taped to the door, my name carefully printed on it in her slanting script.

Luke, I read, *why should I be the one to leave? I've put your things in the toolshed. Call me if you think I've missed something.*

I tried the door but my key wouldn't fit. She'd had the locks changed while I was at work. When I eventually gave up pounding on the door and searching for a window where I might gain access I made my way to the old corrugated iron shed at the end of our garden. Inside were at least fifteen boxes: socks in one, shoes in another, belts and ties spilling out of a third. My T-shirts had been pulled still folded from their shelves; shirts and suits had been thrust into boxes still on their hangers. All my books were there, as was my camera—even a half-empty box of condoms from my bedside table. Despite myself I was almost impressed. She'd been thorough.

For half an hour I lugged boxes from the shed to my car, then gave up when it became apparent that they weren't all going to fit. Some were quite heavy, and I wondered if she'd had assistance. The question was who? Cress had few close friends, only colleagues, and I couldn't imagine her asking her family to help. I wasn't even sure that she wasn't indeed inside the house, though her car was absent and no one had responded to my hammering on the door. Once or twice as I tottered up the driveway I thought I saw a curtain twitch, heard stifled glee. Well, let her laugh. I'd be back soon enough, and she was the one who would be helping to unpack all these boxes.

Meanwhile, though, where was I going to go? I had no desire to involve my family, nor anyone to whom I'd have to explain the situation. I had plenty of friends—people at the office, guys I'd kept up with from school—but how could I tell them that my trophy wife had thrown me out? After some thought, I decided on Tim. We had shared an apartment in our college years, and I knew he could mind his own business if necessary. Joan would be around a bit, I imagined, and her relationship with Kate might make things awkward. But I'd been Tim's friend for years, and surely that counted for something. Besides, it was only temporary.

KATE

·

Cary came back later that night. Much later: around three. He opened the bedroom door and I lay there feigning sleep, terrified of a confrontation or questions I couldn't answer. But he was only checking to make sure I was there, then padded away back down the hall. I heard the CD player being switched on, followed by him gently closing the door to the living room. Such consideration, after all I'd done to him.

He was gone again when I awoke the next morning. Sleep had been a long time coming, then hardly refreshing when it finally arrived. I woke hoping the whole thing had been a dream, that Cary would be already up and in the kitchen as he was every other day, reading the paper and conscientiously chewing his way through a bowl of bran. But his briefcase was gone, the house cold and accusing. He must have left for work in the clothes he'd worn yesterday rather than come into our room.

I didn't go to work myself. I wouldn't have achieved anything, and I wanted to be at home in case he returned. Instead, I spent the day watching TV in my pajamas, checking my cell phone hourly in case Luke had called, starting every time I heard a car in the street. I phoned Sarah but only got her answering machine. She was probably off doing kindergarten duty or at a prenatal checkup, and for the first time such a straightforward life appealed. I tried to think about the whole sorry situation, to work out what I should do or say or what I even wanted. But it was all too hard. Easier to let the daytime soaps wash over me, to lose myself in a world where adultery was once again about passion and excitement, not this constant nausea at the back of my throat.

I tried to apologize; really I did. At night, in the dark, when I couldn't see his face, on the one or two occasions Cary came back to our bed. I'm not sure he even heard, never mind believed me. Soon after that he started sleeping in the spare room. Though it was all a bit late in the piece to be thinking of Cary, I really was sorry. He'd done nothing wrong, and it wrenched my heart to see his face cloud over every time our eyes met. I'd barely cried myself, too numb to shed the tears. Besides, I still wasn't sure what I was mourning—the loss of Luke or of my marriage.

After three days I went back to work. It was getting awkward to be away any longer and it was time I got on with my life. Luke hadn't called, and I suspected he wasn't going to. Cary came home every night, but usually after I had gone to bed, leaving again before I got up the next day. If I made him dinner I found it untouched the following morning, as if he were afraid I would poison him. I left him notes that he didn't answer, even went to the hospital to try to talk to him there. But nothing got through, and after a week we settled into a routine of living like estranged roommates.

Of course, all the love I'd ever felt for Cary flooded back as soon as I saw how upset he was. That was predictable, I guess, but what I hadn't anticipated was that it didn't stop me from loving Luke as well. . . . I spent my days going through the motions, hoping that one would call while simultaneously wishing that everything could be smoothed out with the other. Walking around bleeding from two wounds.

LUKE

•

If I had wondered how I was going to break the news to Tim I needn't have bothered.

"Hey, mate," I began as I called him from a pay phone en route to his apartment. The recharger for my cell phone was one thing Cress had neglected to deposit in the shed. "I was wondering if I could stay with you for a week or so. Cress and I are going through a bit of a rough patch. . . . "

"Yeah, sure," Tim replied, cutting across my carefully thought out explanation. "I've been expecting your call. Cressida told me that she changed the locks."

"She did?" I couldn't keep the surprise out of my voice.

"And that's some rough patch. You had an affair!" He didn't hide the accusation in his tone. I fell silent, stunned. A beetle crawled toward my foot, searching for food or a mate. On impulse I lifted my shoe and smeared it across the pitted concrete.

"Luke? Are you still there?"

I didn't answer, still stung. Tim had never questioned me before. Our entire relationship was based on him being the straight guy and me the maverick, right from the moment I'd first taken pity on him at school. We'd moved on since then, but I guess I still thought of him as one would a younger brother: pride, tolerance and condescension mixed in equal quantities. And I certainly didn't like him criticizing me.

"If it's too much trouble I can go somewhere else." I strove to keep my tone light, as if it didn't much matter.

"Don't be like that. Of course you can stay." Tim spoke as one would to a child, and a sulky one at that. I was tempted to tell him to stick his tiny apartment, his morals and his outrage, but just then the coins ran out. I stood there furiously pondering other options, the receiver whining to be replaced. Fuck it. Tim already knew; it might as well be him.

I hadn't gotten the first box in before he was asking me what happened. Well, not what happened exactly, but why.

"I just don't understand. Cressida's gorgeous, she's smart and she adores you. What on earth would make you have an affair?"

He was lugging boxes up the stairs as he spoke, panting slightly. Tim had a spare room but he used it as a study, with a futon in one corner. "Nothing made me," I tried to tell him, "it just happened." Hadn't he ever met someone he desired so greatly, wanted so much, he just had to have her, regardless of consequences? Tim looked skeptical. I doubt he'd ever done anything regardless of consequences. Nevertheless, I pressed on. What about when he met Joan? I probed. Couldn't he remember that feeling, the tidal wave of lust and longing and eventually love that must have engulfed him? I could tell by his face that I was closer to the mark, though he wasn't having any of it.

"Maybe, but I wasn't married when I met Joan," he replied, as straight as ever. "And isn't that what you felt when you met Cressida?"

I thought about it. Yeah, possibly, but that was so long ago and this was now. I was suddenly sick of talking about it, sick of being interrogated. Sure, I'd screwed up, but I'd made the honorable decision in the end, and I didn't seem to be getting any credit for that. All I really wanted to do was have a beer and watch football: anything to forget about it for a while.

Tim waited for an answer, then gave up, heading back down the stairs for another load.

"Anyway," he called back, "she called while you were driving over here. Had a message for you."

"She did? Who?"

"Cressida, of course," he replied scornfully, waiting for me to catch up to him.

I was momentarily disappointed. "What did she say?"

Tim removed a piece of paper from his pocket and studied it carefully, as if he hadn't already memorized the words.

"That if you ever want to move home again it's contingent upon attending counseling with her and having some tests."

I was confused. "Tests?"

He blushed. "HIV, gonorrhea, that sort of thing. She said she'd e-mail you a list."

Tim refolded the note and returned it carefully to his pocket, glancing at me as if I were crawling with vermin before heaving another box from the trunk. Jesus—I'd never felt more at a loss. Counseling and an STD checkup? I couldn't decide which would be worse.

CRESSIDA

•

On one of my wards, a young boy was dying. Just ten years old, his life barely dipped into, yet winding down with each labored breath. I wondered if his parents felt the way that I did: the grief, the injustice, the loss of control. Death, infidelity—it's all the same, except one is more humiliating. Daily I suffered as if I were dying too.

I found myself thinking again of Emma, and more specifically her parents. I had been so angry with them for neglecting Shura while her sister's life hung in the balance, but I'd had a change of heart. I understood now that when something you love dies, everything else is secondary. There is only room for so much emotion. Nothing mattered anymore; for a while everything I experienced was uniformly bland, equal in its ability to delight or repulse. I finalized details of my fellowship as if filling out a tax return; I closed the eyes of dead children and wondered what to get for lunch.

Eventually, though, I started caring again. It was inevitable, I suppose, though I'd rather I hadn't. While it lasted, the first gray shroud of grief was easier to live with than its successor, anger. I could tranquilize grief, exhaust it into submission, subdue it with sleeping tablets and long shifts. Anger was trickier. It erupted in me at inopportune moments, while I was lecturing students or reassuring a mother. Suppressing it took all my self-control, left me shaken and sick. Gradually I learned to retreat to the park or a broom closet after each of these episodes, to find a space where I could scream out my fury in private. It helped for a short while, this bulimia of the psyche, but still the anger kept coming.

I craved details. I wanted to know why it happened, but not just that—the how and where as well. Perhaps that's why I initiated the counseling, for it wasn't as if I really wanted him back. How could I, after what he'd done? To be honest, though, I didn't know exactly what that was. When Cary called he said Kate had admitted that they'd slept together, but that it was over. It was the last part that made me throw Luke out. *Over* implied longevity, a relationship. It told me that whatever went on between them hadn't just happened the once, a drunken slipup or silly mistake. *Over* meant planning and deceit and some sort of commitment, the things I couldn't forgive. Counseling wasn't going to change that, but it would give me the facts: the extent of his deception, how thoroughly I had been betrayed. I needed to know those things precisely so I wouldn't take him back. And for all that he had put me through I wanted to hear Luke say he was sorry, to look into his eyes and see if he really was.

CARY

·

A month after Kate had broken my heart it still felt unmended. Worse: the pain was as sharp as the first day, the anguish all-consuming. Sometimes, late at night, it hurt so much that I fancied the serrated edges of that organ were rubbing together, grinding away scar tissue and the first tentative healing clots.

I didn't hate Kate. I suppose I should have, but I couldn't. I was furious with her, though, enraged at the way she'd screwed up what I thought was a perfectly happy marriage. She was the one who wanted to take all those vows, not me. For what? To end up only three years later lying to me, hiding things from me, letting me naively go on dreaming my dreams when they in no way coincided with hers?

I did hate Luke, though. Kate I could make excuses for, but he had none. Maybe her head was turned by his good looks; maybe he got her drunk, then took advantage of the situation. Somehow I was sure he initiated it all: guys like that always do. I thought about threatening him, but what would it have achieved? Physically, I'm bigger, but I wouldn't mind betting he's been in similar situations and would know how to handle himself. And I didn't ever want to see him again, didn't want to publicize or even acknowledge the situation.

Something else I didn't want was to be told all the details. That would only hurt, and believe it or not, it wasn't the sex that bothered me the most. What is sex, after all, but a physical reflex? I made myself get over that sort of jealousy after I discovered how many lovers Kate had had. It's not the doing that counts, but the feeling behind it. It still killed me that she slept with him, but I knew I could get through it by convincing myself that's all it was. No, what kept me awake at night was the deception and how easily it was achieved. It takes two to tango—maybe I was as much at fault for never questioning her, or ignoring the signs. Sure, I knew something was up, but assumed she was worried about work or having a baby. I tried to be supportive, but it never occurred to me that the rot was of Kate's own making. I thought she had integrity. Now I was disappointed not only in her, but in myself for getting it so wrong.

We didn't speak for weeks. At first every time I opened my mouth to say something I tasted tears instead, so I quickly gave that up. Then I didn't know how to get started again. Despite everything, I still wanted Kate. I kidded myself that it was because I had too much invested in her to let it all go, but the bottom line was that I loved her, even after all this. Why? I don't know. After seven years together maybe that was a reflex as well. All I could hold on to was that she seemed to want to stay too. That is, she didn't move out, though I'd heard through the hospital grapevine that Cressida and Luke had separated. Maybe Kate realized what a mistake she'd made; maybe it *was* only sex.

I lost her, but not completely. She never hummed anymore, never laughed or even drank, never walked in the door scattering shoes and papers, peeling off her clothes as she told me about her day. But still, she was there. Things could be worse. I just needed to work out how to make them better. Talking wouldn't do it, not by itself. Sex was the farthest thing from my mind. I thought about counseling, but it seemed counter-productive. I wanted to move on, to block things out if necessary, not keep rehashing them. Forward was the only direction I was interested in, putting as much distance between ourselves and what happened as possible. My guess was that we needed space and time, a second courtship, a place where we could find our way back to each other. But where?

KATE

•

Cary booked a trip overseas. For both of us: six weeks in France and Italy, as if we were students again with time on our hands, or honeymooners starting a new life together. I found the tickets when I arrived home from work yesterday, over a month since I last saw Luke. At first I'd thought they were for some conference he was attending, but underneath was a carefully typed itinerary with both our names at the top. Mr. and Mrs. Hunter. Cary and Kate. *We sound like film stars*, I'd laughed to him the first time I heard us introduced together. I flipped through the pages, place names clamoring for attention. In truth it should have read Dr. and Mrs. Hunter. Cary has a PhD, but never uses his title. He wouldn't have dreamed of correcting the travel agent, and for some reason that irritated me. What was the use of all those years of effort if you didn't have something to show for them?

The funny thing was that we had never really had a honeymoon. I had been working only a short while at the time of our marriage and hadn't accumulated any annual leave. The museum had grudgingly granted me a week's break, which we spent in a rented cottage in the spa country. A funny choice, when neither of us was into spas or the myriad treatments that went with them. Cary's scientific streak derided the whole idea of taking the waters; I couldn't bear to lie still long enough for the mud packs to set or the masseuse to finish. Despite that, we'd had a wonderful time— going for walks along the lake, browsing in bookshops, eating too much and sleeping in. And making love, two or even three times a day, long afternoons spent in bed while the scent from a nearby lavender farm drifted through the open windows around us. We had lived together for over a year before we married and dated for three before that, so it wasn't as if the sex were new. Yet somehow it felt it. Cary seemed more relaxed, more open to the possibility of simply having fun rather than focusing on his technique or pleasing me. We never talked about it, but I suspect that the gold band on my finger made him confident, banished those concerns about his seventeen predecessors. I hadn't realized how much they bothered him, but to what else could I ascribe the change? Or maybe it was the water after all.

Three years ago a trip to Europe would have been a dream come true. Now it just seemed odd, or worse—a mistake. What was he hoping to achieve? To rekindle some flame? Get me as far away from Luke as possible? To push me off some cliff on the Riviera and then return, feigning grief and tales of holiday tragedy? The last didn't seem as ridiculous as it sounds. Cary was a calm man, but he felt things deeply. On top of that, he hadn't spoken a word to me in over a month; then suddenly here he was whisking us off to Paris. Is that normal behavior?

So I felt a sense of trepidation when I heard his key in the door later that evening. I had been wondering what I was meant to do. Leave him a note? Send him an e-mail? It looked as if we would finally have to talk.

"Hello," I began cautiously as he came into the kitchen. He looked tired, older, and the guilt that was my near-constant companion winched up a notch.

"Hello," he replied, meeting my eyes for the shortest of seconds before turning away to take off his coat. A pause hung between us.

"Have you eaten?" I asked eventually, cursing myself for my cowardice. The tickets lay on the counter between us like a summons.

"Yes, thanks. At the hospital." His voice sounded croaky with disuse and unnaturally polite. Silence descended again while he unpacked his briefcase. This time it was Cary who spoke first.

"Look, Kate," he said, without glancing up from his task, "I left some stuff there for you to see. I know you must have read it. I hope that's okay, but really it's too bad if it isn't."

"The tickets, you mean? You could have at least asked me." I had no right to be angry, considering my own crimes, but for some reason I was. It wasn't like Cary to order me around.

"Yeah, well, there were lots of things you never shared with me either." His voice was weary, but with an edge of determination. And something else—almost hatred but not quite. Disgust. He finished sorting his papers and stood up.

"I guess it comes down to whether you want to stay in the marriage or not. I'm assuming you do, since you haven't moved out. I'm prepared to give it a shot too, and I think this is the best way. Getting away from everything here, making the effort just to concentrate on each other."

It sounded reasonable, but I felt compelled to argue.

"I don't know if my passport's valid."

"I've checked, and it's okay."

"What about leave then, Mr. Organized? You might be owed that long, but I'm certainly not."

For the first time he looked furious, and despite myself I took half a step back.

"Don't be so bloody petty. Any other man would have thrown you out for what you did, but you're quibbling about leave. If you really want to I'm sure you can arrange some time off. Take it without pay, or quit. For fuck's sake, I'm offering you a second chance. Don't you want it?"

To be honest I wasn't sure. As Cary had said, I hadn't moved out, but was that just inertia? I suppose if I'd had to I could have stayed with Sarah or gotten an apartment by myself. It wouldn't have been impossible. Or was it because I hadn't heard from Luke? What would I have done if he'd called sometime in the last few weeks, admitting he'd made a mistake, begging me to take him back? Then there was the remaining possibility: that I still felt something for my husband. Nothing was clear. I took refuge in more questions.

"How can we even afford it? Wouldn't counseling be cheaper?"

Cary didn't meet my eyes as he replied.

"I've been putting some money aside in case we had to do IVF. We'll use those savings. It's obvious we're not going to need them now."

His tone could have been bitter or accusing, but it was neither. Instead the words were just plain sad, laden with grief and longing. I felt so sorry for him that I didn't argue any further. But I couldn't comfort him either, couldn't assure him that his plan would make any sort of difference.

"Okay then," I muttered, giving in without grace. Then I left the room and went to bed.

I couldn't sleep. Lying alone in the darkness, I thought the whole thing felt like a huge mistake, doomed to fail. But what was the alternative? Move out, which I lacked the energy to contemplate? Continue dragging myself to work, though they'd surely fire me soon, I was so unproductive? Hope Luke would call, or call him myself? I felt my teeth clench at the latter. Never. I'd given him the choice and then a chance, and he'd blown them both. I was never going to contact him again.

That left Europe. Still, I vowed, Cary couldn't expect me to be thrilled about it. I was truly sorry I had hurt him. Maybe I even still loved him. But all that had happened was too raw, too fresh to be moving away from. I wanted time to regroup and lick my wounds, not be rushed off to Europe and a fantasy reconciliation. If he was determined that we go I owed him that, but I couldn't pretend. There would be no poring over the atlas together, none of the anticipation that makes travel so sweet. I would leave it all up to him. Six weeks away, departing in less than a month. I should have been excited, but the world felt dulled, as if I were missing a sense.

LUKE

·

Do you know how they do those tests—the ones that Cress insisted on, for AIDS and other sexually transmitted diseases, as if I'd been sleeping with half of Melbourne instead of just one other woman in the past three years? First you take off everything from the waist down, then clamber inelegantly onto some stained examination couch while the nurse snaps on a pair of rubber gloves behind you. Next she's grasping your old fellow between her finger and thumb as if it were a dead mouse, then zeroing in on her target with something that looks like a long cotton swab. Before you can even comprehend what she's going to do with it the swab has been rammed down the eye of your penis like a ferret sent into a rabbit hole. As if that weren't enough it is then rotated—once, twice—and withdrawn with the same breathtaking brutality. I'm not ashamed to admit that the whole procedure almost reduced me to tears.

Counseling was only marginally less painful. If I had to attend I'd wanted us to see a man, someone who might understand my point of view. No such luck. Cress had chosen a woman. Not only that, but a colleague—someone she knew from the pediatric psych department who conducted what she termed "relationship therapy" on the side. I asked our new counselor why at our first session, and she bristled as if accused.

"It's a natural extension of my work with children," she'd said with a sniff. "Every one of us is a product of our childhood; ergo, it makes sense to look for the roots of our adult behaviors and dysfunctions in the patterns of our infancy and upbringing." I almost groaned aloud. Any hopes I had of being done with counseling in a session or two were swiftly dashed.

The appointments were held at the hospital, after hours. After everyone else's hours, that is, Cressida invariably arriving late and distracted or slotting in the meeting in the middle of a shift. Hardly neutral ground or ideal conditions, and I told her so.

"And just what is ideal about meeting to discuss your infidelity?" she shot back, and I retreated. She'd grown a tongue since we separated, developed opinions and a blunt streak I barely recognized in my previously compliant wife. It was attractive, though, probably because it reminded me of Kate. Lots of things did that: the dark-haired girl whom I spotted once at an industry luncheon, a fig tree coming into bloom at the end of my street, the long evenings I would once have filled talking to or spending with her. Funny how things change. A month ago I was dividing my time between Kate and Cress, rushing from one beautiful woman to be with the next. Now, I was beached in the spare room of Tim's tiny apartment, and most nights it was Joan I came home to.

My test results were fine. NAD, to use Cress's hospital parlance: no abnormalities detected. I wasn't surprised—what were the odds? Kate hadn't been with anyone but Cary for the seven years before we took up, and he hardly looked the type to have introduced any microbes of his own. The nurse who gave me the news didn't even smile. It was the same one who had performed the examination, features set rigid with disapproval—I don't imagine many happily monogamous types felt the cool pinch of her latex. Still, I guess it had been a useful exercise, and gave me some hope for the future. Surely Cress wouldn't have asked me to submit to such indignities if she weren't considering that we might sleep together again someday? The thought filled me with anticipation. I missed sex. Oh, I missed Cress too, of course, still hoped the marriage could be saved, but it had been six weeks since I had seen a woman undressed, the longest period of abstinence I had endured since losing my virginity at the age of fifteen. Once or twice I thought vaguely about going back to the bars where Tim and I had hung out before I met Cress, seeing if I couldn't just get some relief for the night. But I didn't follow through. For one it was too risky—if Cress found out she would never speak to me again. The other reason was less comprehensible. Whenever I entertained such thoughts I found myself feeling unfaithful to Kate. Not to my wife, with whom I was trying to reconcile, but to Kate. The one who had caused all this trouble in the first place; the one whom I'd agonized over, but hadn't chosen. Sometimes the feeling was so strong it made me question my decision. I never let myself dwell on it, though, never once gave in to the temptation to grieve or even despair. What was done was done and for good reasons, though I couldn't really remember them now. All I'd wanted from Kate was a year, and she hadn't even granted that. Most mornings I ached for her, but if she felt the same pain surely she would call? Yet the phone remained as quiet as my evenings.

CRESSIDA

●

The first three sessions went okay. Not brilliantly, but okay. I trusted Robyn, our therapist, and thought we could get somewhere—maybe not to the point where I would take Luke back, but could at least start to understand his behavior. I'd arrived at the first session wanting to get straight into it, hungry for details, the whole sordid picture. Robyn's plan, though, was to work up to that slowly, to have us talk about our families and establish a context, as she put it. Once upon a time I would have blindly gone along with her recommendations. Now I found myself wondering somewhat cynically if she wasn't just trying to spin things out to make a bit of extra money. Gain from pain. Someone might as well, I suppose.

I have to admit, though, that what followed was more interesting than I'd expected. My own story was fairly straightforward: youngest sibling in a high-achieving family, all three offspring following in their father's footsteps. We didn't see one another very often, but that was just because of work.

"Your mother," Robyn prompted. "What about her?"

I shrugged. We were close, I guess—she'd acted as both parents when I was growing up, my father so often absent at the hospital. Now she lived a life of genteel boredom, her days spent fund-raising and hankering for grandchildren.

"I wonder if you were looking for a father figure in your own marriage, Cressida?" Robyn mused. I scoffed at the idea. Luke was too virile for any such Oedipal role.

"No," she persisted, "I meant somebody you could look up to, maybe even revere. Someone to set an agenda that you could fall into line with." I hadn't thought of it that way.

Then it was Luke's turn. Another youngest sibling, but this time the yearned-for boy finally appearing after three girls. Robyn's eyes lit up when he told her that.

"He's grown up on a diet of female attention," she theorized, as if Luke were absent or anesthetized. "Maybe that's the only way he functions." I was liking this approach more and more until she turned to me and asked, "Do you think it's fair to expect him to change?" Luke looked smug and I wanted to hit him. I knew he liked women; I'd turned a blind eye to his flirting for years. But he hadn't slept with his sisters, had he?

At the third appointment we talked about sex. Just in general, no specifics—I was still waiting for those. By this stage I was beginning to wonder if it really was such a good idea to have a colleague acting in this way. I'm sure Robyn was too professional to gossip to anyone about our sessions, but even the idea of one person walking around the hospital knowing how I liked it made me uncomfortable. So I lied a little, bent the truth. I told her that I wasn't very sexually experienced when I met Luke rather than admit I had still been a virgin. He glanced over at me quizzically but said nothing, and I could see him saving up the falsehood as future ammunition. I also informed her that we'd had a great sex life, with nothing wrong as far as I was concerned. That wasn't entirely the truth either, though Luke didn't question that one.

Not having anyone to compare him with, I had always assumed that Luke was a good lover. To be fair, mostly he was. But before we separated I had begun to feel that it was all on his terms—we did what he liked, and when. I hadn't had much chance to ever experiment for myself; rather, Luke had taught me his tastes and procedures. Still, I knew my own performance wasn't faultless. I was thankful the session ended before Robyn had a chance to quiz Luke about our connubial compatibility, but I could guess what he would have said. That while I never refused him I never instigated sex either—I was always too tired, or preoccupied with the problems of my day. Sexually speaking, that was our biggest issue, but maybe there were others. Perhaps I was too modest for his tastes, not given to slutty lingerie or screaming out his name loudly enough to wake the neighbors. Perhaps I was too passive, letting him set the pace because I felt gauche and naive in comparison to his obvious experience. Maybe he just got bored. After all, there must have been something missing for him to do what he did.

But missing or not, the session in Robyn's office had obviously put him in the mood. After the hour was up he asked me to join him for dinner, and when I refused he suggested coffee instead. I wavered, glancing at my watch. My shift was officially over for the day, though I had letters to write and charts to update. More to the point, could I bear to be alone with him, a hostage to his charm and our history? It had been two months since I'd thrown him out. The initial shock was gone but the pain was still well and truly there, throbbing darkly in the background of everything I did, malignant as a heart murmur. On the other hand it was only coffee. We'd have to start talking again sometime, if only to work out details of the property settlement. So I said yes, stipulating that I wanted to be back on the ward by eight. He agreed, smiling, though it could have been a smirk.

Inevitably, though, we were still there at nine. By limiting our conversation to purely trivial matters I found I could relax enough to enjoy myself. We talked about our work, the weather, his sister who was pregnant. I told him about a patient with Tourette's syndrome who had insulted all the nurses; he made jokes about the cleaning regimen Joan had imposed at Tim's apartment. It was easy and fun. If I tried I could almost imagine we were dating again. Later Luke insisted on walking me back to the hospital, and when I went to say good-bye he kissed me. For a moment I was stunned, but then I felt some sort of current, some remaining vagal impulse. Despite everything I kissed him back.

You know what comes next. We've all been there and done that—it's not original. Let me say, though, that it was my decision, my initiative. Five minutes into kissing Luke my hands were on his chest, then under his shirt. Another five minutes and I was panting against his neck while his fingers slid seductively from my nape to the small of my back, cradling me against his body.

"Come home," I heard myself saying against his throat.

"Are you sure?" he asked, though one hand was already on his car keys.

I nodded and kissed him again, eyes tightly shut, abandoning myself to the oblivion offered by his mouth. Somehow he disentangled from me and we drove home in silence.

At home I made him leave the lights off. I didn't want to think about what I was doing, never mind have to see it. Oh, I wanted him, but it was as much about pride as lust. I needed to be assured that he still desired me, that I could still arouse and satisfy him. It turned out that I could, but it was a hollow victory. As soon as he'd finished I wanted him out. Of my bed, my house, my body. I wanted to run to the shower and scrub away all the emissions he'd befouled me with—his sweat and semen, the kisses he'd planted like land mines on my throat and face, the very words he'd whispered while invading me. Instead I lay still, willing him to leave. When it looked as if he would fall asleep I shook him gently and asked him to go, explaining that it was too soon for us to be spending the night together. For a second I thought he would refuse or at least lay claim to that half of the house that was legally his. Fortunately he acquiesced, obviously realizing he'd do well to heed my wishes if he wanted a repeat performance.

There was no chance of that. I hadn't felt such physical revulsion since my first dissection as a medical student, gagging when the initial incision produced an ooze of yellow pearls, fat globules spilling from the abdomen onto my gloves and the table. Throughout our coupling I couldn't help but wonder how my body felt under his hands after Kate's. Did I excite him as much as she did; was I moving in the way he liked? Were my breasts the right shape? Had I moaned enough? He seemed to enjoy himself, but there was no pleasure for me. After a while I faked some in a desperate effort to accelerate the proceedings, shuddering with relief when it was finally over. I slept after he left, but only as a form of escape.

The next morning I took off my rings. For a moment or two over coffee the night before I had allowed myself to think the marriage might be saved, but I should have trusted my premonitions. It was as dead as Emma. I didn't want to be single, didn't want the dream-come-true that Luke had seemed to represent to be over. But I knew now there was no way I could go back to sharing a life or even a bed with him. Some things can't be forgotten. Or maybe they can, but not by me. Whenever he touched me I was going to think of her. Whatever he vowed I wasn't going to believe. Maybe he was genuinely sorry that he'd hurt me, but I was beginning to realize that he wasn't sorry it had happened. And if that was the case, how could I ever possibly be sure it wouldn't happen again?

I hadn't removed my rings since my wedding day almost two years earlier, though they slid off without protest. The skin underneath was as pale and vulnerable as the belly of a frog. I tucked the wedding band away in my jewelry box on the dresser, careful not to read the inscription inside. The engagement ring was more valuable and would have to go somewhere else. Maybe to the bank, to my family's safe-deposit box, at least while I worked out what to do with it. But before I thought about that I had another task. I sat down at the computer and drafted a letter accepting the fellowship. For weeks I'd put off giving them an answer, citing personal reasons, but now I had made up my mind. There was no future with Luke. I'd create a new one for myself elsewhere.

LUKE

•

I always assumed that Cress would have me back. That she would throw her little fit—she deserved that—but if I behaved myself and said the right things we would go on as before. That was why I had chosen her, after all: because given that I loved them both, it was simply easier to stay with the one I was already married to. Wasn't a reconciliation what the counseling was about, and all those hideous tests? I wouldn't have agreed to either if I hadn't thought they were prerequisites for getting my foot back in the door. Maybe I should have just kissed Cressida that evening after coffee, left her wistful and wanting in the way that had worked so well before we were married. I could have drawn things out until she was so mad for it that continuing the separation would have been the last thing on her mind. But for once I wasn't working to a plan.

Maybe I should have just kissed her, but the desire I felt for Cress that night was undeniable. Cress is a beautiful woman, and I'd been abstinent for what seemed like years. But the desire was triggered by more than that, by something I couldn't name at the time: relief. Relief that we had been talking so easily, that she was smiling at me again, that the end was in sight. It's a heady aphrodisiac, more potent than I could have imagined. She appeared to feel the same way. Her mouth opened when I kissed her; she was ready for me almost as soon as we got home. Right at the end she cried out my name and quivered with pleasure, something that rarely occurred. I wanted to stay but left when she asked me to, figuring it was just another hoop to jump through.

The next day, though, she canceled the rest of our counseling sessions. Didn't even tell me personally, just left a brief message on my voice mail at work at a time she must have known I wouldn't be in. I tried to call her, but she didn't answer the page. I even dropped past our house that night, hoping to speak to her, but the windows were dark and her car wasn't in the driveway.

Another week went by with no further contact. I reassured myself that it would all be okay, that she was simply playing hard to get. Just in case it was more than that I drafted a conciliatory letter, planning to send it if we still hadn't spoken in a couple weeks. Really, I should have done that in the first place—I've sold more dubious products using such skills. But before the deadline had been reached Tim came home with some news.

I was in the kitchen helping myself to one of his beers when I heard his key in the door. I'd just gotten in from work myself, and was relieved to see that for once he was alone: most nights he showed up with Joan, for whom familiarity was fast breeding contempt as far as I was concerned. It wasn't that she was boring or unattractive, the two qualities I most detest in a woman. It was just that she was loud. Opinionated, rather. Headstrong. Determined that not only should everyone know her views, but they should share them. We'd clashed more than once, arguing about topics ranging from rain forests to rugby, bickering back and forth while Tim stood between us practically wringing his hands. Some of the time I actually agreed with Joan, yet found myself taking the opposite side just for the pleasure of seeing her rise to the bait. It wasn't as if I had anything much else to entertain me.

"Luke," Tim called out in greeting as he unlaced his shoes. Joan had decreed that we all remove our footwear at the door for fear of tracking in dirt.

"Want a beer?" I asked, hastily proffering my own.

"Nah, I'm going out. We're due at Joan's parents' for dinner."

"Big night then. Sure you don't need something to dull the pain?"

"Oh, they're all right," he replied loyally. "Not as fancy as your in-laws, but her mom's a great cook."

I had begun to make myself a sandwich but looked up at that. Tim hadn't mentioned Cress or anything to do with her ever since our conversation when I had first moved in. He sat down on the couch with his back to me, ostensibly flicking through the newspaper. I knew there was more.

"Speaking of which," he continued, choosing his words carefully, "I caught up with Cressida today."

"Oh, yeah?" I replied nonchalantly. Two could play this game. Hell, I could best Tim at any game I chose.

"Yeah. She said she's accepted the fellowship—you know that she was offered it?"

I nodded, though he couldn't see me. It had been something we'd discussed over coffee, though at that time she'd confessed she still didn't know what to do. Her doubt had given me the confidence to make my move.

"Anyway," he said when I failed to respond, "she's off to Michigan sometime next month. It's all happening pretty quickly. I suppose she'll have a farewell drinks night or something."

I almost cut my hand off with the bread knife. Michigan, next month. I couldn't believe she was doing it, and without me. Nice to have been told.

"Luke? You okay?" asked Tim, finally turning around.

"Yeah, great," I replied, quickly shoveling the sandwich into my mouth so he wouldn't expect me to talk. I tried to escape to my room, but Tim hadn't finished.

"I assumed you probably knew," he said with more than his usual lack of insight. "Listen, I don't want to sound rude, but maybe once she's gone you could move back home? I'm sure you're ready for your own place again, and it's getting pretty crowded with all those boxes in the hall. . . ."

I was chewing furiously but I didn't seem to be getting anywhere, as if the bread were made of bubble gum. People were lining up to throw me out of their lives. I nodded in reply and tried to swallow, though the last thing I felt was hungry.

My immediate reaction was to get Cress on the phone and beg her to reconsider. I even went so far as to dial the number, only to hear the answering machine click in as it had every day for the last few weeks. I hung up without leaving a message. She knew I'd been trying to reach her, yet had made this decision regardless; must in fact have made it a while ago to already have a departure date. Then another impulse: call Kate. Throw myself on her mercy, plead that I'd made the wrong decision. Obviously I had anyway. Yet even as I tried to remember her phone number I came to my senses. It had been over two months since we'd spoken, and that hadn't been the most encouraging of good-byes. I'd thought about her every day since; truly I had. But what would that count for against the decision I'd made, the weeks of silence, choosing—eventually—Cress over her? Kate had a fierce pride, and would never settle for being second best. She would hang up before I had a chance to tell her that I still loved her.

I finished my sandwich sitting on the floor of Tim's spare room, my back against the door. I didn't think he'd try to come and talk to me, but I wasn't taking any chances. I didn't want his sympathy. From two to zip, with only myself to blame. My marriage was over; Kate would never speak to me again. She suddenly seemed far away, ethereal, like a dream I once had and had woken up still believing. Cressida was more real, but moving quickly in the same direction. And all I felt was numb, too tired from chasing one, then the other, to realize I'd lost them both.

The light outside had faded, but I didn't bother to get up and close the blinds. I wasn't going to sleep anyway. My agency was looking for employees to relocate to the office they were setting up in the U.S. Morning would come. I'd let them know then.

TIM

•

I hadn't imagined Joan to be a gossip, but she'd been unable to restrain her curiosity about the whole Luke/Kate thing. Ever since Cressida had first phoned a month or so ago, waking us both in the early hours, the topic had never been far from her mind. What did I know? Had Luke done the dirty on his wife? Who started it? When did it end? I suppose I disappointed her with my lack of inside knowledge, the truth being that Luke had never confided in me. In retrospect I was glad of that—Cressida was my friend too, and at least I had never had to agonize over whether I should tell her. Besides, I had pointed out to Joan, she should have been at least as well informed as myself, Kate being an old friend of hers. In return she had just laughed.

"It was our mothers who were friends, not us," she scoffed. "I always thought Kate was too fond of herself, and a shocking flirt. She had it coming."

I thought this was rather callous but said nothing at the time, still struggling to assimilate the terrible news. Now, as we drove home from dinner at her parents', she was onto the subject again.

"So do you think Luke knew about the fellowship?"

I sighed. Dinner had been relaxed, soothing, and now I just wanted to steep for a while in the fading glow of good wine and conversation. It had been hard enough broaching the subject with Luke earlier that evening without having to dissect it all over again for Joan's benefit.

"I assume so. They've been going to counseling together, so it must have come up there."

"Uh-uh." Joan shook her head. "Not in the last few weeks, they haven't. Apparently Cressida ended the sessions."

"How do you know that?" I queried, surprised.

"I asked Luke," Joan replied without looking over. She was driving; she often did if I had a drink or two, though I was nowhere near the limit. It meant she could dictate when we left.

"Asked him what?"

"How the counseling was going, of course." She spoke slowly, as if talking to an idiot. "He told me that it wasn't going at all. Supposedly Cressida had deferred all future appointments. Guess she won't be rescheduling now."

Despite myself I felt a twinge of sympathy for Luke. My beloved was more tenacious than a terrier when she wanted something, and while I knew he had no desire to talk about his personal life, Joan had obviously managed to extract some information.

"You're incorrigible," I mumbled, awed and appalled at her audacity.

"Why?" she asked, sweeping me a hazel-eyed glance of innocence. "He's your friend, so of course I'm worried about him. Besides, I don't know why you're so determined that we tiptoe around this and act as if nothing ever happened. No one died, you know."

"I just figure that if Luke wants to talk about it he will. I read him the riot act when he first moved in. Now I just want to be his friend."

"You? Read someone the riot act?" she asked in disbelief, though her tone was fond. I smiled but didn't react. Joan made the long U-turn onto the Eastern Freeway, concentrating as she changed down through the gears. For all her eagerness to get behind the wheel she wasn't a natural driver, though I would never have told her so. For a few minutes there was silence and I hoped we could leave it there, but as the freeway entrance receded she started up again.

"I mean, just imagine if he hadn't known she was going to go to America. What a shock! I bet the poor sap was assuming she'd want him back."

"I doubt Luke ever assumed anything."

Joan went on as if I hadn't spoken. "Still, it's no more than he deserves, after cheating on her like that. I wonder what's up with Kate and Cary. Have you heard?"

I shook my head. I worried about them too, how Cary had taken the news, whether Kate was still seeing Luke. Funny to be in such a position. A year ago I had envied both couples: their confidence, their direction, their bright, sparkling marriages. Twelve months later all of that had come undone. All those years of love gone, and nothing to show for them except pain.

"You're quiet," Joan remarked, her voice softer, almost solicitous. "Tired?"

"Mmm," I replied, looking out the window. Our exit was still some miles away, but already Joan was changing lanes in preparation. Tired, yes, but it was more than that. Watching everything unfold had lurched me from anger to disgust and finally sorrow, had reminded me that love is fleeting and precious and should never be taken for granted. All of a sudden I felt the need to seize it with both hands, to assure myself that the same pain wouldn't be mine. Joan glanced across, checking her blind spot, and in the lights of the car behind her profile was as pure as a relief on a Grecian temple. She might be a gossip, but she was also forthright and funny and staunchly loyal. It wasn't how I had imagined my ideal woman, but what does ever turn out exactly as we expect? There are so many ways to fall in love, and then after the fall . . .

It was a spontaneous decision, but why not? One thing Luke's little episode had taught me was that there are no guarantees. As we made our exit from the freeway I swallowed once, then spoke.

"Pull over," I said, "as soon as you can. There's something I have to ask you."

KATE

·

We left for Europe on the last day of August. Through the haze of packing and the incessant ache in my chest I wondered if Cary had chosen that date on purpose. There were almost too many portents to ignore: the end of winter, the coming of spring, a season of regrowth and rebirth. It should have been a propitious choice, but when we arrived on the other side of the world I realized that the opposite, in fact, was true. The days were shortening, autumn was coming on. Cary swore it was the best time to travel, free from crowds and the extremes of heat. Instead I found myself feeling miserable in the world's most beautiful places.

I tried not to think about Luke. I couldn't bear imagining him having a life that I wasn't part of. But it didn't work, and I missed him. He turned up in all the obvious spots—in the smile of a Giotto Madonna, in every cool, marbled sinew of the David. But he was also there when I least expected it, the chance encounters leaving me shaken. A furtive cherub in a dusky corner of the Sistine Chapel's ceiling had his eyes; his hands, incongruously transplanted to a gelati vendor in the Piazza Navarone, counted out my change. My body yearned for him. Longing washed over me in a strange sort of sexual homesickness, a melancholy lust. It wasn't the act I missed so much as his physical presence: his hand on my forearm as we talked, his fingers smoothing back my hair. Luke and I had always been touchers, reaching out to make contact with the other regardless of whether we were eating, walking or just in conversation, a reassurance of existence and possession. He still possessed me.

But I missed Cary too. He was right there beside me every hour of the day, but it wasn't like it would have been a year ago. I didn't know what he was thinking, what he wanted, whether he was truly moved by what he was seeing or if, like myself, he was just traipsing from one sight to the next to pass the time. He conscientiously took photos, wrote postcards, practiced phrases that he thought he might need but never seemed to use. What was there worth the effort of saying anyway? "That fish was very tasty, thank you." "Where is the post office?" "My wife is a whore." At dinner we had little to talk about save for planning the next day's sightseeing. Every night the question of sex hung like the drapery from the four-poster beds in the palazzos and pensiones Cary had booked, suffocating and heavy. Nothing happened. Each new bed we encountered was a reminder of my infidelity, of all those other beds I had so recklessly climbed into with a man not my husband. Checking into our hotel made me shudder, listening to Cary stammer out his request for a double room. *Un letto matrimoniale*, the marriage bed. Even the furniture had expectations. We saw breathtaking scenery and ate fabulous food and I had never felt so wretched.

Cary tried; he really did. Tour guide was a natural role for him, our time flawlessly balanced between cultural activities and R&R. The first month was reserved for Italy, with Rome, Florence and Venice segueing seamlessly into France. On our last night we would celebrate our fourth wedding anniversary in Paris. The schedule was as predictable as the diamond he would have bought for me when we got engaged, and I began to feel sick just thinking about the weeks ahead. Some mornings I wondered how I would drum up the enthusiasm for breakfast, never mind days and days of more of the same. Often the only thing that sustained me through those long hours of cathedrals and galleries, the stifling evenings of small talk, was something I had learned from my work: that all pain is erased in the passage of time. Not just *by*, but *in*. Ten decades hence it would be as if nothing had ever happened. There would be no relics, no scars. No jug to piece together, no bone fragments to date. Emotions fade and leave no trace. Only the inanimate remains.

CARY

·

I knew I wasn't the only person who had ever been hurt, though sometimes it felt that way. I found myself wondering if Kate felt pain too. I knew she used to, but I wasn't so sure now as she sat opposite me at dinner, beautiful and distant, or listened attentively to whatever I suggested without hearing a thing.

The trip didn't start well. I wasn't under any illusions that things were going to get back to normal the moment we left, but I was unprepared for how bad they really were. As soon as the plane took off from Tullamarine, Kate took a sleeping pill and knocked herself out. I have no idea where it even came from. She usually eschewed drugs—the exception, of course, being alcohol—but she swallowed the tablet as blatantly as could be, not even bothering to hide it from me. At least, I think it was a sleeping pill. Maybe she just pretended to sleep. I didn't trust anything anymore.

I should have realized it was an omen. Kate was sleepwalking through the first half of our time overseas. There was nothing I could complain of directly, no hostility, no sulks—quite the opposite, in fact. She was too conciliatory, too obliging. The spark was gone, and it was that which had attracted me to her in the first place. I loved her more than ever, loved her in the way a drowning man loves the flotsam thrown up around him, but it was interspersed with great surges of anger. I have never been a violent man, but at times I itched to hit her, and hard. Some days my fingers ached from the effort of keeping them uncurled.

CRESSIDA

•

My sister called early one morning, before I'd even left for work. I guess she didn't have to worry about waking Luke—I'd told my family that we'd separated and he'd moved out. They had offered sympathy but didn't ask for details, each no doubt assuming that one of the others was comforting me.

"Hi, Cress, did I wake you?" she asked without waiting for a reply. It was Carolina, my oldest sister, named after the U.S. state where my father had been completing his postdoc at the time of her birth. She hated her unusual moniker, but my parents must have liked it, at least enough to grace their subsequent children with a comparable combination of letters. All our names began with C and ended with A, as if we were different models of the same car. I complained about it to Luke as we lay in bed one night early in our relationship, but he pointed out that there were plenty of C/A choices that could have been worse. Wasn't I glad that I wasn't a Clara or a Camilla? A Cora or a Cynthia? For a week or so it became a game for him, to see how many his word-happy brain could come up with. I'd arrive home from work to a note on the kitchen table: *Cecelia. Clarissa. Cassandra.* Or receive a message on my pager of just one word: *Carlotta.* It had made me giggle in ward rounds, something I hadn't done in years.

Now Carolina was using another C-word. Cancer, she was saying. Probably started in his liver, though mets had already been found in his lungs and spine. My father. Six more months. He'd never even been a drinker. Just a glass of wine with dinner and a nip of Scotch later. "All things in moderation," he had repeated night after night as he settled before the fire and Mother brought the tumbler in. It had been Waterford, of course. As a child I'd been fascinated by the way it had refracted the light, loosing the odd brief rainbow as he lifted it to his lips.

"You'll have to take care of him. Cressida, are you listening?"

I had hardly said a word, yet still she went on.

"He needs to be nursed. Mother's got no idea about that sort of thing. Cordelia and I were wondering if you could move back in with them. We've got our families to think of, and you . . ."

The words were left unsaid, but the implication was clear. I had no one, just a too-large house that I'd planned to fill with children and empty spots on the mantelpiece where my wedding photos were once displayed.

"I'm moving to Michigan, though, remember?"

Silence on the other end of the line. She remembered.

"Can't you put that off? Just a year or so? Cordelia can't take any leave if she's to keep tenure, and since David made partner we've been so busy I've had to hire another nanny. Mother's counting on you."

Then why hadn't she called me herself? Too struck by grief, or shame? The phone felt like a gun pressed to my head.

"I've got a lot on my plate too, Carolina," I said, stalling for time.

"I know," she replied, sounding almost embarrassed. "But maybe this would be good for you too. You know, for company, someone to talk to."

As long as it didn't have to be her, I thought, nursing our father or comforting me. Coming face-to-face with messy human emotions. No wonder she'd gone into dermatology.

The receiver hummed expectantly, but I wouldn't give her the satisfaction of an answer. I was worried for my father, annoyed at my fickle sister, angry that my own personal tragedy had been pushed aside so quickly.

"I'm going to Michigan," I heard myself say. Then I hung up the phone before she could argue.

KATE

•

We'd been away for almost a month by the time we got to Venice. By that stage Italy was just a blur of paintings and churches, and I hadn't expected to enjoy it any more than Florence or Rome. But to my great surprise I did. The water softened everything, the lack of traffic was refreshing and the galleries were blessedly small. I loved, too, how compact the city was, how you could find yourself among real Venetians and not just tourists only ten minutes' walk from St. Mark's Square, how you never knew if one of the narrow curved streets would open out into a grand piazza or a tiny back canal. Cary hadn't let me out of his sight in the previous cities, but in Venice he relaxed a little. We were on an island; where could I go?

So when he suggested that we separate for a morning I jumped at the chance. There was a fresco he wanted to track down in a chapel past the Lido. He'd mentioned it the previous day, but must have seen my face fall at the prospect of yet another church. Religion meant nothing to me, the relics and vials that Italian basilicas are stuffed with too reminiscent of my own work to be interesting. Instead, I told him, I would go shopping. It was the first thing that came to mind, but really I just wanted some time alone, a break from feeling his eyes on me every minute of the day, silently and continually gauging whether I was happy or sad, amused or bored.

I felt free that morning, free and happy for the first time in weeks. Everywhere I looked Venice charmed me. A small altar set in the brick wall of a public walkway, lit by flickering electric candles; multicolored chocolate bars stacked like the Parthenon in a shop window; three nuns on their way to Mass, the wind toying with their veils. For a while I just walked, taking it all in. Then a display of Murano glass caught my eye, glossy and brittle. Perhaps I would go shopping after all. It was the perfect souvenir, providing it survived the journey home.

I was coming out of the shop with my purchases when I was approached by a beggar, a young girl carrying a baby. Normally I would ignore such requests, but I was feeling so unaccustomedly happy and she looked so young that I reached into my purse for change. To my horror, as I handed her the money she stole my watch—one minute her fingers were on my wrist and the next my watch was gone, all without losing her grip on the child. Then she fled, leaving me alone in a deserted backstreet, still proffering my foolish coins.

The watch had been a twenty-first-birthday present from my parents. That said, I can't say I was overly attached to it. It was expensive, but not particularly unique, and it was insured. All the same I felt like howling. What else could I do? There was no point in going to the police—I didn't speak Italian and such crime was commonplace. So commonplace that every guidebook I had read had warned me to be careful, not to sightsee alone, to pay no heed to beggars. It was my own fault, and twice as hard to stomach for that. I experienced an instant of overwhelming, unbearable grief. For the watch, I suppose, but also for Luke, my thoughts unbidden and irrational. This would never have happened if he had chosen me.

CARY

·

I didn't sleep well in Italy. Maybe it was jet lag, though I'd never suffered from it before. Our hotels were comfortable and quiet, so it couldn't have been that. Admittedly, though, something about being in a hotel makes me uneasy. How can you fully relax knowing that others have a key to your room?

Of course, there were other things on my mind as well. Had Kate slept with Luke? Really slept, I mean—I had to accept that they'd made love. Somehow, though, sleep was more intimate. A surrender, borne out of trust or abandon or exhaustion. Had his lovemaking worn her out? Had they lain in each other's arms? What did they talk about afterward? I disciplined myself not to think about it during the day, but at night, when my defenses were down, and the insomnia kicked in . . .

Kate, however, slept. Every night, without fail, and it bothered me. Was she taking the tablets she had used on the plane? Was she tired from our sightseeing? Could her conscience be that clear? Questions followed one another like conga dancers. At the worst moments, when it was three a.m. and it seemed everyone in the world was asleep except me, I even had my doubts about the whole reconciliation. I didn't actively wish her pain, but she slept so soundly! I needed to see that she was hurting, or felt some remorse—anything but this anesthesia.

Then again, if she had tossed and turned maybe I would have worried that she was missing Luke, or wondering if staying with me had been the right decision. At least while drugged she wasn't reconsidering. And no matter how long I lay awake worrying about Kate, each morning would still dawn the same as the one before it, and the one before that. We were together, and that was all that mattered. I told myself that everything else would pass.

LUKE

·

So I moved. Tim didn't want me, Cressida didn't want me and Kate was gone, so I left for Boston. No point in half measures. Moved, in fact, before Cress's own departure date—just walked into the office, told them I could go, and had a time and a ticket just two weeks later. I'd hoped for New York, but not surprisingly others had had the same idea. Instead, the company offered Boston or Seattle. I opted for the former—I liked that it had history, plus I'd watched my share of *Cheers*. Then, too, I have to admit that somewhere deep in my subconscious I'd also calculated that it was on the same side of the map as Michigan. Maybe Cress would soften away from the scene of the crime, need me to come over and change a lightbulb or dig her out one day. . . . It wasn't until I'd been there a month that I found out she was still back in Melbourne after all. Tim called to tell me, embarrassed for us both. Oh, whatever. Tim and his dingy apartment were behind me now; Cress was trapped in her family home, nursing her dear papa. I should be glad I hadn't had to get involved in any of that.

Meanwhile Boston was opening up to me like a ripe, juicy mango, like a showgirl at one of the gentlemen's clubs on Lagrange, near the Common. I visited one once or twice when I was at a loose end, but it only made me feel as dirty as the city's begrimed sidewalks. I hadn't realized how clean Australia was when I lived there. Even the Charles River, which sparkled blue from my office window, was littered with beer cans and used condoms up close, its surface smeared with a film of sunscreen and boat grease throughout the warmer months. Then there were the sidewalks themselves, littered with dog droppings and drunks, devoid of anything so quaint as a nature strip. Still, that was the price of living in the city. For all its filth I didn't miss the suburbs, loved having the bars and the clubs and the restaurants at hand, no lawn to mow, no gutters to clear. Settling in was easy. I walked everywhere, made friends, saw the sights. Work was no more demanding than it had been in Melbourne. And Melbourne seemed a long, long way away.

KATE

·

The robbery shook me up. My first instinct was to run, to get back to the hotel as quickly as I could and slam the door shut behind me. By the time I was once more in the tourist area, though, I had forced myself to reconsider. *Don't overreact,* I told myself, *don't let this beat you.* I'd already survived worse than the theft of a watch.

So I went to St. Mark's, drawn by the safety of the crowds pushing through the carved portals into the building. Cary and I had already visited the church on our first evening in Venice, just before midnight. Mass was being said and the sanctuary was dark, lit only by candles. The floor, shaped by years of water lapping at its underside, dipped and crested under my feet, causing me to reach out for Cary without even thinking about it. Despite my avowed atheism I was enchanted. I'm not sure what I was hoping for when I entered it the second time—probably to be similarly distracted, to be soothed by someone else's faith. But Venice had been ruined for me that morning, and so was St. Mark's. Tourists oozed over every surface like an oil spill, obscuring the mosaics, soiling the columns with their greasy hands. The uneven floor that had charmed me on our previous visit now seemed dangerous, unstable—proof that everything was flimsy, even this great house of God. All the gilt and the gold were just garish, overdone as a disco in daylight. I escaped to the balcony, but the famous horses were covered for restoration, every available surface swathed in mesh and spikes in an attempt to deter pigeons.

Leaning against the balustrade I looked down at where my watch had been and felt bereft. Against the rest of my tanned arm the newly exposed skin appeared ashen, shocked. Panic swelled inside me and I gripped the rail hard, suddenly afraid I would cry. Then, through my smarting eyes, I saw Cary in the piazza below. It was crowded and I don't know how I spotted him—he doesn't stand out like Luke. Yet there he was, taking a photo for a family on vacation, pulling faces to make the smallest boy smile. Nothing was ever too much trouble for Cary. He would have been happy to be asked. As I looked on, it occurred to me that as smoothly as the thief had removed my watch she could easily have taken my engagement ring too. For the first time in months I lifted my hand to study the blue-green globe intact on my fourth finger, then turned and ran down into the square.

CARY

·

Things began to improve in Venice, where we made love for the first time since I'd learned of Kate's affair. My libido had been one of the casualties of that ghastly discovery, though initially that was hardly an issue. But as the months lurched on I began to yearn to touch her again. Not so much for the sex as to connect somehow, to be somewhere that only the two of us existed. By the time we left for Europe, though, we hadn't even resumed sharing a bed, never mind anything else. Once there, all our rooms were doubles, but something else held me back: the fear of a rebuff, or even worse, a pained acceptance. I couldn't bear the idea of her enduring me, tolerating my attentions, couldn't bear that she might fake something she didn't feel or, conversely, not even bother with that. Every night I would steel myself to approach her, my body homesick for the old silk of her skin, the habit of her mouth; every night she would fall asleep while I was still in the bathroom, or simply turn her back to me before I had even had the chance to frame the question.

In the end it was her decision. It had to be, didn't it? Kate had always set the agenda. One afternoon she suddenly sought me out in St. Mark's Square, tugging my sleeve and whispering, "Now." It wasn't a command or a question, and I couldn't say what prompted it. We hadn't even spent much of that day together—she'd gone shopping while I'd done my own thing. I don't know, maybe she even missed me. I kissed her then, suddenly as shy as in that feed shed more than seven years before. Something made me leave my eyes open, and the look on her face was that of a child at the local pool who has just stepped gingerly off the high board for the first time ever. She clung to me as if she were falling.

Later, at the hotel, it was good. There were no fireworks, but no shocks either. Our bodies remembered what to do and turned to each other like old friends, delighting in their reacquaintance. Afterward I slept soundly, then awoke feeling revived for the first time in months. The best way to describe it is that it was like eating Vegemite toast again after weeks of rich foreign food and complicated sauces—good and satisfying and familiar. I've always loved Vegemite toast.

KATE

•

At first all I could think about was Luke. How he used to touch me, how he would have looked into my eyes and said my name if it had been him I was in bed with. I expected it to be terrible. Well, maybe not terrible so much as disappointing, bland, like fish paste after you've developed a taste for caviar. A little bit later I found myself thinking about my watch, about things lost and found again. It occurred to me briefly that Cary had been robbed too, and of so much more than jewelry. I wondered fleetingly how he could bear the pain. Then I must have stopped thinking about anything—Cary, Luke, caviar, Venice. I was disoriented when I opened my eyes afterward. I guess I even enjoyed it, though not in a way that would have had the people in the next room complaining. Mainly I was glad that it was over, that we'd survived it without inflicting further damage on each other.

I was more relaxed with Cary after that. We'd done the deed; he'd seen me naked; it didn't have to keep feeling like one long first date. Though it was another week before we tried again, things loosened up a little. We spent less time sightseeing, more time asleep or lingering over robust espressos in one of the tiny bars dotting every street. He made me laugh at dinner, pointing out the honeymooners and surmising how well things were going by what they'd ordered. Then he would request scallops and *zuppa di cozze* for our own table, the seafood arriving with the scent of the ocean, fresh from the Venetian lagoon. He noticed my watch was missing and bought me another. More impressively, he made a complaint to the city police, drafting his report into the early hours one morning by painstakingly cobbling together sentences from our meager phrase book.

And he never rubbed my nose in it. There were no long discussions of my infidelity, no accusing glances or betrayed expressions. Just Cary, on vacation, enthusiastic and interested and attentive. Sarah had told me once about a girlfriend of hers whose husband had had an affair. She took him back and they went on with the marriage, but he was never allowed to forget his lapse. The affronted wife was always bringing it up in front of their friends or upbraiding him for his sins whenever she was drunk. She even made him wear a pager so he could be contacted at all times. By contrast, we didn't talk about it at all. I wondered sometimes if Cary was suffering from a kind of posttraumatic amnesia, if he had blocked it out completely, removed the offending memories as neatly as a surgeon cutting away cancerous tissue. He's a scientist; I wouldn't put it past him. The topic just never came up. But at least we were talking again, which was more than we did before we left.

CRESSIDA

•

Of course, in the end my conscience got the better of me. Dr. Whyte was sorry to inform me that the fellowship couldn't be delayed, only declined. On the bright side, though, there was every reason to expect I would be successful again should I reapply next year. My father, he added, as if I didn't know, was a highly respected man, and everyone in the field had great hopes for his recovery, et cetera, et cetera. Even the hospital in Michigan was accommodating, and invited me to get back in touch if my plans changed. It was almost too easy, reversing in minutes all the plans that had taken months to set in place. Had they ever really been destined to come true?

So that was that, all I had ever wanted gone at once: fellowship, marriage, the support of friends or family. For a crazy instant, surveying the ruins, I had the urge to call Luke, to run back to his side. Why, I'm not sure—so I was at least left with something, maybe, even if it was only the devil I knew. He'd always been good at standing up to my family, making sure he got his way. For a second I was tempted enough to lift the phone. Then reality intervened and I replaced the receiver. I already had enough problems.

LUKE

•

There's a girl at work who likes me. Well, not at work but through work, and *like* isn't what it's really about. I've a fine antenna for such things, something that never atrophied during my scant few years of marriage. I don't suppose I gave it a chance, but like that reputedly durable cycling ability I wonder if such a sense ever really goes away. I can see myself at eighty, in a nursing home, knowing full well which of the female residents—or nurses, if I'm lucky—fancies me and which will be more of a challenge. People say you lose interest in that sort of thing as you get older, but I can't imagine a life without sex in it somewhere, even if it is just thinking about it.

Mind you, I hadn't done more than think about it since I'd moved to Boston. Maybe it was because everyone I met was from work, and it's dangerous to get involved there, or maybe it was that I didn't have the energy for the hunt after the upheavals of moving and divorce. Still, think about it I did: the way Kate writhed when I cupped her buttocks; Cress's small sigh as she let herself go. Some mornings I would wake up sure I was with one of them; most nights I went to sleep wishing I were.

Memories, however, can take you only so far, and as winter tightened its hold on the city I needed more than those for warmth. So I guess I was ripe for the picking when the PA of a client started flirting with me over the phone. We'd never even met, but she must have liked my accent or something. . . . Pretty soon I was making up reasons to call her boss and hoping I wouldn't get straight through. We'd talk about her roommate, my new car, what she was wearing that day. This went on for a few weeks, with our conversations becoming less and less professional. "Would you like to hold?" she'd ask, and I'd say with a leer, "Hold what?" Pretty juvenile really, but it was as much as I was getting.

The adolescent nature of our exchanges was explained when I finally met her at a pitch to the client. As I came into the conference room there was a voice I recognized but a girl I didn't, and for a second I struggled to reconcile the two. She couldn't have been more than nineteen, twenty at the most. Theoretically I was old enough to be her father, or at least to know better than to date teenagers. She was pretty, though, in that air-brushed North American way, and throughout the meeting I kept catching her looking at me when she should have been taking notes. Once I'm sure I saw her lick her lips.

As soon as we wound up she was by my side.

"So how do you like Boston?" she asked.

"It's certainly different," I replied, damning with faint praise and won-dering if she would be sophisticated enough to take offense. She just laughed.

"You'll love it once you get to know it better."

"Oh, yeah?" I asked, knowing where this was heading, daring her to take it there.

"Yeah," she replied, with more confidence than someone of her age should have. "Why don't I show you some spots that only the locals know about?"

I'd been in Boston going on four months by this time, but that was no reason to turn down such a generous invitation. There were always new spots to be seen.

CARY

·

We made it to France and ended up staying, extending the trip a further six weeks. Things between us weren't brilliant but they were improving, certainly enough to make continuing worthwhile. Kate still had moments of impenetrable silence, and I still found myself worrying about where she was or what she was thinking while she sat opposite me on trains or at breakfast, staring into the distance, opal eyes blank. But she was also laughing more often, and as we left our hotel on our first night in Paris I'm sure she was humming softly as we crossed the Seine.

Nonetheless, I was nervous about suggesting the extra time, fearful of her rejection or disinterest. I agonized over it for an entire evening through dinner, managing to dredge up the courage to ask only minutes before she fell asleep. For a moment Kate didn't reply and I feared the chance had been lost. Then out of the warm darkness next to me I heard her sleepy voice.

"Sure. Why not?"

I suppose her response could have been more animated but I didn't care. She'd said yes—I lay awake all that night too excited to sleep, plotting where we might go, what we might do. Beside me Kate slept on. Asleep, probably uncaring. But there.

"So where do you want to go?" I asked her over breakfast the next morning.

"Today?" she asked, pouring a cup of the *chocolat chaud* that had appeared at her elbow as soon as she had sat down. We'd been at the same hotel for four days. The waiter was obviously paying attention. "I thought we agreed on the Louvre?"

"Not today. I mean in the next six weeks." Six weeks! Forty-odd days, a month and a half. I felt almost giddy with delight, and something else. Relief. It was as if I were inhaling again after months of holding my breath.

"Oh," she said, looking up almost shyly. "I wasn't sure if you were serious." For a second I panicked, but she hadn't finished. "I haven't thought about it. Do you have any ideas?"

I'd focused so completely on convincing her to say yes that I hadn't dared settle on a destination. We could go to the moon for all I cared.

"What about Egypt?" I asked, thinking on my feet. "You could see all the clay pots you like there."

"Too many terrorists, and I'm over clay pots. Besides, there's more of that sort of thing in the British Museum than Cairo and Rome put together."

"London then?"

"Too cold. And too expensive. God, I'm starving," she said, reaching for a plate of croissants almost before they had been placed on the table.

"Somewhere warm then. Turkey?"

"Maybe." She shrugged, dismembering the pastry in a spray of buttery flakes. "But wouldn't I have to wear a veil there?"

I thought again.

"Somewhere warm and licentious then. Greece. Temples for me, beaches for you. And judging by their statuary you could probably walk around topless if you wanted to."

She looked up and smiled, then went back to licking her fingers. "No temples. We'll see what you want to in Paris, but after that we're having a vacation. God knows we need one. No churches, no museums, no galleries. I just want to lie in the sun for a very long time." Kate looked suddenly tired. Exhausted even, her face collapsing into a series of lines and shadows. For a moment I thought she might cry, but as soon as I noticed the slump it was gone, features pulled back into line with an effort. She was quiet for a moment, as if concentrating on the transformation, then finally spoke.

"Spain."

"Spain?"

She nodded. "Maybe I could work up the energy to go out for tapas now and then."

"¡Olé!" I replied, and we both laughed like drains, though it wasn't the slightest bit funny.

I faxed the hospital as soon as we had finished breakfast. They weren't thrilled at my request for extra leave, but it was owed, so what could they do? Theoretically I knew I was supposed to take no more than four weeks at a time; realistically I was sure that my department respected my work too much to fire me. Still, I wouldn't have bent the rules a year ago. I managed to find a conference to attend to give my request some validity, but though I registered and paid the fee I never showed up. I don't think we even got to that city. Luckily Kate had thrown in her own job when we'd left, citing personal reasons as an excuse to evade the required month's notice. I think she told them her mother was ill or something; I didn't get involved. Let her put her duplicity to good use for once.

CRESSIDA

·

Instead of settling into Michigan, I spent October watching Father die. It seems I do a lot of that: watch people die, and always from cancer. It's so often the same . . . the drawn-out suffering and gently graying skin, the panic in the eyes, the putrefying breath. I found myself beginning to long for a stroke or an aneurysm, a car crash even. Anything but this prolonged decline.

I grieved for my father; of course I did. But he wasn't all I was grieving for, and the endless days of turning and toileting him, administering morphine and adjusting drips, left too much time to think. My mother hovered outside the door to what was once their bedroom as if waiting for an invitation. At least five times a day she would ask me, "How is he?" and my response was always the same: "The same." *He's dying*, I wanted to scream; *how do you think he is?* Frightened, I imagined, angry and penitent and defiant. But she was frightened too, so I held my tongue. I suppose this was the first death she'd seen.

Then one day something changed. Father was deteriorating quickly and his oncologist suggested that he be moved to a hospice. I could give him drugs, but I couldn't lift him or propel him back to bed when he was agitated. He was becoming incontinent, and occasionally delirious. We tried hiring a nurse, but Father, a doctor to the end, was so contemptuous of her skills that she soon resigned. After that, Mother and I alternated nights getting up to take care of him, though at the end of the first week it was obvious to all that she wasn't up to the task either physically or psychologically. A family conference was called. Cordelia made the decision and no one dared argue.

The first time I went to the hospice to visit there was a middle-aged man bending over Father, dressed only in jeans and a T-shirt. Mother asked him sharply what he was doing, then was immediately apologetic when he introduced himself as the chief physician.

"It's designed to make the place more like home," he said, holding out his hand to her. "I'm Paul, Dr. Paul Mahoney. We've found that too many white coats can be a bit intimidating for both the patients and their families. Besides, it's not as if they're really necessary."

Mother twittered something about maintaining standards and hospitals being different in her day.

"Yes," he said placatingly, not at all ruffled by the criticism. "I'm sorry to have confused you, but you'll soon get to know us all."

"I wanted to introduce something similar on my own ward," I said, "so the children wouldn't be scared of the staff. But the hospital authorities wouldn't have it—said it was a security risk."

Dr. Mahoney looked at me for the first time then.

"Oh, so you're a doctor too?"

I nodded, foolishly pleased. When I mention working at a hospital most people assume I'm a nurse.

"Where are you based?"

"At the Royal Children's normally, in pediatric oncology. I'm on leave at the moment, though."

"She's been nursing her father," my mother interjected. "Heaven knows what I would have done without her. We would have ended up here a lot earlier, I suppose."

I was so stunned by this public display of gratitude that I could only stare at the floor. Too many kind words might reduce me to tears.

"Good on you," said Dr. Mahoney with quiet approbation. "It's very hard to tend to someone you love, to watch them deteriorate while you stay well. Guilt, pain, anger and all that." Then he added, "I cared for my wife when she was dying of breast cancer. Luckily we didn't have children. As you'd know, it's a full-time job."

I caught him looking at my hands. My left hand specifically, the empty fourth finger. He saw me notice and smiled unapologetically. I found myself smiling back, amazed that my face still remembered how to do so.

LUKE

·

Our date began with dinner at a small Italian place on Long Wharf, followed by a jazz club nearby. But really, who cares? She was sending out all the signals, and from the moment we met at the restaurant I knew where we were ultimately headed. The only question was whose place we'd end up at.

Hers, it turned out. From what I could see, it was barely a rung above student accommodation, all sticky-tape-marked walls and bikes in the hallway. For an instant I couldn't help but compare her apartment to the house I'd shared with Cressida: classically neutral furnishings always arranged just so, the towels in the bathrooms replaced as soon as they were damp. Then the lights went out and any further interior design evaluations fled my mind. She was as ready for it as any woman I've slept with, almost pushy in the way she hauled me into her bedroom. I was more than ready too, pent-up and aching after six months' enforced celibacy. My only initial concern as her hands roamed smoothly from my chest to my groin and her impatient nipples dug into my rib cage was to make sure I lasted. Usually I'd try to spin things out, to savor the experience rather than bolting from start to finish, but it was a battle I was losing. Her fingers were on my belt, then beneath it; her mouth followed suit. As it did she guided my hand beneath her own clothes, where instead of underwear all I felt was skin, soft and damp and drawing me in like a siren. I lowered her to the carpet, pushed up her skirt and went suddenly soft.

I was mortified. This had never happened before; I had never even dreamed of it happening. I stalled for time, suddenly diverting to other techniques that I usually couldn't be less interested in with a woman spread like warm butter on the floor in front of me, praying desperately as I did that it would all be okay. Never before had I realized that there was such a disadvantage to being a man. If a similar thing had happened to my partner—complete and catastrophic loss of desire, along with all anatomical correlates—she could have just carried on as before and no one would be the wiser. But I licked and I probed and I manipulated and nothing happened, just a question mark where there should have been an exclamation point.

Eventually I had to give up. We were both getting cold, and I was hideously embarrassed. She said all the right things—that it didn't matter, it meant nothing, we could wait awhile and try again—but it didn't help. I knew I couldn't do it. She invited me to stay the night, no doubt hoping she'd get lucky in the morning. I waited until she was asleep, then got out of there as quickly as I could. Our agency lost the campaign two weeks later and I never had to speak to her again.

The worst bit was that I didn't know why it had happened. I didn't have too much to drink; I hadn't taken drugs; I swear I wasn't thinking of my twin regrets ten thousand miles away. Maybe it was her peculiarly raised vowels or those winter-upholstered thighs, just a little too heavy for someone her age. But afterward the episode did make me think of home, and specifically Kate. I felt stupid and anxious and furious at her. What had gone on in that Boston high-rise only underlined to me how well Kate and I had been matched, how right things were between us. Yet she'd forced me into some artificial decision, refused to hold on with both hands to something unique. A year, that's all I'd asked. What's a year in the scheme of things? Worse, she'd assured me she would leave Cary, but had ended up staying with him. I wondered if she'd even told him the truth, that she chose *me*, that he was just the default. She'd gotten off scot-free, the coward, while I'd paid the price for us both: impotence and exile.

Seven months of rising as reliably as yeast whenever I saw Kate, and now this. She was still comfortably ensconced in her marriage bed, while I couldn't even service a teenager. Alone that night back in my apartment I cursed both her and Cary. I hoped my ghost was with them every time they lay down together for the rest of their lives.

KATE

•

We went to Spain and gradually I fell in love again. No, that's too strong. Returned to love? Accepted love? Settled for love?

The thing is, I fell in love with Luke, not Cary. Fell for the sheen and the sweat, the adrenaline of the hunt. Faltered, reeled, collapsed. There was no falling with Cary. Loving him was gradual and logical, inevitable as the path of a glacier. But Luke was a thunderclap, appearing out of a clear blue sky, soaking me to my skin, then moving on, leaving everything looking different. And post-Luke nothing was the same.

Not a day went by that I didn't think of Luke. Had the cards fallen differently, however, who's to say I wouldn't be pining for Cary in the same way? I knew now what I'd miss: his patience, his enthusiasm and easy smile. His forgiveness.

Despite my initial misgivings, I adored those months in Europe. No, *adored* is also too strong. . . . I enjoyed them, more with each passing week. Cary and I stayed in some beautiful places, saw some wonderful things. Yet once we had made our peace with each other my thoughts started turning to home. I found that I longed for Melbourne's vast sky, clear blue and lucid, uncluttered by souvenirs or cathedrals. I missed our clean, straight streets, the logic of our planning. I missed Sarah. I missed understanding what people were saying; the tacit empathy that came from speaking the same language. Europe was glamorous and fascinating and exotic, and it had been good to us. But it wasn't home, and I was ready to go home.

CARY

·

We arrived home in early December, six weeks having turned into just over three months. All my leave and most of my savings had run out, but it had been a more than worthwhile investment of both. Things weren't back to normal, but they were approaching a new kind of normal. We talked; we laughed; we made love on occasion: a future had been salvaged. Admittedly, I still hadn't spoken to Kate about her affair. Somehow there had always been a reason for putting it off, though I had planned to discuss it. *Why?* I wanted to ask her. *What was missing that you had to get from him? Was it just better or different sex*—I could live with that—*or something more fundamental? What did he give you that I don't? And how can I be sure it won't ever happen again?* The last one occupied my thoughts particularly. At the end of the day, why had she stayed with me? I hoped it was love, though neither of us had dared utter the word the whole time we were away. Had she loved Luke? I didn't even really know why they had broken up. Cressida had seen them kissing and confronted Luke, but how much longer would it have gone on if she hadn't been a witness? And where would it all have ended?

The questions formed themselves hourly to start with, then perhaps a little less frequently as our trip wore on. Yet still I didn't ask them—fearing the answers, perhaps, or reluctant to upset our fragile truce. Kate certainly didn't volunteer any information—acting, in fact, as if the whole thing had never happened. Perhaps that was the best approach. It was certainly the one I seemed to be taking.

But the strategy was shot as soon as we got home. There, amid the pile of bills and junk mail that had accumulated during our absence, was a wedding invitation from Joan and Tim. Kate glanced over my shoulder as I opened it.

"I didn't even know they were engaged," she exclaimed, then flushed. Of course she didn't. We'd been away. Why should she?

"Mmm," I replied, staring at the card, unable to meet her eyes. My heart thudded in my throat. Even seeing Tim's name rattled me. How much had he known?

"Here's the phone bill. And oh, we missed the council elections. I suppose they'll be after us now for failing to vote. Remember when Simon next door didn't vote and he had to do community service? I think he had to spend a day planting trees with people who'd held up shops and stuff. It seems a bit ridiculous, doesn't it? He said—"

"Kate," I interjected across her prattle. I recognized the symptoms—a patina of chatter to mask her unease. "Should we go?"

"I don't want to go," she said quickly. "I haven't seen Joan since . . . since the trivia night, and . . ." She was blushing again and winding up to talk some more. I held up my hand to stop the flow.

"I didn't ask you if you *wanted* to go. Do you think we *should* go?"

Kate sagged; her eyes lowered. We both realized that Luke would be there and probably Cressida as well, assuming she could get back from Michigan. Of course she would be invited; Tim had always adored Cressida.

"It's up to you," she muttered, my forthright, opinionated wife, the one who had made all of our decisions with little more than a nod in my direction. Things change.

My initial reaction was to decline. Kate and Joan weren't that close anymore, so why on earth would I put myself in the situation of being in the same room as my faithless wife and her relatively recent ex-lover? Yet the more I thought about it—and I thought about it a lot, at work, in traffic, while Kate slept beside me at night—it seemed that maybe here was the answer to my questions. If she still loved Luke, if she had ever loved

Luke, it would be obvious. Kate was emotionally transparent: grief, joy and anger showed up on her features like makeup. The whole time she was having the affair I'd known something was wrong, just not what. If she still wanted him it would be apparent, and I knew she wouldn't be able to resist speaking to him if there was anything left to say. I sent our acceptance.

Did I do the right thing? The wedding was slated for February, another three months away. There was still time to pull out if necessary. Did I really want to put myself through such a reminder? But reminders were evident everywhere anyway. The fault lines in the relationship were there for good now, acutely visible, though I hoped in time they'd fade. For a while it seemed that every time I turned on the TV or opened a book adultery was featured. Songs on the radio fantasized about it, denied it, celebrated it. The subject came up in jokes or conversation, the evening news. Not long after we returned a prominent athlete was found to have had a fling with a teammate's wife and was subsequently forced to resign. The ensuing scandal led to a whole new slew of e-mailed gags—more uncomfortable reminders. Had it always been like this? Was the whole world so obsessed with sex, and forbidden sex in particular, yet I had somehow failed to notice? There seemed nothing more powerful, even when meaningless.

For all we could pretend the affair hadn't happened, things, it seemed, would never be the same. Still, the baby would have changed them anyway.

LUKE

·

I opened the envelope with a sense of foreboding. Tim and I had hardly spoken since I'd left for the U.S., yet here was something suspiciously thick and creamy with his handwriting on the front. It wasn't as if we'd had a falling-out, more that there just hadn't been anything to say. He didn't approve of what I'd done with Kate; that much was obvious. He didn't approve of my moving to Boston either, though I failed to see how remaining in Melbourne would have won me any points. And I didn't approve of Joan, though I'd been less up-front in conveying my emotions. It was none of my business, a lesson he would do well to learn. He drove me to the airport and we'd shaken hands. Since then we'd exchanged the odd e-mail: I'd forward the latest joke doing the rounds of North America; he'd write back and tell me about his job or Joan, as if I'd asked.

I knew they were engaged. It had happened before I left, further hastening my departure from his apartment. Through lawyers, Cress had proposed that we sell our house. We were both moving overseas at that point and neither could afford to buy the other out. I agreed without thinking about it much. It was too big for me to live in, and she was right not to want the bother of tenants and maintenance from the other side of the globe. I returned a few times before my departure to collect my designated half of the furniture and get the place ready for the auction. With both of us gone it looked vulnerable, smaller. For a minute or two I allowed myself to feel some regrets, then put them aside. I hadn't even chosen the place;

had never wanted to live in the suburbs anyway. Why start tearing up about it now?

As expected, the letter contained a wedding invitation. But there was worse: Tim had attached a note, asking me to be his best man. To tell you the truth I had been planning to skip the whole event, say with deep regret that distance and work commitments, yada, yada, yada. The guest list scared me. Tim was still in touch with Cressida, so there was every chance that she'd be there, and Joan, I knew, had once been friendly with Kate. Why on earth would I fly twenty-four hours to endure that?

Yet Tim's request made a refusal difficult. I suppose I should have anticipated it, but I'd assumed Tim's nose had been so put out of joint by my debauchery that I was no longer up for the role. Instead, it seemed that he was bravely going to put friendship and loyalty above my disgrace. What could I do? Tim was still my friend. He'd been best man for me; he'd given me a room when Cress threw me out. By then I would have been away for six months anyway, so it was probably time I paid my family a visit. I booked a ticket.

CRESSIDA

·

The wedding invitation included Paul, for which I was grateful. I'd moved in with him only two months after we met, and not everyone was as accepting of the relationship. I could almost hear the whispered phrases when I returned to work or walked into a room at either of my sisters' houses: *rebound, impulsive, can't cope without a man*. Really, though, the decision made sense. The sale of my married home had been arranged when I thought I was taking the fellowship, and since my father had been moved to the hospice there was no real reason to continue living with Mother. Oh, my sisters said I'd be company for her, but she spent most of her waking hours at my father's bedside. I was no longer needed. Time to go back to my job, to find another place to live, to make a second attempt at a life of my own.

Paul was part of that. It was certainly convenient that he'd asked me to move in, but that wasn't why I had accepted. We got along well; he made me laugh, he listened, he valued my ideas. He was nineteen years older than me, but that was about our only significant difference. Perhaps best of all, he was as passionately involved with his work as I was. He understood the late nights, the middle-of-dinner pages, the responsibility I felt for my patients. He never apologized if plans had to be changed if he was needed at the hospice, and he didn't expect me to either. I had been dreading going back to work and facing the gossip of the hospital, but found to my surprise that I was enjoying my job more than ever, feeling free to throw myself into each shift without always watching the clock or wondering guiltily if I cared too much. My moving in was good for both of us. He'd been lonely since the death of his wife; I'd begun to resent my family's claim on my time. Acquiring a partner, no matter how hastily, gave me back some status in their eyes. Yes, he probably was a bona fide father figure this time, but so what? It hadn't worked out the traditional way. And it wasn't as if I had promised to marry the man. We were just living together, seeing what happened, allies as much as lovers. Matrimonial refugees, as Paul once laughingly described us. We both knew that no matter how much a commitment was meant it could still be undone. Better just to live from day to day.

My father was holding on, though just barely. Often if Paul was paged into work while we were at home together I would go in with him and spend the time in an extended paternal visit. Father was almost always cataleptic with painkillers, but that didn't matter. In many ways it was better. He asked no awkward questions about my failed marriage or the divorce settlement; he didn't sit in judgment on my career or life choices. He would have approved of Paul, I'm sure, but it was a relief not to have to seek that out.

Some days, if Paul had the time, he would help me bathe him. There was a nurse for such tasks, of course, but that didn't seem to stop him. I fell in love with Paul in these moments, my heart defenseless against the tenderness with which he shaved my fallen father or soaped his atrophying limbs. At other times Paul would help me feed him, wipe his mouth or his bottom when it was needed. Luke would never have done such a thing. He would have thought it beneath him, obscene. I replied to Tim's invitation, joyfully accepting for us both.

KATE

•

I couldn't find a damn thing to wear to that wedding; nothing, anyway, that didn't make me look fat or frumpy. I'd reached the four-month mark of the pregnancy, an awkward time when it was obvious I was putting on weight, but not yet that I was expecting. Everything I tried on stretched too tight across my abdomen or hung tentlike from below my bust, hardly the look I was trying to achieve. But what was I trying to achieve? I didn't want to go anyway, would never have agreed if Cary hadn't insisted.

I had realized I was pregnant just before we left Europe. For the previous week all the symptoms had been there: nausea, fatigue, aching breasts, though I was thankful I'd never gone the complete Hollywood route and fainted. At first I thought I was just tired, then that I'd eaten something that disagreed with me. When I finally did my math the grim truth dawned on me, and was quickly confirmed by a trip to the drugstore. Pregnant! I couldn't believe it. What were the odds? I'd stayed on the pill, at least up until the prescription had run out, a few weeks after ending things with Luke. I'd meant to renew it but was too depressed or distracted at the time. It had felt like I'd never have sex again anyway, so what was the point? The thought crossed my mind when I finally slept with Cary in Venice, but I could hardly stop him. As far as he was concerned I hadn't been taking it for a year, and was probably infertile. I didn't want to get into any deep discussions about family or future at that time anyway, and the risk of conception seemed so slight. It wasn't as if we were going at it night and day, even after that tentative reconciliation. I'd just tried not to think about it, crossed my fingers instead of my legs, hung on and hoped for the best.

But pregnancy was something I couldn't ignore. As if to prove the point, the morning sickness that would be my companion for the next ten weeks kicked in as soon as we got home. I vomited all through Christmas, a very different Christmas from the last. As I doubled over the toilet for the third or fourth time on the morning of Christmas Eve it suddenly occurred to me to wonder if the heart I'd carved into the fig tree in the botanic gardens one year ago was still there. I wasn't doing anything special that day, but I didn't have the energy to go and look.

I'll admit I wasn't too thrilled about the situation on any number of levels. It was too soon. We weren't ready. Cary and I were barely talking to each other normally; now we were having a baby. I'd hardly proven myself reliable, but before long something was going to rely on me. I wasn't even sure I possessed a maternal streak. I kept waiting for it to show up, but all that arrived instead was nausea, regret and anxiety. At night, when the worry kept me awake, I imagined the little one inside me, shipwrecked in such a hostile environment, and hoped that I'd learn to want it.

But in another way I guess the pregnancy was for the best. It closed all other options. Right through everything, through Europe, through being able to look Cary in the eye again and not pull away when he reached for me, I still wondered if just maybe . . . I knew Luke hadn't chosen me; I knew Cary had and that I was better off with him, but every so often I'd find myself wondering if things were truly over. This baby said they were. Utterly. No other man would ever want me now, and from what I'd seen of Sarah's life I'd hardly have time to think of anything else anyway.

Cary, of course, was thrilled. He cried with joy when I told him the news, and slept each night with a hand on my stomach. He had even started thinking about names, e-mailing me his ideas from work almost hourly for the first trimester. And I guess the timing was appropriate—I was thirty-three and didn't even have a job I had to resign from. It was time to grow up and get on with things. And that meant attending this damn wedding, if I could ever find a dress.

LUKE

·

I flew into town the day before the wedding. Why arrive any earlier? I had dinner with my parents that night, dropped into the rehearsal and planned to fly out again on the Sunday morning after the big day. No point using up too much precious annual leave.

After the rehearsal I tried to tempt Tim into coming out for a drink. He wavered for a minute, then declined as Joan swooped over to claim him.

"Hello, Luke." She gave a polite nod in my direction, then took his arm. "Come on, Tim, we still have to staple the wedding programs."

He smiled ruefully and allowed himself to be led away. My disappointment surprised me. I could have done with the company. For some reason I felt on edge, was more jittery than I had been the night before my own wedding. Exactly why I couldn't say, though it obviously had something to do with the thought of seeing Cress and maybe even Kate again. Still, I didn't anticipate any scenes, and had no intention of causing them.

As it turned out, they were both there—one ignoring me, the other eating me up with her eyes. I couldn't look during the first part of the ceremony, but later, from my vantage point at the altar as Tim signed his life away, I had a chance to study them both. Kate was near the back, dark head lowered, uncharacteristically subdued in navy blue and somewhat heavier than I remembered. To be honest, it took me a few seconds to spot her, and I would never have thought that of Kate. But when I did finally locate her and my gaze lingered it was as if a message had been sent.

She looked straight up, straight into my eyes, almost devouring me with her hunger. The impact was such that I nearly took a step back; then Cary touched her arm and she dropped her face again. Cress, by contrast, wouldn't even glance in my direction. She looked great—creamy shoulders, upswept hair, pink lips—though I couldn't work out who the older man sharing her hymnbook was. Maybe a friend of Joan's parents whom she'd been saddled with and was too polite to ditch.

I didn't see either of them again until much later in the night. There was the service, of course: promises and confetti flung around with comparable ease. Then there were the photos that dragged on for an hour, and parading in ahead of the happy couple with the chief bridesmaid on my arm. Neither Cress nor Kate was seated near the bridal table, and I spent the evening making polite conversation with the bridesmaid and Tim's mother while surreptitiously scanning the room for both of them.

It was Cress I had expected to feel bad about. She was the one I'd betrayed, after all, the one I'd promised to forsake all others for, an oath I'd managed to keep for less than a year. But to my surprise and slight pique she looked fine. Happy even, and genuinely so. She smiled as she danced, whispered and giggled to the old man next to her all through my speech, something the decorous doctor I'd always known would have frowned upon. I was sorry I'd never seen that side of her.

Kate, though . . . Kate was drowning in the noise, in the music, in that terrible blue dress she was wearing. I could see her going under, opal eyes flashing a distress signal every time she looked my way. But did I dare approach her? I knew her fierce pride, the anger and humiliation she would have felt when I elected to stay with Cress. Twice I got up to go to her; twice I sat down again. Maybe she just wanted to have it out with me, and I couldn't face that here.

I was jolted back from my thoughts by the bridesmaid tugging at my arm, looking slightly green.

"We have to dance," she hissed, gesturing toward the floor, where Tim and Joan were already shackled in their bridal waltz. Tim couldn't dance, I thought, as I watched him shuffle around the floor as if he were wading through mud. I allowed the bridesmaid to lead me up to join them, hoping she at least knew what to do with her feet. For a moment we managed all right, but then I felt her clutch me and put her head to my chest.

"What's wrong?" I whispered, alarmed. Her arms had gone around my neck, and I felt her going slack.

"I'm not well," she moaned quietly. "I think I've had too much to drink. Or maybe it was the oysters. Or both." She belched softly, and I could smell the main course.

"Do you want me to take you back to the table?" I asked, our feet slowed almost to a stop.

"Yes," she murmured, all her weight on me now, head buried in my neck.

We'd gone only a step or two, though, when I felt her body tremble, heard that shallow cough. She was going to vomit, so instead of heading back to the bridal table I quickly steered her straight outside, past the surprised eyes of the guests and into the cold night air. The last thing I saw as we left the reception was Kate, her eyes naked with want. I knew that look. I'd seen it a million times, every time we'd made love, or said good-bye: every time I looked up and saw her coming across the gardens, the pub, the forecourt of the museum.

As the bridesmaid retched into the rosebushes I urged her silently to hurry. I *knew* that look, and it was still there. I thought Kate would never forgive me for not choosing her—it was why I hadn't called after Cress threw me out, sorely as I'd been tempted to—but maybe I was wrong. Maybe we still had a chance. As soon as this girl had finished being sick I was going to go straight back in and find out.

CRESSIDA

•

The wedding was fun. I'd found I loved being anywhere public with Paul, loved showing him off and basking in his attention at the same time. Whenever Luke and I had gone out—to parties, trivia nights, what have you—I would barely see him all evening. I don't think that he was already being unfaithful, though the possibility has crossed my mind. He never articulated a reason for his absences, though I understood it well enough. Coal to Newcastle, bananas to Africa. Luke may have loved me, but I was old news. Why stay with your wife when there was a whole room full of fresh people to charm? Paul is different. Grown-up, dare I suggest, and sure of his choices. He talks to others, but I'm the one who really captures his attention, whose company he plainly prefers. It's new; I'm new; maybe that will wear off. Somehow, though, I don't think so.

Luke was at the wedding, of course. I had wondered how it would feel to see him again, but when I did there was nothing—no pain, no longing, just some embarrassment at how blatant he was with that girl. I sensed him watching me once during the service and looked away. The other person I avoided was Kate, for obvious reasons. She didn't seem all that great, actually, staying in the background and not even drinking, as far as I could tell. That wasn't like the old Kate. She looked puffy, worn-out, and didn't once get up to dance. Despite myself I felt a stab of triumph. I hoped she hurt; I hoped she saw Paul holding me close and wondered who he was. I hoped they both wondered. My turn to sparkle.

But though I wouldn't look at Luke, Paul did—curious, he said, to see what sort of fool would throw away someone like me.

"He's quite the player, your ex-husband," he observed as we danced together.

"What did I tell you?" I asked.

"Yes, I know," said Paul. "But I hadn't expected him to be quite so . . ."

"Good-looking?"

"Out-there," he responded firmly. "Oh, okay, then, handsome," he amended, pulling me closer, completely unperturbed by the fact. "He's bloody gorgeous, isn't he? I imagine every woman in the room is hoping he will ask them to dance."

I shuddered slightly, remembering another wedding. For a moment or two Paul and I watched as a bridesmaid threw herself at him and he bent down to whisper in her ear.

"See how he does it?" I found myself hissing at Paul. "Next he'll be kissing her in the middle of the floor, or slipping off somewhere for a quick grope."

As I said the words I realized I was angry, an emotion I thought I was through with. So there wasn't quite nothing after all. But it was only anger, and I could live with that. No sorrow, no regret.

KATE

·

We left the wedding early. Three hours into the reception I couldn't stand it anymore and told Cary I felt ill. I had been suffering morning sickness for the past two months, so I knew he wouldn't question me. The balance may have shifted since the whole Luke thing, but when it came to this pregnancy I still held the ace.

Luke was there, of course. I'd been half hoping he wouldn't be, unsure what reaction the sight of him would provoke. Anger? Lust? Regret? Only half hoping, though, because a part of me yearned to see his face again, to catch his eye and his attention, if only for a moment. Loving Luke had been the most powerful experience of my life, yet between his dismissal and Cary's silence sometimes I wondered if I'd dreamed the whole thing up. I needed to reassure myself that he existed.

I got my wish. I saw him, all right—how could I miss him, standing by the altar with the bridal party, beautiful in black tie and drawing every eye toward him instead of Tim and Joan? I felt drab and dowdy in return, took Cary's hand for solace without even meaning to. While the marriage certificate was being signed I watched Luke scan the congregation for Cressida. She in turn ignored or was unaware of him, deep in conversation with a silver-haired man on her left. And then he was looking for me; I was sure of it. . . . Suddenly terrified, I ducked my head and stared at the pew in front of me, but the heat of his gaze upon me drew my face up again. Our eyes met, and for a second there was a jolt of recognition, of acknowledgment. But it wasn't enough. When he looked away I hungered for more.

I was distracted and restless throughout the rest of the service and dinner, annoying Cary as I toyed with cutlery at the table. I needed to see Luke. That I couldn't do so easily made me feel trapped: by the event, by my condition, by the gold band still on my finger. I'd vowed never to speak to Luke again, but what was the point of that when everything in me craved him once more? Finally the speeches were over, and I got up, ignoring Cary's questioning glance, got up with the intention of going to Luke. I don't know what I intended to say, but it wasn't simply hello.

Only he was busy. He was leaving, actually, with a bridesmaid, their arms around each other, the intent clear. She was clinging to him, and he in return was holding tight to her, hurrying toward the exit as if he couldn't have her quickly enough. It was all unbearably familiar. I knew how he left functions—he'd left one with me once before.

Shattered, I sat down again. All of a sudden I found myself alone at our table, the others dancing or deep in conversation elsewhere. Something rose up in my throat, and with horror I realized it was panic and tears. The room contracted and I closed my eyes, willing myself not to cry. Inside I felt the strangest thump—my heart breaking, perhaps. Just then Cary materialized. "Are you okay?" he asked, and I shook my head no.

"Come on then," he said tenderly, and took my arm. "Let's get you out of here."

I'd never been so glad for his touch. We left immediately, through a side door, without saying good-bye or wishing the happy couple all the best. It was probably rude, but I didn't care. Would I ever see them again? I hoped not. For better or worse, that part of my life was irrevocably over, gone the minute Luke had swept that bridesmaid out of the room. Cary steered me out into the calm of the evening and I took great gulps of air, breathing as if emerging from a long time underwater. I felt better by the minute, though the thumping continued. It wasn't until we were halfway home that I realized what it was: the kicks of our child, resonating through my body for the first time.

CARY

•

The wedding? It was okay as far as weddings go. Tim is a good guy and I wished him well. For all that had ensued since the last nuptials we attended, it was actually pretty straightforward. Kate was subdued and stayed close to my side. Luke was best man and made a fool of himself with a bridesmaid. I almost felt sorry for my wife and the ease with which she had been replaced. Tim looked ecstatic and Joan triumphant. Cressida just looked great, beaming and beautiful and cared for. Watching her with her new partner, it suddenly occurred to me that maybe, just maybe, it was her I should have pursued after all, back when it was just us and the hospital we both loved, before either Kate or Luke had thrust themselves into our lives. She came over to say hello and was so gentle, so warm . . . but it was only for a minute, and laughable, really, with Kate wan and pregnant at my side, mine inside and out. Really, the whole thing was far easier than I'd imagined. I'm glad we went.

It's hard to remember much now. These days we stay home a lot more, and that suits me. That wedding was the last big event we attended before Joel was born. Kate might miss going out, but I don't. Finally, I have everything I want: my wife and our child, faces that turn toward me when I come home at night.

They look up when I enter the room, lamps lit behind them. Kate is so beautiful as she nurses Joel that the burst of happiness is like a knife in my side; the lump in my throat feels as if it will choke me. My joy is magnified by the pain it has taken to achieve all this, the way hunger improves the taste of a meal.

Joel looks just like her, except his hair is bright blond. Mine was too as a child, though it's much darker now. Sometimes I catch her stroking that hair, fingers tangled in its silkiness, her face a mask. I ask her what she is thinking about and she smiles slightly and says she never has time to think anymore. After the life Kate was used to I wonder if the days feel long, but she doesn't complain. I call her to chat, but lately she's never home, or doesn't answer if she is. Maybe she's turned the phone down so it doesn't wake the baby. Perhaps I should get her a new cell phone.

Occasionally and against my will I find myself thinking about last year. Silly things remind me—seeing Cressida's name on a roster at work, Kate not answering though I ring and ring. Really, she's probably taking Joel for a walk. The bottom line is that she's mine again and we're happy. We're together. It's pointless to dwell on anything else. Picking away at scars only reopens them.

And besides, all that's in the past, and that's not the direction I'm headed.

ACKNOWLEDGMENTS

•

After the Fall has benefited from the guidance of a number of remarkable women. In particular, I wish to thank my agents, Pippa Masson in Australia and Stéphanie Abou in the United States, for taking me on and for all their enthusiasm and assistance along the way. For their wisdom, advice, encouragement, and attention to detail, I am also deeply indebted to Jackie Montalvo of Doubleday and Jane Palfreyman of Allen & Unwin. My sincere gratitude to all—it has been a pleasure and a privilege to have worked with you.